HOT
PURSUIT

HOT PURSUIT

To Catch a Thief
Book 1

Kay Marie

All Works By Kay Marie

To Catch a Thief
Hot Pursuit
Stolen Goods
Off the Grid

The Love Match
The Love Rematch
The Love Lie

Confessions
Confessions of a Virgin Sex Columnist!
Confessions of an Undercover Girlfriend!

To my family for their unconditional love,
my friends for their overwhelming support,
and my fans for their incredible enthusiasm.
Thank you from the bottom of my heart.

- 1 -

Jo

The kitchen resembled a war zone. Flour hung in the air like a slow-motion explosion. Dirty bowls littered the counter. Crumbles of dough spotted the floor. Whisks and spatulas floated in the water-clogged sink. But Jo hardly noticed. She was transfixed by the little mounds rising higher and higher in the oven.

Her newest creation.

The pookie.

Jo pursed her lips, thinking. Something about that wasn't quite right.

Or maybe the cookie-pie?

What about the cook...ie...

No, wait. She shook her head. *That doesn't work.*

The coopie?

Jo chewed her bottom lip as she watched the pie crust start to brown. The sugar-butter glaze she'd decided to add at the last minute had been the perfect touch. Now she just needed a name. It was all in the name. Jo still held that she invented the cronut long before it became the newest fad. But she'd called it the doussant. Because, well, it was a doughnut and a croissant... a doughnut-croissant... a doussant.

Long-festering resentment brought a sneer to her face. *The freaking doussant!*

If only she'd flipped the words around...

If only she'd called it a croissant-doughnut...

If only—

Jo sighed.

Cronut. So simple. So annoyingly catchy.

The oven dinged.

Jo leapt from the marble counter of the center island, sending another wave of flour into the air as she landed on her feet and rushed across the tile floor to open the stainless-steel door. A wave of tangy-sweet goodness hit her nose, making her eyes flutter closed with pleasure.

The coopie.

Simple.

Catchy.

Perfect.

Her lobster oven mitts were still on her hands, so she reached into the heat and grabbed a baking sheet in each claw, then nudged the oven closed with her hip. And though she knew she should wait, her impatience won out—as it usually did.

Hot, hot, hot!

Jo juggled the coopie in her palms, shifting it from one to the other so it could cool for a moment before she took a satisfying bite. Sinking her teeth through the flaky pie dough, she sighed as the ooey-gooey chocolate chip cookie stuffed inside hit her taste buds like a blissful, sugary explosion.

Oh. My. God.

Her mind spun with the million directions she could take this. Pie crust stuffed with caramel apple bars. Pie crust stuffed with rainbow sprinkle sugar cookies. Pie crust stuffed with molten chocolate brownies.

Jo dashed to a stool and hopped onto the seat as she slid her laptop across the counter. She flipped the screen open and immediately began typing.

@TheBakingBandit: Guys, guys! Are you awake? Are you there? I have it. I have the idea for my future bakery. This is it. For real this time!

There was no response.

Jo glared at the screen as she took another bite, then perked up when a thought bubble appeared on the group chat.

@TheGourmetGoddess: That's what you said the last time…

@TheBakingBandit: I know, I know, but I mean it this time!

@TheGourmetGoddess: Sure you do…

@Sprinkle-Ella: I'm here! I'm here! What's the new idea?

@TheBakingBandit: Wait for it…

@TheBakingBandit: …

@TheBakingBandit: drumroll please…

@TheGourmetGoddess: Spit it out!

@Sprinkle-Ella: *slapping my hands against my cutting board*

@TheBakingBandit: The coopie!

A huge grin spread across Jo's face as she typed the words, giving her creation a life outside of her own head and this isolated kitchen sitting smack-dab in the middle of nowhere. Well, not nowhere. The kitchen, and by definition the house, sat on a ten-acre private island off the coast of the Bahamas—her father's personal paradise. They'd lived there for over a decade, ever since her mother passed away the summer just before Jo entered high school. Her childhood hadn't exactly been normal. But her father was Robert Carter, one of the world's most renowned art thieves, and Jo, for lack of a better word, was sort of his protégé. So normal had never been in the cards anyway.

She frowned at her computer.

Waiting.

Waiting.

@TheBakingBandit: GUYS!

@Sprinkle-Ella: Um...I love it!

@TheGourmetGoddess: What the hell is a coopie?

@TheBakingBandit: I thought you'd never ask :) The coopie is a miniature pie crust stuffed with a delicious cookie! Currently munching on chocolate chip coopie goodness, but my mind is spinning!

@TheGourmetGoddess: I never thought I'd actually say this, but that is a GREAT idea!

@Sprinkle-Ella: OMG! Love! Send us your recipe so we can test it out!

@TheBakingBandit: Sending now...

Jo reached for the papers scattered across the countertop and gathered them into a pile, scrambling to put the recipe into a more coherent format. A smile widened her lips, tugging at her cheeks and spreading them until it was almost painful. But she loved moments like this—when her creative juices were flowing, yes, but also her time with these girls. Cyber friends, sure, but they were the best girlfriends she'd ever had.

The three of them had met almost two years ago in an online forum for fans of *The American Baking*

Championship. They'd bonded over their obsession with the runner-up (Jo still contested he'd been absolutely robbed! The little old lady who'd won had been the fan favorite by a landslide, but Jo knew an act when she saw one. Granny had evil-genius in her eyes, no doubt about it.). And well, the fact that they were the only three women under forty in the forum. After the show ended without being renewed, she'd invited them to their own little group chat, and the three of them had been swapping recipes and gossip ever since. @Sprinkle-Ella's real name was Addison Abbot, and she worked at a cake shop in South Carolina, specializing in wedding cakes and fairy-tale dreams, obviously. And @TheGourmetGoddess was really McKenzie Harper, a trust-fund baby who'd forsaken the family expectations to become a pastry chef, and a fabulous one at that. She worked as a sous chef at a Michelin-starred restaurant in New York City.

And Jo?

Well, they knew her as Jo Carter, Florida resident working in the family business, dreaming of something more. Mostly true, though the best lies always were. Her full name was Jolene Carter. The Bahamas were sort of close to Florida... Close enough, anyway. And they didn't need to know that the family business was crime, just that one day she hoped to be free of it, doing what she'd always wanted—owning her own bakery instead.

The Coopie Factory.

Eh, needs a better name than that...

What to call it...?

What to—

Just Desserts!

The corner of her lip perked.

Now that has a nice ring to it.

Jo finished typing up the recipe and pressed Send, then drummed her fingers against the counter as she waited for a response. Her eyes wandered to the edge of the screen, and she practically fell off her stool when she noticed the time.

It's almost two!

Shoot!

Her father and Thad, the son of his late partner and one of her best friends, would be back in an hour and she hadn't done any of the recon she'd promised. The coopie had taken over her entire weekend.

Jo jumped from her seat and raced toward the French doors on the other side of the kitchen. Her gaze flew across the pool deck, down the boardwalk, and along the entire length of the dock, then froze on the empty slip all the way at the end. She breathed a sigh of relief. They weren't here yet. She had time.

Jo glanced over her shoulder to the stack of coopies fresh out of the oven, ripe for the taste testing. Then she reluctantly tore her attention away, shifting it to the second laptop sitting on the kitchen table, the one she used strictly for business. Her father was an artist, and forgery was his greatest skill. But Jo hadn't inherited any of his craft. No, her specialty was something very different—hacking. She hadn't even realized it was a skill, or, well, a crime, until she'd been caught breaking into the middle school mainframe to change her schedule around, skipping French and Biology while adding extra sessions of Home Ec and Computer Science. She'd never seen her father so proud...or her mother so pissed.

Now, at twenty-five, she'd graduated to more sophisticated techniques. And ever since that first punishment—a week-long suspension that, truth be told, felt more like a vacation—she'd never been caught red handed again. Pink, maybe. But she didn't mind living on the edge.

In fact, she thrived on the edge.

Which was why her focus shifted back to the oven, still hot, and the many recipes flitting across her mind. An hour. An hour. Was there time? Did it matter? She just wanted to try one more recipe before her father and Thad got home, and then she'd focus. Then she'd get to work. Just one more...

Jo turned her attention back to the window, to the empty dock. Only, this time, something in the water caught her eye.

A boat.

Not her father's.

A boat she didn't recognize. And it could only mean one thing. Well, two. A lost fisherman—a really, really, incredibly lost fisherman.

Or the Feds.

Again.

- 2 -

Nate

"Do you think we're getting a little close?" Nate called over his shoulder, eyes locked on the shoreline rapidly approaching.

Thump.

"Ow!" A yelp sounded below deck, followed by the rapid slap of feet on steps. Leo, his partner, emerged from the tight staircase rubbing his forehead and wincing. "Shit, man. Sorry."

He ran back to the wheel and kicked the engine into high gear. The water at the back of the boat bubbled as they fought the current pulling them toward the island.

Nate grinned. "I told you that jerk chicken looked questionable."

He didn't have to see his partner's eye-roll to know it was there. "I was hungry. I grew up on chicken shawarma and tacos from the food trucks down the block. I thought I could survive anything."

Nate snorted and shook his head.

"We didn't all grow up in Pleasantville, Parker," Leo half joked, half groaned.

His partner had a point. Leo had grown up in a crime-riddled area of Houston, the oldest of two boys, raised by a single mom. His only way out had been to enlist, using an ROTC scholarship to pay for college. Nate, on the other hand, had been groomed for the FBI since the day he was born. His father had been a high-ranking agent, they'd lived in a cushy suburb outside of Washington, DC, and he'd received the best education the nation had to offer.

But that didn't mean his childhood had been all roses. There'd been hard times too.

Impossible times…

A smile. A wave. Then pop! pop! pop! *The screech of tires. A scream. The burning heat at the back of his throat. A ruby patch spreading wider and wider across the freshly mowed lawn, spilling into the driveway, a red river flowing down, down, down to the drain. The stark stains on his fingers as he tried to hold it in, the wet heat beneath his palms, growing colder and colder and colder.*

Nate's chest pinched.

He shoved the memory of that dark day back into the farthest reaches of his mind, locking it away like he always did, burying it. His lips smoothed to the focused line they'd been in moments before as he swallowed the emotions back and turned to his work for solace, grabbing the binoculars from the table. Nate lifted them to his eyes and searched for movement through the tinted windows.

He caught motion. The shadowy form of a body paced inside the house—tall and thin. He couldn't make out anything else, but he had his suspicions about who it might be. They'd been tracking Robert Carter for months, and there was very little Nate didn't know about his target's personal or professional lives. The figure inside had to be his daughter—Jolene Carter.

Auburn hair.

Jade eyes.

Expert hacker.

And trouble with a capital T.

"Any update from the onshore team?" Nate asked, dropping the binoculars away to rub at the bridge of his nose, frowning.

"Carter and Ryder landed at the airport in Nassau about twenty minutes ago. They're on his private boat now. He had a black briefcase with him, but no confirmation of what's inside. We lost the satellite feed for about an hour when they were in Cuba meeting with the Russians. By the time it was back up, the deal was done."

Slippery bastard, Nate silently cursed.

The bureau had been close to catching him so many times—*so close!*—and this operation could be their last chance. Rumors were circling with Nate's informants that Carter was thinking about retiring from the business of crime after this one final trick he'd been planning for months. Some people said he'd been grooming his protégé, Thaddeus Ryder, to take over the business. Others said he wanted to lie low for a few years, something to do with his health. More said the rumor was a joke, and there was no chance a man like Robert Carter would ever change his ways. But Nate had learned a long time ago to never believe the gossip—listen to it, take note of it, and then leave all the options open.

He and Leo had only been assigned to the Carter case for a few months. Neither of them worked for the art crime unit, but over the past few years, Carter's business had taken a decidedly darker turn—one that made him a person of interest to the organized crime unit where Nate and Leo worked. They tracked a branch of the Russian mafia operating mainly in illegal arms deals for almost two years before coming across the name Robert Carter. One of their undercover agents had let slip that the mafia was using a stolen painting as collateral against a deal—a stolen painting that had been attributed to the great Robert Carter, infamous art thief since the seventies. Once Nate and Leo started digging, they couldn't believe all the threads they found tying the two seemingly separate criminal enterprises together. No proof, of course. Life wasn't that easy. But counterfeit money and forged bank bonds with Carter's signature style, as well as a refined selection of stolen art discovered during a raid, were enough to pique the bureau's interest.

And Nate's.

Because to him, this wasn't just business.

It was personal.

Personal enough his application for the organized crime unit had almost been denied. Personal enough he'd had to argue his way onto this case. Personal enough he'd caught the way the boss's attention had lingered for a few minutes before he'd given them this assignment, the question if Nate could control himself circling in those wise, hazel eyes.

But he could.

He would.

"Parker, you seeing what I'm seeing?"

Nate blinked at the sound of Leo's voice, clearing his vision and turning his attention back to the house.

He nearly fell out of his chair.

"What the…" His voice trailed off as he snatched the binoculars from the table and lifted them to his eyes.

"Is she coming over here?" Leo asked, flabbergasted. "Should we do something? Should we move?"

"No, hold steady," Nate said, blinking rapidly, unable to quite believe what he was seeing.

Jolene Carter.

In a bikini—a red string bikini.

Riding a jet ski.

Headed straight for their boat.

With...

Nate squinted.

Is that a Ziploc bag of cookies in her hand?

He shook his head, stifling a smile at the sheer audacity of this woman. And then he dropped the binoculars away and squared his shoulders, trying not to focus on the fact that the grainy pictures in his files definitely hadn't done Jolene Carter justice.

Not even a little bit.

Not even at all.

- 3 -

Jo

This was probably a stupid idea. Then again, the best ones usually were.

Besides, the Feds weren't exactly being discreet, showing up in a boat outside her very private, very isolated island. Their desperation for information was showing.

I mean, they aren't even trying. Not bothering to set up fishing poles off the back? That's just lazy! Jo thought as she gripped the handles of the jet ski tighter and her eyes slipped down to the bag dangling beneath one palm. *And I really do want an unbiased opinion of the coopie.*

A wicked grin spread across her lips as she shifted her gaze, zeroing in on the small boat rapidly growing larger and the two blurry figures scrambling on board. This was going to be fun.

"Hi, boys," she called out when she got close, trying unsuccessfully to keep a teasing tone from her voice. Jo whipped the jet ski around and cut the engine, sending a splash over the edge of the boat as she came to a stop parallel to their port side. "You lost?"

"Morning," the man in the back drawled, leaning against the control panel, chest hair visible through the gape of his shirt as he offered her a devilish smile of his own. Dark hair. Golden eyes. Bronze skin. A little short, but strong and clearly confident enough to pull it off.

Yet Jo found her gaze slipping to the man in front, sitting stiff as a board by a small table with his white shirt buttoned all the way to the collar. He had those classic good looks that never went out of style. Sandy brown hair. Bright baby-blues. An all-American type with a strong jaw and, Jo couldn't help but notice, a rather impressive set of biceps, since he sat with his arms crossed, eying her warily, not attempting to be friendly. Little did he realize his taut lips and standoffish expression only served to present a challenge Jo couldn't keep herself from accepting.

"Could you hold this?" she asked, overly sweet, before tossing the bag of coopies right at his face, forcing him to unfold those arms or be smacked in the forehead. He smoothly lifted one hand and caught the bag with hardly any effort at all.

Nice reflexes, she admired silently.

The edges of her lips twitched with amusement as he gently placed the bag on the table and glared a brooding sort of scowl in her direction.

Before either man had time to react, she hopped over the side of the boat with her jet ski tie in hand and fastened a quick knot. Leaning against the ledge, she folded her arms in just the right place to perk her medium-sized breasts into optimal position.

Two sets of eyes dropped.

Then rose.

Then slipped down for another instant.

And finally returned to an alert, straightforward position.

The red bikini was a good choice, she noted, watching Mr. Stiff clench his jaw and take a noticeably tight swallow. Her gaze dropped to the table in front of him, cataloging what she saw—binoculars, notepad, cell phone, map—then darted around the rest of the boat. Another phone. A two-way radio. More papers. A stack of manila envelopes secured with two thick rubber bands. Cameras. And two holsters with handguns piled in the corner.

Jo pulled her focus back onto those baby-blues. "Two lost fishermen with no fishing poles?"

He shrugged. "Lunch break."

"I see," she murmured, drawing that last syllable out as though it were its own sentence. The silence stretched while all three of them took note of the clear lack of food, aside from coopies, anywhere on the boat. Both men shifted uncomfortably. "Is oxygen the new fad diet? I must be getting a little out of touch on this isolated island."

Neither answered.

Jo couldn't stop a light giggle from slipping out as she pushed off the side of the boat and stepped toward the table, snatching her bag of coopies. "Well, boys, maybe we can help each other out. You look hungry, and I have a bit of a conundrum. You see, I've just created what I'm sure will be the biggest thing in baking since the mini-cupcake—I'm calling it the coopie, for now— but I've got no one to taste-test. At the moment, I'm all by my lonesome in that big old house, as I'm sure you're well aware, and since I know we're both waiting on the arrival of the same person, I figured you might have a few minutes to spare to help me out."

They kept watching her, unsure. Mr. Stiff drew his brows together, creating a deep and somehow intriguing groove down the center of his forehead, keeping his lips in a smooth line. His friend looked at her, face going a little green as Jo opened the Ziploc bag, pulled a coopie out, and dropped the rest back on the table. Before she could open her mouth, he turned and fled down the stairs, the *smack* of a closing door the only sound in his wake.

Hmm…not the reaction I was hoping for.

"Guess it's just us," Jo said and turned back to the grump with what she hoped was an irresistibly charming smile, offering him a coopie.

He didn't move.

His gaze flicked back and forth between the coopie and her face, as though trying to decipher some hidden agenda. To be fair, she couldn't blame him.

Jo was almost always working some sort of angle. But this one time, no matter how much her words seemed to dance and dart around the unspoken, she really did just want an honest opinion about something she cared more about than almost anything else in the world—her food.

Her smile drooped for an instant.

She stretched her hand a little closer.

"I don't bite," Jo commented. His lips softened. His muscles relaxed. He almost—almost!—reached out to accept the coopie, until she couldn't stop herself from adding, "Unless you're into that sort of thing, of course."

She wriggled her brows and flashed her teeth.

A pink flush rose on Mr. Stiff's cheeks as he jumped to his feet.

Tall, check.

Broad, check.

He stepped past her, reaching down to deftly untie her jet ski from their boat. Jo let her gaze drop for a moment.

Very grab-able ass, check.

As though he could hear her thoughts, he jerked upright and turned, holding the black rope in his more-than-capable hands and offering it to her. "Have a nice day, Miss Carter."

Jo cocked her hip to the side, staring up at him for a moment before reaching her palm forward. She let her fingers linger on his warm, tanned skin as she took the rope from his hands, loving the way her stomach clenched, how a little flurry of sparks exploded in her chest. Mr. Stiff...hopefully in more ways than one.

He pulled his hand back, but she clenched her fingers and held on, forcing him to meet her eyes.

"You can call me Jo."

- 4 -

Nate

He didn't want to notice the perfect O her plush lips made as she said her name, but he couldn't control it…or the immediate reaction his body had at the sight. Nate froze, jaw clenching as he fought to control the blood rush coursing to a very distinct place.

Jo leaned closer, tightening her grip.

His gaze darted to those jade eyes staring up at him, vibrant and sparkling with hidden mirth. He'd always had a weakness for green eyes. And women in barely there red bikinis…

He jerked back, shaking free of her hold.

Jo folded her lips together for a moment, holding back a smile, before licking them slowly. A single brow arched. "You have a name?"

Nate frowned, cleared his tight throat, and nudged his chin in the direction of her jet ski. "I said good day, Miss Carter."

"No fun," she sighed with a pout, then smirked. "You know I can find out if I want to, right?"

She can't seriously be... Nate shook off the thought and pushed his brows together in question. "You wouldn't be implying what I think you're implying, would you?"

Her smile widened with an unspoken challenge. "What if I am?"

Nate straightened his spine and crossed his arms over his chest, funneling his disbelief into a stern, scolding expression instead. "Breaking into a government database is a federal crime," he said calmly, the edge of a threat laced through his tone. "Class B felony, punishable by up to twenty years in prison."

The flames in the centers of her eyes brightened. "Only if you get caught."

Unbelievable...she's unbelievable.

No shame.

No remorse.

No...no...

"Can I tell you a secret, Miss Carter?" Nate murmured, not really sure why he was playing along, but the words tumbled from his lips before he could stop them. Her eager expression intensified. An almost childlike sense of wonder was etched into the grooves of her face as she nodded. He leaned in, just to prove to himself that he could, and forced his rebellious pulse to remain even. Her auburn hair tickled his face as he pressed his lips close enough to feel the heat of her sun-kissed skin. Something in his chest hitched, but he didn't back down. "Eventually, you always get caught."

She sucked in a breath. He leaned back just enough to stare into her eyes, not at all liking the defiant golden sparkles dancing at the centers of her irises, flickering like sunshine through a dark forest, brilliant and burning.

The air between them was tense.

A silent battle of wills.

Neither backing down.

Both fighting for the win.

She opened her mouth to speak, drawing his gaze, and—

Static cracked loudly over the two-way radio.

"Parker, Alvarez, do you copy? Are you there? Satellite feed says Carter should be in sight momentarily."

Nate snapped upright.

Jo didn't move except to perk one corner of her plush lips, watching him unflinchingly, victory simmering in her eyes.

"Parker, are you there? Do you copy?"

She turned her head toward the sound and shrugged. "You going to get that?"

Nate took a slow step back, eyes never leaving her for a second. His gun was four feet behind, resting next to Leo's on the control panel. But his phone was on the table, along with his notes. All within reach of her thieving hands.

A pulse of static coursed through the radio again.

Nate lunged for it. Pressing the button to speak, he kept a laser focus on Jolene Carter, trouble personified. "Here, Boss."

"Parker, do you see Carter?"

A small smile danced across her lips as she mouthed, *Parker.*

Nate stifled a groan and turned his attention to the horizon. A white spot in the distance caught his eye, bright against the endless blue. "Carter is in sight, I confirm. Carter and Ryder are in sight."

Jo spun. Her entire body froze for a moment, and then in one deft move, she flung herself over the edge of the boat and landed smoothly on the jet ski. Her long, toned legs straddled the seat, muscles clenched tight. Her chest was angled forward, fingers gripping the handles. A gust of wind blew her hair to the side, revealing the graceful curve of her neck. She revved the engine once.

Nate jolted at the sound.

"Anyone tell you it's not polite to stare, Agent Parker?"

He gritted his teeth. "Anyone tell you it's not polite to trespass?"

"Sure. I just don't care." She shrugged and flashed him a grin, her gaze sliding down his chest, all the way to his toes and back up, pausing on the collar of his shirt. Amusement obvious, she pulled her lip in and bit down as the corners of her mouth stretched wider. Finally, she found his eyes again. That damn sparkle was back. "That's the difference between you and me, Agent Parker. I'm fully aware that some rules are made to be broken."

Jo revved the engine again, but this time raced forward, completely in control as she circled his boat at a breakneck speed, bouncing over waves, creating wakes that made the floor shift beneath him. But Nate had grown up on boats. On the weekends, his father had taught him how to sail. So, he planted his feet wide and kept his arms crossed, perfectly balanced as she completed the arc and sent a splash over the edge, wetting his feet.

"See you around, Agent Parker," she called over her shoulder as she sped away.

Nate watched her go, drawn like a moth to a flame. Her golden skin was radiant in the afternoon sun, and that auburn hair blazed like the streaks of a fiery comet, flying in the wind. The bright-red bottoms of that barely there bikini goaded him. The sound of her laughter was a soft echo in his ears.

Dangerous.

Dangerous.

Dangerous.

The *snap* of a door caught his attention. Nate blinked and shook his head, tearing his eyes away and turning his attention to his partner, the one slowly crawling up the stairs, clutching his stomach.

"Oh man, that rocking did not help things," Leo muttered as he stumbled his way to the control panel and collapsed back in his chair.

Nate jerked his head in the direction of the yacht growing larger on the horizon and then tossed the radio in his hand to his partner. "Carter and Ryder are here. Boss is on line one."

After a juggle or two, Leo secured his grip on the radio and turned the wheel to give them a better view of the approaching vessel. He grumbled not so silently the entire time, but a bad round of food poisoning mixed with some seasickness wasn't enough to stop Leo. The two of them had been through worse together. Much worse than this.

Nate dropped back into his seat by the table and grabbed the binoculars again, shifting his notepad closer. One quick glance through the lenses told him it would be a few minutes before the yacht was close enough to get a good look at anyone and anything on board.

A sweet, buttery scent wafted into his nose.

He sighed and dropped the binoculars to his lap as his gaze fell on the bag of—*What the hell had she called them? Coopas?*—resting open on the other side of the table.

His stomach growled.

The muscles in his abdomen clenched.

Nate swallowed and frowned.

No. Stop.

He shook his head and looked away. This wasn't a bake sale—it was a stakeout. And those were from a wanted criminal—a brazen wanted criminal. Sure, Carter and Ryder had never been violent. They had no reason to attack an FBI agent, had never hurt civilians, and had never been suspected of so much as firing a gun. Their skills were different, more refined, steeped in subterfuge rather than threats. The mobsters they worked with were the ones who relied on terror, on violence. But there was a first time for everything, a first time—

A breeze brushed softly against his cheek, carrying that delectable fragrance to his nose once more, making his mouth water and his empty stomach ache. It had been a few hours since his last meal, and it could easily be a few more hours until his next.

Nate's defenses lowered as his hunger rose.

One bite couldn't hurt... he reasoned as he slid his palm over the smooth surface of the table and dipped his fingers into the bag. But he paused, focus darting to the woman in the distance who was now standing at the edge of the dock, watching the horizon. She was bold—that was a given. Curious, maybe. Taunting, definitely. But not threatening. The cookies were nothing more than a way for her to get inside his head, a way to distract him...and apparently, they were working.

That's it.

Nate defiantly grabbed a cookie, determined to meet her silent dare head-on. He was done going in circles, done with the mind games. And if they really were contaminated, then, well, he deserved what he got for not reading the suspect clearly.

He bit down.

And groaned, closing his eyes.

God damn, this is good.

Not that he'd ever tell her.

Jolene Carter.

Daughter of his target.

Expert hacker.

Criminal herself.

Nate sighed as the image of her plump, rosy lips filled his mind.

Jo.

- 5 -

Jo

Jo held her palm over her eyes to block out the sun as she watched the yacht grow larger and larger on the horizon. It was small enough to be manned by one or two people, yet large enough to still look impressive as it slid slickly through the bobbing waves, gleaming white in the sun. The windows were dark blocks of opaque ebony, but Jo didn't need to see through them to know who was inside. One glance at the words painted across the outside in crisp cursive was all she needed.

My Susanna.

Named for her mother. Only three people were allowed on board, and one of them was standing here.

Unable to stop her curiosity from taking over, Jo slid her gaze from the familiar to the deliciously new. The small fishing boat was far enough away that she could no longer make out anyone on board, but her imagination had always been rather robust, and it didn't take much for her to imagine Mr. Stiff, shirt buttoned to the collar, light-brown hair ruffled in the breeze, full lips drawn in a determined line as he watched her.

Agent Parker, what am I going to do with you? A small grin pulled at her lips as she shook her head. *I wonder if you gave in and tried one of my coopies yet...*

Jo sighed and pulled her focus away, letting it drop to the shimmering aqua water lapping up against the dock as her mind jumped to the two people she actually should be concerned with, her father and Thad—the two people who would not be at all amused by the state of the kitchen or the state of her assignment.

It's okay. It's okay. I'll get everything done tonight. I'll say I was worried. My father couldn't possibly stay mad at me if he thought I was worried. Thad, on the other hand...

Well, Thad would see right through her. He always could. Just one of the many, many reasons they'd never worked out as anything more than best friends.

"Jo!" a deep voice called.

She snapped her gaze up. "Thad!"

He jumped over the edge of the yacht, as graceful as a panther. Before Jo knew what was happening, she was in his arms, wrapped up in a bear hug. Her feet came off the dock as he lifted her into the air and spun her until she was dizzy.

"Okay, okay," she half griped, half laughed, slapping Thad's muscular shoulders until he put her down. Jo leaned back, meeting his teasing eyes. His gray irises were usually the color of a storm rolling in over the sea, but every so often, they shone for her, the glinted edge of a steel knife, beautiful and a little bit dangerous. His sinfully dark chocolate hair was matted and tussled, yet somehow on him, it always managed to look just right. Jo grinned. Thad did the same. As always, she couldn't stop herself from wrinkling her nose and pressing her pointer fingers into his dimples, one perfectly charming spot in each cheek.

"Jo Jo," he pleaded, the only one to ever get away with calling her that nickname.

She dropped her arms with a satisfied smirk and stepped back. "How was the trip, Thaddy Bear?"

He grimaced, thunderclouds gathering in his gaze.

She'd never quite gotten away with using his nickname…the one she'd crafted at the ripe old age of six, after he'd stolen her favorite stuffed bear to give to his terror of a dog and she'd decided to simply use him as a replacement. Jo had spent the rest of the summer chasing him around, and he'd spent it running away, until the morning neither of them would forget. The morning his mom up and left, seven months pregnant with a sister Thad had never met. He hadn't minded the nickname or Jo's incessant pestering after that.

Not really.

"The trip was successful," an authoritative yet somehow warm voice interrupted.

Jo spun.

It was her turn for a full-frontal assault as she spread her arms wide and launched into the air before she had time to process. But even though her father was an older man, he was still sturdy and strong, and he caught her easily in his arms, pressing a loving kiss to her brow as she held him tight. After all these years, their homecoming ritual had never changed.

"Hi, Daddy," she murmured.

"Hi, pumpkin," he whispered for only her to hear. When she was a toddler, her hair had been a bright-orange mess of curls. Now it was a more muted auburn, but the name stuck for most of her childhood, and even now, on occasions like this, it snuck out of hiding. But Jo loved it because for a brief moment, she was a little girl again, not a care or a worry in the world, safe in her father's steadfast arms.

She stepped back and looked into his face. Before they'd moved to the isolation of this island, her friends used to tease her by calling him a silver fox. In middle school, the idea had been met with mortification. But now, at her slightly more mature age, she could understand what they meant. His black hair was a salt-and-pepper gray, combed over the crown of his head and set off nicely by the perpetual tan on his freckled skin. Her hair had come from her mother, but her eyes were all Robert Carter. Bright green and filled with mischief, just like the ones staring at her now.

"Any particular reason for the enthusiastic greeting, Jolene?"

Jo grimaced. *Damn.* "No, not really…"

"Because I could have sworn I saw a jet ski racing toward the dock not even ten minutes ago."

Thad snorted behind her.

Jo turned to make a face at him, but he was focused on tying knots and securing the yacht to the slip. She turned back to her father. "I just went over to say hello."

"To the Feds?" he scolded as his attention slid to that old fishing boat, lightning flashing in his gaze. "They've been tailing us for days."

"It's nothing new." Jo shrugged. "Just thought I'd try being friendly for once, not that it made any difference. They had a map and some binoculars and a whole heap of frowns for me, nothing more."

Much to my chagrin, she silently added as Agent Parker's scowling face came to the forefront of her thoughts. Somehow, he made grouchy look charming. Remembering the scratch of his calloused palm on her arm and the little flash of desire in his eyes, well…it made her heart do a little flip in her chest. Jo was the queen of wanting things she couldn't have—and a federal agent hunting her father, her best friend, and probably her as well? Yeah… He was at the top of the bad idea list. Number one. Underlined. In bold.

Jo did a mental shake, clearing her head and her heart, then returned her attention to her father. "So, how *was* the trip?"

Thad and her father had gone to the mainland to meet with a few of his former business associates and finalize the details for their upcoming trip to New York. As per usual, Jo had been left behind to man the fort. Not that she minded a few days on her own—after all, it was her only time to hunker down in the kitchen and bake to her heart's content. But something had felt different about this trip, something she couldn't quite pinpoint, a nagging fear she'd spent the past few days burying in the back of her mind.

Her father had promised her this would be his last trick. He'd promised that after this trip to New York, they'd both be done.

Free of the shadows.

Finished.

Jo wanted so badly to believe him. But she couldn't help but notice how neither he nor Thad would meet her eyes or answer her seemingly simple question.

"Successful, like I said," her father muttered, gaze cutting to the small boat in the distance then returning to her for a split second before dropping to the briefcase he held made of dark, polished leather. "We'll discuss it more when we're inside."

Jo swallowed her complaint and knelt to help Thad with the knots. Her father took off down the boardwalk, leaving the two of them alone. They worked in silence for a while, washing the salt from the deck and tidying the interior of the boat. When her father disappeared inside the house, Jo collapsed onto one of the leather sofas in the main cabin, worn out and exhausted even though it was hardly past midday. Her coopie energy was rapidly depleting, and the idea of spending the rest of the evening reviewing plans and catching up on the recon she was supposed to have finished days ago sounded more and more daunting with each passing second.

"Is there anything I need to know?" she asked as she dropped her head back against the seat, letting it roll to the side as Thad emerged from the lower level with a suitcase in each hand. He put them down before dropping into the seat beside her, then grabbed her hand in his strong fingers and ran his thumb over her palm.

"Don't worry about it, Jo Jo. That's my job," he murmured. "The plan hasn't changed. We fly to New York. Go to the gala. Grab the painting. In. Out. Back in a blink. One last hurrah before we send your dad into a much-deserved retirement. Leave the rest to me, okay?"

Jo bit her lip but nodded.

A few minutes with her computer and she knew she could uncover whatever it was they were hiding from her. And yet, she had no desire to do so.

Instead, she trusted his words.

His promise.

Because Thad had never broken a single one he'd made her.

He stood with a sigh, rolling his shoulders once before snatching the bags from the floor. Thad found her gaze again, this time with more life in his eyes. A smile widened his lips, digging those squeezable dimples back into his cheeks. "Besides, you have more important things to worry about. Your dad and I took a quick look at the security cameras on our way home. What in the hell were you doing all morning?"

"Crap!"

Jo jumped to her feet and raced past him, out the door. The kitchen was a disaster. The oven was still on. Her precious coopies were still cooling on the countertops. And, worst of all, her personal laptop was still open to the chat with her friends—and the dreams her father knew absolutely nothing about. Dreams to leave this island. To follow her own passions. To have her own life. Dreams he would never understand.

"Relax, Jo," Thad called after her. "I told him to go the long way through the front entrance."

She stopped cold and spun, relief flooding her chest. She should have known Thad would have her back. He was the only person aside from her online friends who knew anything about the bakery she one day hoped to run, and he'd always protected that hope as though it were his own, just like he'd always protected her.

"I know." Thad winked as he jumped off the boat and landed smoothly on the dock. "You love me. I'm the best. What would you do without me?"

"I don't know," she said and leaned up to kiss his cheek. "I really don't."

He rolled his eyes but didn't protest. Jo took one of the bags from his arms, sparing a moment to glance over her shoulder at the boat still bobbing on the other side of the breaking waves. Then she closed her eyes tight, shook her head, and pushed all thoughts of those blue eyes from her mind as she followed Thad home.

- 6 -

Nate

"You going to come up for air, Parker?"

Nate jerked upright. The sudden movement caused a lump of dough to lodge in his throat, so he thumped his chest and coughed a few times to clear his airway. "What?"

A spew of crumbs may or may not have been released along with the word.

Nate wiped his mouth and spun to face his partner, resisting the urge to slap the grin from Leo's lips.

"You've had like five of those things in ten minutes."

Nate dropped his gaze to the table, noticing that the bag of cookies was half-empty and he himself was feeling a little light-headed from all the sugar. Stubborn until the end, he just shrugged. "I'm hungry."

Leo's lips twitched. "I see that."

Nate clenched his teeth and turned back around, lifting his binoculars to his eyes. Jo and Ryder walked down the dock, looking rather cozy. He had one arm draped across her shoulders, holding her close as he leaned down to whisper something in her ear. Jo's head dropped back as her entire body shook with unabashed mirth, auburn hair cascading over her shoulders, a trail leading down the curve of her spine all the way to that bright-red bikini that barely covered anything at all.

"Jolene Carter," Leo said with an appreciative sigh.

Nate banged the binoculars back on the table—a little too hard—and lifted his fingers to the bridge of his nose, rubbing at his skin.

"Do we know if she's going to New York with Ryder and Carter?" Leo continued, unaware of the way his words grated like nails on a chalkboard, making Nate's shoulders writhe. "I wouldn't mind tailing her for a couple of days. Not at all. Might be—"

"She's a wanted criminal," Nate interrupted. *Suspected of hacking into a government database, a private security firm, a museum archive, and probably a million other places we don't know about yet.*

"She's a fine piece of—"

Nate shot a glare over his shoulder. "Of what?"

"Of a woman, Parker," Leo finished. "You'd have to be blind not to notice. Or, you know, a straitlaced stickler who only sees the world in black and white."

Leo pointedly lifted his brows.

Nate ignored the teasing jibe, because oh, he saw it.

He saw it all right.

"She's beautiful, and she knows it," Nate admitted, keeping his voice even. "A woman like that can be…" He paused, drawing out the syllable as he searched for the right word. "Tricky, in our line of work. She knows how to muddy the waters, how to blur lines you thought were drawn with steel."

"I was trained to withstand torture," Leo argued with a laugh. "I think I'll be okay." And then his eyes narrowed. He focused on Nate, one brow lifting as his lips puckered, holding back a grin. "Unless I'm not the one you're worried about. What exactly happened up here, Parker, while I was busy puking my guts out in the bathroom downstairs?"

"Nothing," he grumbled, turning around in time to see Jo disappear behind the tinted windows of the house. Ryder followed close behind.

"Hmm…nothing?"

"She jumped back on her jet ski and took off."

"Leaving her, uh, cookies behind?"

"Apparently."

There was a distinct pause in the conversation.

"Did that red bikini leave an impression, Parker?" The words carried an unmistakable undertone of laughter.

"Leo."

"Oh, you're Leo-ing me, are you?" His partner snorted. Nate could imagine him shaking his head, not bothering to hide a wide smile. The very idea made him wince. "I have to say, I didn't give thieving little Jolene Carter nearly enough credit if she stole her way under your skin in less than five minutes."

Just as Nate turned to offer his overly cheerful partner a death glare, the two-way radio sparked to life.

"Parker, Alvarez, update?"

Saved by the boss…

"Carter and Ryder arrived," Leo spoke seriously into the radio, back to business in a heartbeat. Nate turned around, folding his hands in the space between his knees. "The daughter was waiting for them on the dock. They had a short greeting, but we couldn't see or hear anything. Within a few minutes, Carter was inside the house, carrying a black leather briefcase with him, likely the one you spotted when they exited the plane in Nassau. Ryder and the daughter lingered for a while. They appeared to be cleaning the boat, and then they disappeared into the house, both holding small rolling suitcases."

"Did you get anything off the mic?"

Nate resisted the urge to curse under his breath.

Leo didn't. "Shit."

"Shit, what?" their boss drawled.

Nate jumped to his feet and grabbed the radio from Leo's hand. "We had some complications, sir."

"What complications?"

Robert Carter's private island was immune to FBI penetration. A cleaning woman who came by once a month was the only other person allowed inside the premises, but she wasn't an American citizen, and there was only so much they could do to try to turn her into an informant. After their failed attempt, it hadn't gone unnoticed that a couple hundred thousand dollars miraculously appeared in her bank account the following week—a presumed gift for her loyalty. They'd tried bugging food deliveries, but Carter was a magician at locating the devices. With an elite security system run through satellite feeds and a computer genius for a daughter, so far nothing had worked.

If Carter really was using this job as his last hurrah before retirement, they had to nail him before it was too late. Discretion be damned. So, they were going old school. A boat parked outside and a handful of specialized microphones—parabolic mics that could pick up sounds at a distance of one thousand meters and laser mics that could detect sound vibrations off a window. "Agent Alvarez ate a bad batch of jerk chicken before we left the dock this morning, and I didn't get the laser mic set up in time. All we got through the parabolic was static. Too much wind."

Leo's eyes bulged accusingly.

Nate took his thumb off the transmitter. "Do you really want him to think we were distracted by Jolene Carter instead?"

Leo hesitated for a second before relenting.

"Get the mics set up, Parker. All the mics."

The boss is not amused...

"Will do, sir. Immediately."

"There's still too much we don't know. See what you can get. I'm keeping you stationed there until the target leaves for New York. I'll send a crew out tonight with supplies that should last for a few days. We can send some more if you need it."

Leo groaned audibly behind him.

The sea hadn't been kind to him so far.

But Nate thought he had it worse—they were sharing the bathroom. And the only other room downstairs was hot, windowless, and full of all the advanced tech they'd wanted to keep out of plain view.

Guess I'll be sleeping under the stars. Please, for the love of God, don't let it rain. Just for a few days.

That's all I ask.

He closed his fingers into a fist, holding back everything except for a quick, "Yes, sir."

The line went dead.

Nate looked at Leo.

Leo looked at him.

Without speaking, they launched into work, setting the mics up, getting the recording devices together downstairs. The two of them had been partners long enough to do so silently, tossing things back and forth with little more than a sparse word here and there, grunting complete sentences. The afternoon heat gave way to cool twilight before they were done putting the system together.

Nate enviously eyed the sleek yacht bobbing in its slip as he wiped the sweat from his brow, the irony not lost on him. Criminals lived the high life—zipping around on private jets, in luxury cars, on glitzy yachts— while the upstanding citizens trying to bring them to justice were relegated to what by the end of the week would quite literally be a floating pile of shit if his partner didn't start feeling better soon. The Lord only knew what amount of wealth was sequestered on Robert Carter's private island, hidden behind those tinted windows and an impenetrable layer of security. But Nate was determined to find and seize every last bit of it, no matter what red-haired, green-eyed woman batted her eyes at him.

Leo disappeared below deck, but Nate remained in the fresh air, used to the salt and the sea, not at all bothered by the rocking motion. He reached for his binoculars again, ready to do one final check before he called it a night.

A flash of light caught his eye.

The door to a small balcony opened, bright for a beat, before the yellow ray disappeared. It took a moment for his eyes to adjust. When they did, he nearly choked.

Jolene Carter.

Bathed in soft moonlight.

Wearing nothing but a semisheer negligee and a grin.

Nate resisted the urge to chuck the binoculars across the boat, and instead gently placed them back on the table before collapsing against the makeshift bed he'd thrown together. Closing his eyes was no use—the image still burned.

Nate shook his head and focused on the stars instead, distracting himself by studying the tapestry painted across the clear sky. Just as it started to work, a whisper came through the parabolic mic aimed at the house.

"Good night, Agent Parker."

A soft trill of satisfied laughter followed the words.

Nate squeezed the ridge of his nose as he groaned.

It was going to be a long couple of days.

Scratch that.

It was going to be a long operation.

$$- 7 -$$

$$Jo$$

There was no room on the entire island Jo hated more than the vault. Underground. No windows. Dark. And dank. Free from any form of technology aside from the stand-alone security system used to get in and out. Black walls. Black ceiling. Black floor. Spotlights shone on her father's most prized possessions. A Monet. A van Gogh. A set of Warhol's famous prints. A drawing attributed to Leonardo da Vinci. Along with a handful of other works Jo never bothered to memorize. And hidden at the end of a long narrow hall was his studio, full of stolen paints—some with the distinct signatures of a dozen different renowned artists, others specialized pigments stolen from historical archives to throw off any carbon-dating techniques—and a wall of brand-new tubes in every shade of color imaginable.

Thad considered it a sacred space.

Jo just found it uncomfortable.

Down here, there was no place to pretend. Her father's profession, her profession, it was thrown in her face, a mirror reflecting all their illegal activities, unable to be ignored. The black walls and bright lights made her squirm.

But soon it would be over, and she could have her own sanctuary.

Her own bakery.

Her *Just Desserts.*

"Jolene." Her father's voice punctured her unease.

She looked up from the surface of the polished mahogany table edged in gold leaf—a relic from Versailles that had been taken during one of the French revolutions and eventually purchased by her father on the black market. A bit gaudy for her tastes, truth be told, and the chairs weren't even comfortable. But it had been their meeting table ever since she started working in the family business. "Huh?"

"Did you hear me?"

No… Jo ran back through the past five minutes, trying to remember what they'd been talking about before she'd started drafting a recipe for an oatmeal raisin coopie and completely zoned out. "Oh, um, the alarm system. Right, right. I think I have it figured out, no worries."

"No...worries?" her father repeated, frowning.

Jo rolled her eyes. "Have I ever done you wrong, Daddy? I've got it under control."

He didn't look overly confident.

Jo leaned forward, resting her forearms on the table as she ran through the plan quickly. The job was a relatively easy one. Simple insurance fraud. A rich guy with a penchant for shady business dealings realized he could get almost twice the payout for a stolen painting than he could by selling it to an auction house. The infamous Robert Carter got wind and offered to take the priceless work off his hands, through covert channels, of course. They'd never spoken. Never met. Had absolutely no visible connections. Her father got a priceless work of art, and the rich guy got his insurance claim. Mutually beneficial.

Like she said, easy.

"We've got the blueprints for the house," Jo thought aloud with a shrug. "The blueprints for the security system, and the locations of all the sensors. With a few tricks, I should be able to plant a virus that will give us remote access. Thad and I will be in and out with"—she paused to smile—"no worries."

Her father pressed his lips into a thin line but nodded regardless.

If there was one thing the two of them had in spades, it was trust. After her mother passed away, they'd only had each other to count on, to lean on, to believe in. The illness had come swift and quick, ruthless in its devastation. Within four months of discovering the cancer, her mother was gone. They'd both been in shock. In anguish. Grief wasn't a strong enough word to fully encompass the sight of the empty chair at the kitchen table, the absence of her laughter, her smile, her touch. The void had been a thick, palpable thing. A constant lump in Jo's throat that would have choked her if not for her dad. For his sturdy arms when she was crying. His warmth when she was cold. His silent steadfastness at a time when there simply were no words to say.

Robert Carter was an infamous art thief to the rest of the world. But to Jo he was simply her rock.

He'd come clean that summer. Promised never to lie to her again. Told her all about his past and his present. Where the money had come from. What her mother had known and surmised. Everything he'd done and planned to keep doing. She'd only been fourteen, but she'd known what a criminal was. She'd known legal from illegal, but more importantly, she'd known right from wrong. Right was sticking by her family no matter what. Wrong was losing both of her parents in one swift yank. So, they'd moved to the island with Thad and his father. She finished high school through an online course and began her education in other things. More nefarious things. Things she hoped she'd be free of soon.

"So, you leave for New York tonight. The plan is set. Everyone's ready?"

Jo glanced up, meeting her father's eyes. They were the color of money. The color of greed. The color of envy. But also of life, of regrowth, of renewal.

"Ready," she confirmed, voice steady.

"Ready," Thad agreed, tone deep and rich and thrumming with confidence.

The two of them were going to New York alone to finish the job. Her father's role for these past few years had been mostly in the setup rather than the execution. Not that he was too old or anything, of course not—at least Jo would never suggest it to him. But it was safe to say that Robert Carter didn't have quite the getaway skills he once did should the need for a quick exit arise. And he never liked to leave the island unattended, the perfect excuse for her and Thad to convince him to remain home.

Her father nodded once. "Don't say another word until you get to New York and can establish a safe zone."

Jo and Thad looked at each other, fighting the instinct to roll their eyes or shake their heads. He'd already told them that about five times in the past two days—they weren't idiots. The first thing she'd done after walking back into the house was a sweep of the security system, the internet connection, the phone lines, anything and everything, but there were no bugs or viruses that she could find. And if she couldn't find them, they didn't exist. Which meant Mr. Stiff and his partner were relying on more limited techniques.

Satellite feeds. Thermal imaging. Long-range mics… Jo paused at that last one, unable to stop the grin tugging at her lips. Toying with the Feds probably sounded like a bad idea to most people. But to Jo, it was too much fun to resist. What was the harm in prancing around in some sexy lingerie at night? Or lounging by her own damn pool in a teeny-tiny bikini? Or going for a run on the beach in nothing but a sports bra and spandex shorts? Or, her personal favorite, belting nineties ballads at the top of her tone-deaf lungs? They didn't have to watch or listen if they didn't want to.

Well, technically they probably do.

Jo closed her eyes and shook her head, trying to wipe the smile from her face as she imagined the way Agent Parker must have growled when she spent forty-five minutes in the kitchen yesterday, singing along to her favorite soundtrack, *The Bodyguard.*

Whitney Houston had the voice of an angel.

Jo had the voice of a dying parakeet. But it was all about confidence, which for some unknown reason, she seemed to have in abundance.

Thad tossed her a curious expression as they got up from the table and made their way back upstairs, leaving her father to who knew what in his studio.

"What's that face?" he murmured.

Jo shrugged. "What face?"

"That self-satisfied, wicked little grin."

She hip-checked him and pushed through the door first. "Wouldn't you like to know."

Thad sighed behind her. "No, I really wouldn't."

"Why?" Jo spun on her heels, stopping so short he almost banged into her. But Thad was nimble. In one move, he grabbed her hand, twirled her around, and laced their elbows together so they walked arm-in-arm.

"Because, Jo Jo. I've seen that face. I know that face. And it means trouble."

"Thaddy," she cooed, leaning her head on his shoulder.

"Don't *Thaddy* me," he teased, nudging her off as he deposited her at the base of the stairs up to her room. He turned to look at her, expression more somber than she'd expected. "Go pack and do whatever you have to do to get focused. This, this—" He cut off and darted his gaze to the window, remembering the rules. "*This* is important. More important than you realize, okay?"

Jo opened her mouth but clamped it shut before any questions came tumbling out. Questions that could get them both in trouble. Instead, she flicked her gaze between his eyes, searching for the information he clearly wasn't telling her. His irises were tumultuous storms, inscrutable and intense.

What aren't you saying, Thad?

What else is going on?

She could have dragged him back down to the vault and demanded answers, but she didn't. Because deep down, she wasn't sure she wanted them.

"Okay," she murmured. "Okay."

He held her gaze a moment longer and then walked down the hall to his room. Jo watched him until he disappeared behind his door, questions churning. But the *smack* of slamming wood jolted her from the trance.

Jo raced to her room.

Thad was right. She needed to stay focused. To keep her eye on the prize. This was her last job, their last job, and there was no way she'd let herself be the reason any of them got caught so close to the end.

Still though, when she entered her room, her gaze went straight to the window and the boat still parked right beyond the breaking waves. Ever so slowly, her attention shifted to the CDs stacked in the corner of her room—her precious collection she'd never give up no matter how outdated it became. There was Britney, Christina, Beyoncé, NSYNC, the Backstreet Boys...all the classics, really. Then a few favorites she'd stolen from her father—Johnny Cash, Loretta Lynn, Kenny Rogers, and of course, Dolly Parton. "Jolene" had been her father's favorite song long before it became Jo's name, and it held a special place in their family lore. According to her mother, her father had first introduced himself by sauntering across a bar, smug and self-assured, saying, *With hair like that, it's a wonder you were born with brown eyes.* Not the best pickup line, since her mom had taken it as a complete insult and promptly turned her back. But her father was nothing if not persistent, and he'd put on the roguish charm after that, sweet-talking her mother into a proper first date.

The story brought a smile to Jo's lips. She blinked a few times, clearing her eyes, and refocused on the stack of CDs, landing on the perfect option.

The Spice Girls.

Jo's eyes went so wide they felt as though they might burst, a quick shift in emotion. She clamped her hand over her mouth to catch the laugh spilling out as she realized her father wasn't the only Carter known for having a stubborn side. Jo did share the same blood after all. So, not thinking twice, she raced across the room, carefully opened the case, and slid the disc into the player.

Agent Parker is going to love it.

- 8 -

Nate

Leo was humming. Again.

Nate hadn't noticed it at first. They were parked on the side of a busy New York City street, waiting for Jo to emerge from her hotel. A cacophony of car honks, curse words, blaring radios, and the intermittent rumble of a subway passing below filled the air. Without even realizing, Nate began to nod his head and bounce his leg to a beat. A few seconds later, high-pitched female voices with British accents started telling him what they wanted and zigging and ah-ing.

Nate snapped his face to the side. "You've got to stop it, man."

Leo jerked upright, turning to Nate apologetically. "God, sorry. I swear I didn't even realize it this time. That song is fucking catchy, Parker. I can't shake it."

Nate grumbled under his breath.

Two and a half hours.

Two and a half fucking hours.

Jo played the same Spice Girls album on repeat, singing at the top of her lungs, if her screeching could even qualify as such.

Mental torture.

The woman had a gift for mental torture.

Nate had thought maybe, just maybe, he'd be free of her once he got off the boat. But Leo kept humming that damn song. And after listening to the recordings on the mics and realizing Robert Carter was staying behind on the island, the boss decided that Nate had built some sort of rapport with the daughter, so he assigned them to be her tail for the rest of the operation.

Ryder was off gallivanting around New York City, probably setting up meetings with his Russian contacts, and Nate was stuck here, waiting for the princess to emerge from her tower.

"Hey," Leo murmured, sitting up and nudging him with his elbow. "I think that's her."

Nate narrowed his eyes and nodded.

He'd recognize that body anywhere. That walk. She had a way of straightening her spine and swaying her hips, something sultry yet elegant at the same time.

A saunter.

No, a strut.

"Wait until she gets to the end of the block before you start the car," Nate said, tearing his gaze away before his mind wandered too far astray—wandered to long tan legs, skimpy nighties, and the memory of her fingers slowly tugging the knot on the back of her bikini free as her hair tumbled down her shoulders just before she'd disappeared through her bedroom door.

He shook his head and blinked.

Goddamn that woman.

Nate opened the folder on his lap and sorted through some papers. They had two separate teams working the operation—one focused on Ryder and one on Jo. They also had three possible heist locations: a premier auction house holding its yearly modern art sale, a museum launching a new special exhibit, and a private home hosting a fundraising gala. They'd found viable evidence for all three spots, and each one was dripping in fine goods ripe for the taking.

Leo flipped the ignition and eased from the curb, dropping his chin to speak into the mic clipped to his shirt collar. "This is Alvarez. Do you copy, sir?"

The boss came through both their earpieces loud and clear. "Copy."

"We have Jolene Carter in sight, and we're following about a block behind. Can everybody hear us? Do you copy?"

"Copy," a few scattered voices affirmed.

They had men on the ground nearby in case she dipped into the subway or they got stuck in traffic, all dressed in street clothes. Leo focused on the road, while Nate did something he'd become annoyingly good at these past few days—stared at Jo.

"Jolene Carter is wearing what appears to be a button-down top in light blue, maybe jean, and white shorts," he spoke into the mic hidden by his wrist. "Her hair is pulled up into a knot. And large-rim sunglasses are covering her eyes. She's also got a bag hanging from her shoulders, canvas or linen, something beige. Large enough for her computer and a small gun. Do you copy?"

"Copy," the team chimed again.

Nate nodded, even though no one could see.

"Where do you think she's headed?" Leo asked as he glanced over his shoulder to check for a car before switching into the next lane over, a little closer to Jo.

Nate met his eyes, brows scrunched. "I don't know."

All three of the possible locations were uptown from Jo's hotel in Greenwich Village. But she was walking south on Seventh Avenue, in the opposite direction.

"Possible fourth location?" Nate wondered aloud.

Leo sighed. "Eh."

"A gallery, maybe?" Nate mused. Greenwich Village was littered with them.

Leo shook his head. "Apartment? Meeting with someone?"

"It's possible." Nate shrugged, keeping his gaze sharply glued to the back of her head, not letting his focus wander any lower. "Are there any internet hotspots around here? Public? Something it'd be hard for us to trace if she established the right parameters?"

"I'll ask the tech guys to run a search."

Leo mumbled into his mic. Nate pursed his lips into a thin line as his jaw clenched.

Where are you going?

What are you doing?

Who are you meeting?

They followed her for another ten or so blocks, completely confused about a possible destination. Jo paused and reached into her handbag. Nate grabbed the camera by his feet and lifted it to his eyes before zooming in as far as the lens could go.

"What's she grabbing?" Leo asked, gaze darting back and forth between their target and the traffic, which had suddenly decided to speed up. "I'm gonna get too close if she doesn't start walking again."

Nate scrunched his eyes. "A phone, it's a phone." He lifted his wrist to his mouth and spoke into his mic. "Did we get the warrant for Jolene Carter's cell phone, sir? Can you tap in and see what she's doing?"

Keyboard clicking came on the line, then muffled voices, and finally his boss. "Grab the tablet in your dashboard. The tech team will send you the live feed."

Nate opened the glove compartment, unable to believe their luck. A cell phone? She was using a cell phone? Surely she had to know they'd been able to get the warrant for remote access. It was the oldest trick in the book. For a computer whiz, the move was almost impossibly naïve.

The light ahead switched to red. Leo let out a relieved breath as he pressed the brake, stopping the car about ten feet behind the target—a little too close for comfort. Nate balanced the tablet on his lap, watching as the feed started coming through the screen, live updates of the apps she was accessing, any and all data the provider had been able to give them access to through their warrant.

"Okay, looks like she's pulling up a map, typing in some directions," Nate read aloud for Leo's benefit. "The address is…189 Spring Street."

He lifted his wrist to his mouth. But before he could get the question out, a technician came on the line. "Place called Dominique Ansel Bakery. Pretty famous. The guy invented the cronut. Was a craze for a while. It's about a block and a half to the left. You should see a line of people waiting to get inside pretty soon."

"Do they have seating? Wi-Fi? Could she be meeting someone there?" Nate questioned. He turned to his partner. "Take the next left, and let's see how close we can get."

"On it."

"One of the guys on the street, can you get inside? Or by a window? I want eyes on her while Leo and I try to find a place to pull over."

There was a pause for a few moments. Then, "I'm in position."

Nate lifted the camera back to his eyes, refocusing the lens as Jo dropped the phone back into her purse. She jauntily strode across the street, weaving through stopped traffic, jaywalking without a care in the world and with a smile on her lips.

What was it like to feel so untouchable?

So above it all?

The rules.

The world.

The light turned green. Leo cut a taxi off to change lanes, earning a prolonged five-second beep. Some pedestrians paused and turned, tourists probably. Most kept on walking, including Jo. His brows scrunched. Something about her was too... He didn't know. Too something. Unaware? Aloof? For a wanted criminal fully cognizant of the fact that the FBI was on her trail, she was a little too oblivious. The hairs on the back of his neck stood, a sixth sense that something wasn't right. Something was off. But what?

Jo disappeared around the corner.

Leo followed.

The street was packed. A line wrapped around the sidewalk, stretching a few blocks down, leading to a yellow awning in the distance. Nate nudged his chin in that direction, but Leo was already on it. He scanned the road.

"I don't see any place to park."

Nate sighed. "That's because there is no place to park."

"There's a side street right there, smaller, less crowded," Leo said, tilting his head to the right. "Let's wait there and listen to the comms."

Nate clenched his teeth but nodded. There was no other choice. He lifted the mic to his lips as they drove by Jo, moving with the flow of traffic. Her eyes never once turned in his direction, which was either a very good or a very, very bad thing. "Okay, Leo and I are stuck. We're pulling around the corner to park. I want eyes on and updates when you have them."

"I'm here," one of the street agents murmured. "Flashed my badge and cut the line to get inside the bakery."

Nate turned in his seat, straining to see Jo over his shoulder. But it was nearly impossible with the crowd.

"Do these people really line up like this every day?" he muttered.

Leo shrugged. "I would if I had the time. My brother's office got a personal delivery of cronuts when they were at the peak of their buzz, said it was like eating little bites of heaven. I've been dying to try one."

Nate rolled his eyes.

Leo's younger brother was a software engineer for one of those major companies, though Nate could never remember which. He lived out in San Francisco and earned the sort of paycheck normal people could only dream of. But he was a good kid. And he knew how much Leo had looked out for him when they were teens, getting in fights to protect him from bullies, keeping him out of trouble and far away from the gang violence pervading their community. Last Nate heard, Leo's brother had bought their mom a new house in California, moving her out of the dangerous neighborhood where he and Leo had grown up.

"I don't care how good it tastes," Nate grumbled, turning back around and dropping his gaze to the tablet, hoping something might pop up on her cell phone feed.

"Jolene Carter just walked inside the front door," a staticky voice came through the comm. Whispering always made the signal weaker. Nate leaned forward, focusing on the sound. "She's walking to the counter. She's in the preorder line. Three people are in front of her, but she doesn't seem to be communicating with anyone."

He tapped his thumb on his knee, jittery.

"Two people now."

He clamped his palm around his thigh to stop the fidgeting.

"One person."

Nate swallowed.

"Okay, she's at the counter. Reaching into her purse. Appears to be a wallet. Taking out a credit card. The cashier is handing her a box. It's sort of a tangerine orange. She's smiling. He's smiling. He handed her back her card. She took the box. I can't see anything unusual about it. She's turning. She's walking out. She's leaving. Not sure I can follow without my cover being blown."

"I'm outside," another voice jumped in. "Across the street. Eyes on. She's walking through the door now. Hold on, she's stopping. She's reaching into the box. She's taking something out, it's a...a...oh. It's just a doughnut or something. Oh wait, she's reaching into her purse now. Pulling out...her cell phone again. I don't see any contacts close by, but it's crowded. She's looking at the screen. Lifting it. Maybe searching for a signal."

Nate zeroed in on the tablet in his lap.

What app was she opening?

Was she trying to make a Bluetooth transfer?

Was she trying to call someone?

Was she—

"I think she's taking a selfie."

Nate closed his eyes, squeezing tight as he lifted his fingers to the ridge of his nose.

That was exactly what she was doing.

A selfie.

A goddamn selfie.

Was this what his life had come to?

"I can confirm, she opened the camera app on her phone," Nate said with a sigh, trying to remove the aggravation from his tone.

Leo snickered.

"Okay, yeah, she put the cell phone back in her bag," the agent continued, a little bit of the energy gone from his voice. Nate dropped his head against the back of his seat and closed his eyes as every single life decision he'd ever made ran through his thoughts, making him wonder how he'd gotten here, to this assignment.

Patience, Nathaniel. His father's voice cut through his thoughts.

Patience. Patience.

The one lesson Nate hadn't had enough time with him to learn.

"The target is back on the move. She's crossing the street. Heading east. Turning a corner. I lost visual. I repeat, I lost visual."

Wait…

Heading east?

Turning a corner?

Nate's eyes flew open.

A gentle knock drummed on his window.

His head fell to the side slowly, reluctantly.

"Morning, Agent Parker, Agent Alvarez," Jo said with a wave, looking at them over the rim of her sunglasses, a grin across her red lips. "Want a cronut?"

- 9 -

Jo

If she could have bottled this moment to save it for later, she would have. His face was priceless. Absolutely priceless. The perfect mix of stony contempt and unabashed admiration, perhaps a little heavier on the stony contempt. But Jo took the fact that she was getting to him as an unintentional compliment—it would've been far worse if he'd shown no emotion at all.

After a brief pause, he lifted his hand and pressed a button on the door.

His window rolled down.

"Miss Carter," he half growled, half greeted.

Jo smiled cheerily. "Cronut? They're delicious."

And they were, they really freaking were—much as she loathed to admit it, professional jealousy and all that. But the cronut was nothing like the doussant she'd invented ten years ago during that first long, lonely year on the private island. This was perfect. Flaky. Fried. Doughy. Dipped in sugar. Filled with cream. Finished off with a light yet necessary glaze that tied the entire thing together. Dominique Ansel was a god, and Jo was a mere mortal.

Though, hopefully, my coopie will help change that!

Jo stretched the box closer to the window, letting the smell of the pastry fill the small car, trying to hold back a smile. She'd woken up at the crack of dawn two weeks ago to place a preorder for a full box of six cronuts, refreshing the web page over and over in a frenzy until her order processed. Sure, she could've hacked her way into the system to place an order, but sometimes, doing things the hard way was more fun. And the payout was even sweeter.

Jo met Agent Parker's exasperated gaze. "You know you want one…"

He didn't move. His partner, however, lunged across the seats and reached into the box.

"Leo." Agent Parker whipped his head to the side.

His partner shrugged and took a massive bite, eyes closing in blissful joy as he chewed. It was hard to tell with his mouth full, but Jo was pretty sure she heard him mumble the words, "So good."

She looked back at Mr. Stiff, leaning down so her elbows rested on his windowsill, putting their faces about a foot apart. He swallowed and narrowed his eyes but didn't say anything. Jo shook the box.

"No laws were broken during the procurement of these cronuts," she teased, letting her voice drop to a low, sultry whisper. "I promise."

He held her gaze, not moving.

So, Jo did the same thing right back.

He frowned.

She smiled.

The moment stretched on and on and on, until—

"I'll take another one…in case he wants it later," Agent Alvarez, or Leo, as Mr. Stiff had called him, reached back across the seats to grab another pastry from the box.

Jo waited until he was done before shrugging and breaking eye contact with Agent Parker. She stood, folded the box back together, and dropped it into her purse. Then she lifted her arms over her shoulders with a sigh, letting her head fall back, basking in the sunlight as she stretched. She'd practiced the move in the mirror earlier, fully aware of the exposed stretch of skin flashing at just about eye level to Agent Parker right now, a few inches of smooth, flat stomach.

She dropped her arms. "There's nothing like New York on a hot spring day."

Agent Parker curled his upper lip and let out a derisive puff of air.

Jo stared down at him, curious. "Don't you just love being surrounded by so many people?"

Jo did. She spent too much of her life alone. She thrived on the crowd, on how easily she could disappear into the folds and pretend to be normal, how easily she could blend in, just another tourist.

Funny how at home, she so often felt lost despite knowing exactly where she was. But here, in these swarming streets, dependent on a map to get around, she'd never felt more alive, more found. Though, maybe that had more to do with the fact that she knew someone was paying attention.

"No." The grumpy word slipped through Agent Parker's mouth. Jo folded her lips to keep from laughing as he twitched slightly at the sound and then lifted his gaze to meet hers. "Too much traffic."

"But there's such a vivacious energy," she said, inhaling deeply, as though the air were a drug and breathing a high all its own.

He wrinkled his nose. "There's a smell."

"Well," she countered, cocking her hip to the side and raising her brows in challenge. "If you stepped outside that stuffy car, you might think differently. I've got a few more bakeries on my list and not a soul to share them with. Interested in going for a stroll? Or would you prefer I continue on my merry way and pretend I don't see you following me?"

"I'm quite comfortable where I am, Miss Carter," he said, leaning back into his seat and folding his arms, shifting his gaze to the front window instead of her face, literally staring at a brick wall instead of her.

"Never thought I'd see the day that a good southern boy from Virginia would pass up the opportunity to accompany a lady…" Jo prodded, sharpening her tone ever so slightly. Oh, she could flirt and play nice, but she wanted him to remember she wasn't some silly girl he was dealing with. And she didn't plan to go down without a fight. "I guess chivalry really is dead."

His gaze snapped toward her.

She winked.

Yeah, that's right, Agent Parker—or should I say Nathaniel Parker. I did my research.

Agent Parker was the son of a former FBI agent who died almost twenty years ago while undercover. He was the oldest of three children. His mother still lived in the 1892 center-hall Colonial where he'd grown up. He graduated top of his class in high school and college. Earned a master's degree in criminal justice. Joined the agency young and quickly rose to the top ranks, gaining a highly sought-after position in the competitive organized crime unit. All of which led Jo to wonder how in the world he'd landed here, hunting an art thief and his daughter.

Agent Parker clenched his jaw, refusing to respond.

"Suit yourself." Jo shrugged, letting the carefree tone slide back into her voice. Then she finally let her lips break out into the wide, brimming smile she'd been suppressing for the past few minutes. "Just try your best to keep up."

She spun on her heels and slapped her palm against the roof of their car twice, drowning out any response either agent might have muttered. And then she took her phone out of her bag and proceeded to do exactly what she'd told them she would—visit three more bakeries while chatting with her girlfriends to keep herself entertained.

@TheBakingBandit: You'll never guess where I am...
@Sprinkle-Ella: Where?! Where?!

Jo sent the selfie she'd taken with her cronut.

@Sprinkle-Ella: OMG! Jealous! I want to go to NY so badly!
@TheGourmetGoddess: Ugh. Still can't believe the one weekend you come to NY is the one weekend I'm out of town. What are the chances?

Pretty good, Jo thought, chewing on her lip. Because well, McKenzie, the Gourmet Goddess, was speaking at the annual American Pastry Chef Association conference being held in California for the next few days. And Jo may, or may not, have had something to do with introducing her name to the organizers. If she had, for argument's sake of course, it would have included hacking into one of their computers and planting her friend's information into the conference files. But McKenzie totally deserved the recognition, so Jo hardly considered it a breach of the rules, and it hadn't really been about her friend anyway.

Keeping the two vastly different sides of her life from ever crossing paths was of vital importance to Jo—baking was baking, crime was crime, and never the two should meet. Which was why she refrained from divulging personal details in their chats, keeping the conversations focused on craft, and went out of her way to ensure they'd never meet in real life, planned or accidental. Digital deceit was one thing, but Jo never wanted to put herself in a situation where she'd have to look her friends in the eye and lie to their faces. They were her escape from this life, and she planned to keep it that way.

@TheBakingBandit: How's the conference??

@TheGourmetGoddess: Great! My panel isn't until tomorrow, and the food tents don't begin until the weekend when the conference opens to the public, so right now I'm just enjoying myself and trying not to freak out. Get back to me in the morning.

@Sprinkle-Ella: You'll be amazing!! And so will your food!

Wish I could be there!

@TheBakingBandit: Agreed! No need to freak!

McKenzie was an eternal perfectionist, something she vented to Jo and Addison about all the time. It was one of the reasons she'd been drawn to pastries—all the precision and calculations. Jo and Addison, on the other hand, were a little bit freer with their baking. Okay, Jo was a lot freer…and sometimes it gave McKenzie anxiety. But it was all part of how their odd little threesome worked. Addison's eternal optimism, Jo's unfailing enthusiasm, and McKenzie's endearing snark.

@TheGourmetGoddess: So, Jo, what's the verdict on the cronut? Tasty enough to end your unrequited grudge?

@TheBakingBandit: Maybe…

@TheBakingBandit: But if he starts selling a coopie, it's back on in a heartbeat! That goes for all of you…

@TheGourmetGoddess: Shaking in my Louboutin boots.

@Sprinkle-Ella: I'd kill for Louboutin boots, watch out!

@TheGourmetGoddess: You couldn't kill a fly, let alone me :)

@Sprinkle-Ella: I just got commissioned to bake a black wedding cake…black! My lethal instincts have increased since the last time we spoke.

@TheBakingBandit: Black?! Sounds fun!

@Sprinkle-Ella: You would say that… It's tragic.

@TheBakingBandit: It's unique! A challenge!

@TheGourmetGoddess: If you need a recipe for a great ebony fondant, let me know. I have two go-to formulas, one using cocoa powder for a chocolate flavor, and one for vanilla that uses a perfect ratio of different dyes to get a deep, rich color.

@Sprinkle-Ella: Please send! The struggle is real. My boss said I needed to step out of my comfort zone. But I ask you, what is wrong with sugar flowers, lace piping, fondant ribbons, and a gold accent here and there? Nothing! Nothing!!

@TheGourmetGoddess: Relax, killer. Don't bust a tiara…

Jo snorted at McKenzie's comment and popped the last bite of macaroon through her lips, sighing with satisfaction as the nutty almond and sweet coconut flavors exploded in her mouth, perfectly accented by the hints of lavender in the jelly. Her food tour of Greenwich Village had not disappointed. She was high on the sugar, her stomach ached from being too full, and every calorie had been absolutely worth it. With all four of the bakeries she'd wanted to visit crossed off her list, it was time to get to work. She was supposed to meet Thad in forty-five minutes, which left just enough time to lose her tail and catch a subway uptown.

Jo turned to glance over her shoulder.

Agents Parker and Alvarez were parked three cars back at the other end of the street.

She waved.

Nathaniel dropped the binoculars, and even from this distance, Jo thought she noticed a frown across his alluring lips. At first, she'd been toying with him for the fun of it, for the entertainment and the challenge. But Jo had to admit, she almost respected his steadfast loyalty to the rules. There was something admirable in it. Something undeniably charming, almost sexy, in the way he refused to give in to her taunts, to her game. Something—

Jo shook her head and turned back around. *Something I shouldn't be feeling or thinking about. Not now. Not ever.*

She took a deep breath and grabbed her bag, then stood, reluctant to leave the peaceful spot where she'd been sitting for the past twenty minutes—a chair outside of a small coffee shop, situated directly in the warm sun, right next to a little park. Nothing went better with macaroons than a fresh latte. This was New York City at its best.

Now I've got to be me, at my worst.

Jo stepped back through the glass door to the café, making for the bathroom. Once inside, she let her bag slip to the floor and crouched, searching through her things for the small set of precision screwdrivers she kept with her at all times—meant for making jewelry, but they worked perfectly for picking locks, or in this case, popping her cell phone casing open. Jo kept the device for purely personal reasons—social media for her baking blog, chatting with her friends. But she wasn't a fool. She knew the FBI could track her location—heck, could probably see everything she was doing, maybe even record her voice through the microphone if she wasn't careful. So before meeting Thad, it had to be off. Not just turned off, but battery-out off. Completely dead and undetectable. A turn of the screwdriver, a pop, a twist, a quick unplug, and she was good to go.

Jo walked out of the bathroom, keeping an eye on the man in the corner who'd been working on his laptop—an undercover agent, she suspected, judging by the way his hoodie was pulled up to cover his ears and the casual glances he'd been sending her way.

They made eye contact briefly.

Yup. Definitely undercover. And probably just alerted that my cell phone went offline. Jo didn't stand down. She held his gaze, waiting for him to look away, and then smirked. *Well, boys. Let the games begin.*

Jo cut through the back hallway, past the kitchen, not caring as a voice called that she wasn't supposed to be back there, that it was for staff only. She'd looked the building plans up a few days ago and picked this bakery as her last one specifically because it had a back door that opened to a small side street, close to the West Fourth subway station, which had enough platforms and enough staircases to lose the Feds.

Jo slipped through the door and into the street, then shifted into an all-out sprint. Turning one corner. Then another. The streets were smaller down here than they were in midtown where the city was mostly in a grid, which gave her the advantage. Within two minutes, she was running down the subway steps, taking them two at a time. The Feds followed her, she was sure. She hadn't lost them yet, but she just needed to stay one step ahead, and she'd be fine.

After paying for the ride, she followed two more sets of steps down until she reached the bottom level of tracks, and then slipped around to the back side of a staircase, pressing herself against the concrete wall, which was wide enough to hide four of her.

Because it was New York, no one stared as she pulled a black wig from her bag and slipped it carefully over her bun, pressing any straying auburn strands under the edge. Then she pulled a brown dress over her head, tugged the cotton sleeves all the way down to her wrists, and spread the black hair over her shoulders to hide any bits of blue from sight. Large black-rimmed glasses with rose-tinted lenses went over her eyes. And then she opened a compact and held it around the bend, looking into the reflection to see if any bodies came running down the steps after her.

Two men in street clothes barreled through the crowd. Jo shut her mirror and dropped it back into her bag, the only thing she hadn't camouflaged. But it was beige, hardly enough to stand out, and she kept it by her knees just in case.

Two minutes went by, during which Jo stepped far enough away from the concrete steps to not be so obviously hiding behind them, but close enough to still have cover. The agents split. One ran right by her as she kept her chin ducked, pretending to play with the dead phone in her hands. A train finally came. The agent within sight stepped on, bringing a smile to her lips as Jo joined the line of people exiting the train, molding to the crowd and following the pack back up the stairs where she'd come. Jo cut her way across the station to a different platform and got there right as an uptown train came to a stop.

Easy-peasy. No more Feds.

Twenty minutes later, she found Thad sitting on a bench in Central Park wearing a blond wig and a tailored gray suit, with a sandwich foil open on his lap—the image of an unconcerned businessman taking his lunch break. If not for the telltale dimples digging into his cheeks, she might not have noticed him right away.

"You got away no problem?" he asked as she sat down on the other end of the bench.

Jo smiled. "Obviously. You?"

"No problem." He took a bite and paused to chew, keeping his eyes on the field spread out before them, searching for anyone who might be glancing their way. "They had undercover agents parked outside the museum, the auction house, and the townhome. I took a long walk, letting them see me go by each one, not stopping long enough to take note of anything of importance. Then I lost my tail, got in disguise, and circled back to the target. There are two traffic cameras that might have the front door of the house within view, and another where we're planning the getaway, not to mention the private security we already know about."

Jo shrugged. "Easy enough to deal with."

"My thought too," he said with a nod and took another bite. "There were trucks parked outside, starting to set up for the gala. I pretended one of the movers bumped into me and started an argument on the street, behind the side of the truck where the street cams couldn't see. In the commotion, I slipped the router you wanted me to plant onto the underside of one of the tables."

"Good."

The device wasn't a router, per se. That was just the easiest way she'd been able to explain it to Thad and her father. In reality, it sent out a signal only her computer could detect, allowing her to easily hack her way through the firewalls by turning her foreign device into one recognized as internal by the system. Highly illegal. But what else was new? When she got back to her hotel, she'd have access to the house's internet, which should let her go into the security system without detection. From there, she could do basically whatever she wanted.

"That agent still on your ass?" Thad murmured, recapturing her attention. Jo grinned. She'd told him about her antics with Agent Parker, and suffice it to say, Thad had not been amused.

"I bet he wishes he were under it," she commented smoothly.

Thad almost choked on his sandwich. "Jo Jo."

"It's harmless."

"It's dangerous."

"It's entertaining."

"It's reckless."

Jo couldn't help it. She broke the rules and turned to stare into his stormy eyes. "Oh please, you can't be serious, giving me a lecture. You've got a girl in every city of this country just waiting for your call. Just try to tell me you slept alone last night. I dare you."

The corner of his lip began to rise, but he forced it to stop. "That's different. They're not cops."

"And nothing is going to happen," Jo bit back. "My flirting is keeping him distracted. It's not only fun, it's advantageous. I might as well use all the tools in my arsenal."

"That's all...?" Thad dipped his chin as he probed her expression.

Jo shifted her head forward again. "That's all."

"The gala is three days away. You do your part, and I'll do the rest. Meet back tomorrow, same time, second rendezvous point."

"Done," Jo agreed.

Without another glance, Thad stood and crumpled the empty sandwich wrap in his hand before tossing it into the trash. Then he paused with his back still turned, but his head angled casually toward her.

"Forgot to ask—how was the cronut?"

Jo released a dejected puff of air. "Ungodly delicious."

A soft peal of laughter escaped his lips before he walked away, shoulders shaking ever so slightly as he disappeared into the crowd. The less time they spent with each other, the better, which was why they'd discussed the plan so elaborately before. But that didn't make her feel any less alone.

Jo waited another half an hour or so before she got up from the bench and hailed a cab. The driver deposited her back at her hotel, where an agent waited in plain clothes in the lobby. She nodded to the woman as she walked by and made her way to the elevator, preparing for a long, lonely night of typing ahead.

- 10 -

Nate

"I think she's going in, sir," Nate muttered into the mic at his wrist. He kept the camera at his eyes and zoomed in as Jo Carter climbed the grand front steps to the Metropolitan Museum of Art. They'd followed her to two more bakeries that morning—Nate for the life of him didn't understand how a woman who ate like her looked like her as well, but that was beside the point. He was still furious about losing her the day before, a failure that was only accentuated by the fact that as soon as she'd returned to her hotel room, she'd found all five of the bugs they'd had a team plant while she was gone. He'd heard them go out, one by one by one, leaving dead silence. Meaning, he had nothing. Abso-freaking nothing. "Should we send someone in? This is about the same time she lost us yesterday."

"Yeah. Beta team already lost Ryder, about an hour ago. There's definitely a meet going down, and I want eyes on this time." Their boss came on the line. Nate met Leo's gaze. They sighed together. Clearly, he wasn't happy with the performance thus far. "I want you to go in, Parker."

Nate choked on his breath. "Excuse me, sir?"

"You heard me, Parker. She seems to like you. Even invited you to join her yesterday. Why don't we give the woman what she wants?"

"She was trying to get a rise out of me, sir," Nate countered. "Nothing more."

He could practically hear his boss shrug through the comms. "Even so, she might talk to you, if you ask the right questions. You might be able to distract her enough to cause her to slip up. Just put on some charm, Parker."

Nate curled his upper lip. "With all due respect, sir, if you want charm, we should send in my partner."

"Hey now," Leo cut in, speaking directly to Nate and not into his mic. "Don't drag me into this."

Nate shot a glare in his direction while the radio buzzed with static.

"Let's go, Parker."

"But, sir—"

"Parker."

"Sir, I—"

"Now, Parker. That's an order."

Nate squeezed his eyes shut and curled his hands into fists, letting his frustration funnel through his clenched muscles, making his arms tremble. "Yes, sir."

"Good luck, lover boy," Leo chimed as Nate reluctantly shoved his door open and eased from the car. "I'll grab you a hot dog from the vendor down the street."

At that, Nate did turn. "Don't even think about it, Leo."

"You've got to get over this aversion to street food—"

"Not in this lifetime," he grumbled and shut the door behind him, cutting off Leo's retort.

Nate darted around the traffic as the light switched to red and then cut through the crowd gathered outside the museum, eating lunch on the famed steps. Taking the stairs two at a time, he rushed for the front entrance, skipping the line and heading directly to the security guards just inside the front door. A flash of his badge was all it took for them to let him through the metal detectors and into the museum. The grand atrium was lined with columns, topped by sweeping arches that soared across the giant two-story foyer. Clumps of people stood by the information counter in the center of the room and at the ticket booths on either end. A whole line swept along the far wall, people waiting to deposit bags and coats in the check, and that was where a spot of auburn caught his eye.

"Excuse me, excuse me," he murmured politely, cutting through the crowd, not using his badge this time but the pretense of familiarity. "Excuse me, yes, I'm with that woman up there. Thank you."

On and on, until the sound of his voice finally filtered into her ear. Jo turned slowly. Her red lips puckered, caught between a smile and a self-satisfied smirk. She put her hand to her chest and raised her gaze to the ceiling for a moment, shaking her head ever so slightly.

"Be still my beating heart. Nathaniel Parker, here to see me," she cooed.

"Ask and you shall receive," he murmured, doing his best to be charming.

Ugh, charming.

He hated that word. He'd rather be real. Authentic. Truthful in the fact that Jolene Carter and everything she stood for disgusted him.

She raised a dubious brow, almost as though she could read the thought running through his brain, and leaned into his chest. Stretching onto her tippy-toes, she brought their faces close together, far too close, and pressed her lips against his ear. Voice low and laced with innuendo, she whispered, "What exactly will I receive?"

Nate clenched his muscles and held his body stiff as a board, keeping his stance wide and his arms by his sides, not giving in to the taunt. His spine was straight. His every nerve was on high alert, prepared for two very different kinds of assault—and he wasn't quite sure which one he preferred in that moment.

Jo released a throaty chuckle as she patted her palm against his chest. "Loosen up, Agent Parker, or you'll give the game away."

"Next," an attendant announced.

Jo sighed reluctantly and dropped her arm. Nate released a long breath, watching as she stepped up to the counter and plopped her large tote bag onto the surface. After a few seconds of rummaging, she tugged a smaller shoulder bag free and slipped it over her head. The attendant took her things and handed her a ticket. Nate strained his neck trying to read the number, but when she turned back around, Jo saw. She arched a wry brow and deftly flipped the paper in her fingers, presenting him with the black block letters.

"Ticket number one hundred and eighty-two," Jo murmured and then reached for his hand. Easily finding his mic, she brought it to her lips. "In case you were wondering. Though I think you'll be disappointed with what you find inside."

Nate shook her off with a frown as his gaze dropped to the smaller bag securely strapped to her body, resting snug against her hip. Not big enough for a computer— the computer. The one that if he could just for a minute get his hands on, would have all the evidence he'd ever need to get Robert Carter put in jail for life. Agents had spent an hour searching her small hotel room for it yesterday, and again this morning, to no avail. But though she was bold, he hardly believed she had the audacity to leave a laptop full of illegal activity at the coat check.

"I couldn't make it too easy for you, Parker," she murmured, eyes sparkling with silent mirth, silent challenge. "What would be the fun in that?"

What, indeed... he thought, holding her gaze, trying to read the secrets swirling in those smoky jade eyes, bright yet opaque and inscrutable. And then he sighed. *Charming. Charming. Try to be charming.*

"So, what brings you to the museum today," he asked, changing the subject and lightening his tone, shifting to something more conversational.

Jo blinked into his face.

Once. Twice.

And then her entire body convulsed with laughter. She doubled over, clutching her stomach around the middle as her torso shook, then raised her hands to her lips to catch the bubbling noise.

"What?" he questioned, honestly confused.

Jo stared at him, still trembling, mouth covered by her fingers.

"What?" His tone was a little sterner this time, a little more defensive.

"What brings me…?" She barely got the words out before her voice filtered off into breathy glee. She shook her head, auburn hair falling over her cheeks, and then took a deep sigh. "Art, Agent Parker. Art brings me to the museum today. What about you? Just out for a stroll and decided you wanted to take in some ancient artifacts, maybe a Roman sculpture or two?"

He ignored the jibes, something he was becoming all too skilled at. "Art, huh?" He paused, frowning. "We both know you're not the artist in the family."

Jo shrugged. "I'm broadening my horizons."

Then she spun on her heels and walked across the atrium, fully aware he had no choice but to follow as she cut through the crowds, swerving between bodies, bumping into one or two. Nate kept his gaze sharp, but he didn't see Ryder in the swarm. Or any other face he recognized.

A static fuzz came through his comm, followed by, "You're surprisingly terrible at witty banter, Parker."

"Thanks, Leo," he drawled. "Very helpful."

"No, no, keep at it. We were all in need of some entertainment after yesterday. You're doing a great job."

"I'm turning the mic off," he grumbled.

"Don't even think about it, Parker," his boss cut in.

Nate clenched his jaw.

And then clenched it tighter as a snicker came through the line.

Great, just great.

She's turning me into the office joke.

But they were right—witty banter, not really his forte. He lacked the patience and the blasé attitude. Wasting time made his blood curdle. He wanted to cut through the surface, straight to the core. He wanted to cut deep enough to make her pause.

But how? he thought as he followed her up the steps to the second floor. How to cut through smoke and mirrors? How to cut through the façade and see the real woman underneath? Jo hadn't spared a moment to glance back, but he had the sense she knew he was right behind her, that she was just as aware of his presence as he was of hers.

When she eventually came to a stop, the room he found himself standing in was hardly a surprise—the impressionist exhibit. Nate stepped close behind her, leaning down and keeping his voice low as he stared into the painting she'd sought out—a sweeping canvas of pastel brushstrokes, soft and sinuous, depicting crashing waves in the hazy light of dawn.

"You are your father's daughter," he murmured, trying to goad her into discussing something a little deeper.

Jo jolted and then relaxed, the tension seeping from her frame as quick as it'd come. She shrugged. "Monet was a master."

"I've heard rumors you've been far closer to his work than this," Nate hinted, fully aware of the intel that Robert Carter had a stolen painting in his possession. "Had your hands on the gilded frame, in the dark shadows of an underground vault, perhaps."

Jo kept her eyes on the artwork, though a smile tugged at her lips. "Hearsay doesn't hold up in court."

Her walls were up, reinforced with steel.

Mentioning her dad wasn't the way in. At least, not like this.

Jo wandered to the next canvas, another Monet. A classic water lily this time. Though she stared at the swirls and globs of paint, Nate got the distinct feeling her mind was on something else. Especially as her focus shifted and she scanned the room.

"Looking for someone?"

"I already found him." Jo tossed him a sidelong glance, throwing in a wink. "More like, he found me."

Nate sighed. They were back to meaningless flirtations. He wouldn't get anything out of her like this, not that he really thought he had a chance of getting anything out of her at all. But he needed to. The entire operation depended on him. They needed more info. More intel. Anything. Or Robert Carter would slip out of reach yet again, maybe this time for good—and the Russians Nate's team had spent years tracking would slip away with him.

Jo walked around Nate and into another room of impressionist paintings. Her gaze darted over a few canvases before settling on one. Nate followed the path of her eyes, trying to see what had caught her attention. A still life with apples, fruits, and an uneaten slice of pie.

Pie! Of course, pie.

Why didn't I think of that before?

Nate leaned down, keeping his voice casual. "I should have known."

"Huh?" Jo turned to look up at him, honest surprise written across her face.

He nudged his chin in the direction of the artwork that had caught her eye. "You have an obsession with baked goods."

"Obsession?" Jo froze, a thin trace of ire laced through her tone.

It was Nate's turn to force back a grin. He was onto something. Finally, after so many meaningless words, he could tell from her voice he'd finally found something she cared about. And he planned to milk it for all it was worth.

"Yeah, obsession." He emphasized the word, getting a thrill as her nose wrinkled with unspoken protest. "You've dragged me to half the bakeries in Manhattan. Practically tried to force-feed me a cronut and a coopa, or whatever it was you called it."

"Coopie," she corrected, voice clipped, defensive.

"Huh?" He feigned ignorance, pushing a button he didn't realize could so easily be pressed, not with the calculated, confident Jolene Carter.

"Coo-*pie*," she repeated, stressing the second syllable as flames gleamed to life in the centers of her eyes, sparks of angry fire. "A cookie in a pie. A coopie."

Nate shrugged.

Her irises flashed brighter.

The edge of his lip twitched. "Cute."

Somehow he knew that single word would set her off.

He wasn't disappointed.

Jo put her hands on her hips and narrowed her eyes so they burned like lasers. At least, he guessed that was the general effect she'd been going for. Instead, he was amused.

And it's about damn time!

She'd had the upper hand for far too long. He'd almost forgotten what it felt like up here, where the air was cleaner, fresher. Nate took a deep breath, soaking in that sweet, cool scent of victory, letting it fill his lungs as the woman before him continued to fume. He straightened his spine, using his height to his advantage as he looked triumphantly down at her.

"Cute?" she spat with disbelief. "Cute? Mark my words, Nathaniel Parker, the coopie is going to be huge. The coopie is going to take the world by storm."

"So that's the big endgame?" Nate countered, bringing the conversation full circle now that her defenses were down, now that she was, for the first time, edging on vulnerable. "Internationally renowned hacker and wanted criminal turned…baker?"

Jo blinked and swallowed.

For a moment he swore, he *swore*, uncertainty flickered in her gaze.

Nate pressed the advantage. "Can I ask you a question, Jo? How is that going to work? The Feds will never stop hunting you. We're not in the habit of letting felons go gentle into that good night. Ride off into the sunset. Live happily ever after."

Jo stared at him. Her chest pulsed with heavy breaths, stretching in and out, rising and falling, filling the space between them with something new, something that almost felt the slightest bit like fear.

"We catch you," Nate continued, hammering the final nail in her coffin. "And we put you in jail."

- 11 -

Jo

Jo sucked in a slow breath. He didn't know, he *couldn't* know, that he was dangling her greatest hope and her greatest worry right before her eyes, a careful balancing act that teetered on the precipice of all the things she was too scared to dream of and too scared not to.

She had to regain control of the situation.

She had to hit him where it hurt.

Jo swallowed and tried to wipe the stress from her features, the little cracks in her façade that gave him a view to a place she didn't want a Fed to have access to— her heart. "Haven't you ever had a dream, Agent Parker?"

Good, she thought to herself as the words slipped out, calm and collected and verging on dismissive. Not heady and full of unspoken desires.

He narrowed his gaze. Those baby-blues darted across her face, trying to dissect every line etched into her skin, the reflective glass of a microscope as it zoomed in. Then he shrugged. "I'm living mine."

He answered like she thought he would.

A gift presenting her with the perfect opening.

Jo raised her brows and cocked her hip, leaning her weight to one side as she shifted a little closer, getting into his personal space. His eyes dropped to her chest, rose to her lips, then settled on her eyes. Proximity was an underestimated weapon.

"Ah, yes… Taking after dear old Dad." She said it like an accusation, making her voice breathy and seductive, reaching for any trick at her disposal to regain the upper hand as her words fired like a bullet straight to the center of his chest.

Agent Parker's gaze hardened to cut sapphire as a blaze of pain passed over his irises, quick as lightning, gone in a flash, leaving glass in its wake. "My father was a hero."

His voice was raw.

Hurt.

The sound made Jo pause.

She'd known the jab would pinch, but she hadn't thought it would land as true as it did. Actually, she'd found surprisingly little information about the entire incident, even with her very specialized skills. His father had died twenty years before, killed while on active duty, leaving Agent Parker's mother to raise her three children alone. But now, staring into his eyes, Jo had to wonder if there was something more—something that had never made the news, something the bureau had helped bury.

Jo thought of her own mother. Lost to cancer. Just another statistic to an outside viewer, yet a decade had gone by, and the wound still bled. Open and aching. The sort of cut that never healed, no matter how much time had passed.

Idiot. Idiot.

Guilt churned in her gut. She never should have said anything. She never should have brought it up. Never should have used that lowest of the low blows against him.

"I—" Jo started to apologize, but Nate cut her off.

"At least my father is someone I can be proud of."

Jo's hackles immediately rose. *And I was about to apologize to this oaf!* "I'm proud of my father."

"Proud of a criminal?" Agent Parker scoffed.

Jo pressed her pointer finger into the center of his firm chest. "Proud of a man who took care of his family in the only way he knew how. Proud of a man who pushed his own grief aside to ease mine. Proud of a man who has done everything within his power to keep the people he loves safe from anyone who might wish us harm, including you."

"Me?" He guffawed. "Safe from me? Do you have any idea who your father even is? What he's done? He's a bad person, Jo. The worst kind. I'm trying to keep other people safe from him."

Something in his accusation made her heart thunder in her chest. The disbelief in his tone. The earnestness. The conviction.

Why? she almost wanted to ask. *What for?*

Her father was a crook, a thief. He stole art. He sold forgeries. He had a lot of money he probably shouldn't. Sure, he wasn't the role model of the century, but there were worse people in the world. Dangerous people. Real criminals. He wasn't hurting anyone. Not really.

...right?

Jo licked her lips as her mouth went dry.

"You and I have different interpretations of the word 'bad,'" she murmured, trying to brush his accusation aside. But the hoarse tone of her voice was unconvincing, even to her.

"There's only one interpretation."

"Oh really?" she charged, letting her frustration carry her forward. Anger was so much easier than doubt, so much easier than fear. "A man goes into a grocery store and gets caught stealing a jar of peanut butter and a loaf of bread, good or bad?"

"Bad," Agent Parker answered immediately, no hesitation.

"Okay. A man who just got laid off from work goes into a grocery store and gets caught stealing a jar of peanut butter and a loaf of bread, good or bad?"

He shrugged and again answered easily. "Bad."

"Fine. A man who just got laid off from work, who is drowning in debt from his late wife's medical bills, goes into a grocery store and gets caught stealing a jar of peanut butter and a loaf of bread, good or bad?"

Agent Parker swallowed, pausing for a moment. "There are other ways…"

"Good or bad?" Jo pressed.

He shifted his feet, but a challenge sparked in his gaze. "Fine. Bad."

"Okay. Now a man who just got laid off from work, who is drowning in debt from his late wife's medical bills, who has three children at home who haven't eaten a real meal in three days, goes into a grocery store and gets caught stealing a jar of peanut butter and a loaf of bread, good or bad?"

"A crime is a crime," he responded firmly.

"That's not what I asked," Jo countered. "I asked if he's a good person or a bad person."

"The law works in black and white."

"Well, maybe it shouldn't." Jo shrugged. "Not when the world is awash in shades of gray."

Agent Parker threw up his hands as he grunted and shook his head. "What does this have to do with anything we were talking about? We were talking about you. About your father. Not some poor victim of circumstance."

"Well, here's another hypothetical for you," Jo answered. Deep inside, her better sense screamed at her to shut up, but she couldn't. Because she didn't want to be seen as the bad guy, as the villain. She didn't want him to see her that way. "A fourteen-year-old girl who doesn't have a care in the world aside from boys and school and her Easy-Bake oven finds out her mother has an aggressive form of cancer and only has a few months to live. Her father chooses the night of her mother's funeral to come clean about his true profession, asking for forgiveness, asking for love, for loyalty. So she gives it. And she keeps giving it, pushing all her own dreams aside, because they are all each other has in the world. Good person or bad person?"

Agent Parker's face softened.

His shoulders dropped from their tense position around his neck. He lifted his hand, as though to stretch it across the space separating them, and then paused. "Jo."

She stepped back and arched a brow, holding on to the challenge in her voice, to the fight, to the fire. This man wanted to lock her in a jail cell for the rest of her life, wanted to put her father away, Thad, everyone she loved. No baking. No friends. No life. And maybe she deserved it. But she had to hold on to the idea that she didn't—or she would crumble. "Good person or bad person, Agent Parker?"

His jaw clenched.

Those stern brows pressed together, hard.

"Bad," he answered finally, forcing the word through his lips, making it sound almost like a confession.

Jo released a sad puff of air as she raised her brows for a moment and held his gaze. "Then I guess we're done here."

She turned and walked away.

Let him try to follow.

The museum was a maze of small rooms and open doors and crowded hallways, giving her the obvious advantage as she slipped from one spot to the next. Jo had planned to meet Thad in front of the Monet, one of his favorites, but they'd made eye contact the second she'd walked into the room, and he'd fled immediately. Knowing Thad, he hadn't gone far. Jo just needed to give him a chance to catch up to her in a place Agent Parker couldn't see. The meet today wasn't a long one, just a quick exchange, over with the briefest sleight of hand.

I only need to lose you for a minute, Jo thought, glancing behind to find Nathaniel Parker in the crowd, eyes sharply focused on her. Luckily, he was tall enough to stand out, making him easy to spot, and broad chested enough to bump into people, slowing him down.

She grinned and waved.

Never let them see you sweat.

Jo turned, kept her head down and pressed on. Cutting through a door. Swerving through another. Drawing confusing circles. Then down a flight of stairs. Through another hall. Into a room. Out of another. Quick. Quick. Quick. Until she reached the spot she wanted to go to, the one she assumed Thad would also gravitate toward—the Temple of Dendur. Practically given its own wing, the temple stood in the center of a massive vaulted room, surrounded by a shallow moat of water. A two-story wall made entirely of windows looked out at the park. The sheer size of the space made voices echo and carry, and the sheer number of people inside made it ideal. The room was by far the most popular one in the entire museum, an easy place to get lost in the crowd. Not to mention it was close to the exit, which made for an easy way out.

Jo moved toward the temple, climbing the handful of steps up to the platform. Keeping her head forward, she was careful not to be obviously searching for anyone in the crowd, but also made herself visible enough to be easily spotted. She reached into her purse and found the thumb drive at the bottom of her things, next to a tube of lipstick. She clutched both in her fist. Idly observing the ancient temple, Jo freshened her red lips and then put the makeup back into her bag, discreetly holding the drive against her palm with her thumb so no one would see. To the casual observer, nothing would have looked unusual. But if Thad was there, it was the signal.

A moment later she felt a presence at her back.

A warm breath on her neck.

"Jo Jo," the softest whisper.

She breathed a sigh of relief and turned her palm. Thad's fingers brushed against hers, taking the thumb drive and pressing a small paper into its place.

Then he was gone.

Jo slid the paper into her pocket and continued on her merry way, barely having stopped for a minute. Nate caught back up with her while she was waiting in line to retrieve her bag from the coat check, but he didn't come up to her this time. He waited from the peripheral, watching, always watching. If he hadn't been so adamant about keeping his distance, he might have noticed that when she handed her ticket over to the attendant, it wasn't the same number as the one still sitting in her purse. And that when her bag slid across the counter, it looked the same from the outside, but the contents were completely different. As it was, Jo just smirked as she left the museum behind and walked back out to the street, feeling invigorated.

Where to next? she thought, surveying the scene. Her computer could wait a few hours. The sun was out. The day was young. And suddenly there was a spring in her step that she didn't want to waste. Jo thought of Agent Parker's smug face. *I know just where to go.*

A wicked smile curved her lips, one she didn't even try to smother as she pulled her phone from her pocket and hunted for a store close by. The two of them were playing a very careful game of chess, and it was Jo's move.

Game on, Nathaniel Parker.

Game freaking on.

- 12 -

Nate

Nate watched Jo scurry down the front steps of the museum and merge into the crowd, as much as any beautiful woman could blend in, which was to say, not much. Her red hair shone brightly in the sun. Her step was vivacious. Without even realizing, she turned heads. And not for the first time, she'd turned his. But in a way he never would have expected.

That hopeful expression.

That frightened one.

The uncertainty. The panic.

Her tone when she talked about her food had come through fueled with passion and yearning. Her voice when she'd given the hypothetical truth of her past had been caged and straining. At the mention of her father, he swore he saw a flash of shame, of doubt, in her eyes.

"Well, you tried, Parker," Leo consoled as Nate dropped heavily back into the car, half falling into his seat as this new theory began to percolate. The very idea of what he was considering had left him dumbfounded and speechless, tasered by the unexpected, because deep down he had the undeniable feeling that it just might work.

"Leo," Nate murmured.

"You look like you've been hit by a bus," his partner responded, not quite able to erase the humor from his voice. "You okay?"

They eased from the curb and merged into the oncoming traffic, following Jo as she continued walking parallel to Central Park, looking down at her phone.

"Leo," he said again, a little louder this time.

"Hey, man, what is she looking at on her phone? Can you check the feed?"

"Leo," Nate stated, loud and firm.

His partner's head swiveled. "What?"

"I think…" He blinked a few times and shook his head before he looked up and over, meeting his partner's somewhat concerned gaze. "I think I have an idea."

"And…?" Leo raised a brow as the corners of his lips twitched. "What? The shock of it has sent your body into hyperdrive?"

Nate frowned. "No, I'm serious. I think—"

"Parker, Alvarez." Their boss's voice came through the comm, interrupting him. "Did you pick up the address the target typed into her phone?"

Nate swallowed the words sitting heavy on his tongue, popped the glove compartment open, and grabbed the tablet. He turned it on, then waited for the live feed of Jo's phone to load.

"Sorry, sir," Leo teased into the mic. "My partner was struck dumb at the first sign of original thought."

"Don't be cute, Alvarez. What's going on?"

"Nothing." Nate half sighed the word as he tapped his leg, watching the feed update. Jo turned on her phone. She opened her GPS app. She typed in *La Perla*.

Nate turned to look at Leo. "Do you know what La Perla is?"

"Uh." Leo shrugged. "Jewelry store?"

Nate drew his brows together. Something about that didn't seem right, but he shook it off and lifted his wrist to his lips. "We have the address, sir, about fourteen blocks south and one avenue over. We'll follow on the road. Ground team can meet us there."

"Good," the boss affirmed. "Now, what's this stupefying idea?"

Nate rolled his eyes. When exactly had he become the office punching bag? He'd really like to know. "I was going to bounce it off Leo, sir, before approaching you."

"I haven't got all day, Parker. Spit it out."

Actually, you do, he thought with a snort. *That's sort of the definition of a stakeout.*

But talking back to the boss was something he'd never do. Instead, he took a deep breath and tried to work his theory out in a way that made sense. "I think, sir... Well, I think when I was talking to Jo"—he coughed under his breath—"I mean, Miss Carter, I saw something in her eyes, something we might be able to use. You were listening to everything, I presume?"

"Naturally."

"Did you notice the change in her tone when she talked about her coopies?"

"Her what?" the boss asked. "Is this some slang I don't understand?"

"No," Nate rushed to say. "No, it's a cookie in a pie, or a pie in a...something. Whatever it is, she calls it a coopie." *And it's damn tasty. Those things probably will take the world by storm, not that I'd ever admit that to her.* "Anyway, I think she's done with the life of crime. I think she wants to bake."

There was a pause. Nate and Leo made eye contact as the line hummed. When the boss finally did respond, the words came out flat. "One of the best hackers in the world wants to retire at twenty-five to bake cookies?"

Coopies, Nate silently corrected on Jo's behalf. *They're called coop—gah!* He shook his head forcefully, dispelling the rebellious thought. *Get out of my head, woman.*

Leo tightened his hands on the wheel to keep them from shaking as his breath wobbled with mirth, as though he could see the quiet battle raging.

Nate glared at his partner as he spoke into his mic. "Did you hear her hypothetical story about a fourteen-year-old girl? It was about her obviously. She's only doing this because she loves her father. I don't think she knows anything about what's really going on with the Russians. Maybe that's why Ryder and Carter left her behind when they went to Cuba. She's in the dark."

The boss took a deep breath that sent a wave of static through the line. Then, "Go on."

Nate released a relieved puff of air as his mind wandered to Jo's words, about shades of gray, and black and white, and making the system match the world. And then, he just spit it out. "I want to offer her a deal."

Leo turned to Nate and studied him.

"What sort of a deal, Parker?"

"I don't know, sir. That would be up to you," he said, holding Leo's gaze. His partner nodded in agreement—silent approval of his new plan. The act gave Nate an extra ounce of assurance. "Get her to disclose everything she knows about Ryder and Carter, get her to turn over her computer and any documents in her possession, maybe get her to wear a wire into the island compound to get her father on tape, whatever you want. And in return, we give her immunity."

"Immunity?" the boss practically shouted into the phone.

Nate winced. "I think it's the only way, sir. The deal would need to be compelling enough to hand over her father and someone who to an outside viewer appears to be a best friend, or a brother figure. She wants to be free to pursue her own dreams. We give her that, and she might give us what we need."

Leo pulled to a stop at the end of the block as Jo disappeared into a store. From their angle, Nate couldn't make out the name or see into the front window, but he assumed it was the place she'd typed into her phone. He leaned back into his seat as an agent in plain clothes came through the comm, saying she would get a better vantage point.

"What makes you think she'll turn on her own flesh and blood?" the boss asked once they got the undercover agent into position.

"I'm going to show her that they turned on her first," Nate answered, thinking back to that moment in the middle of the museum, surrounded by crowds yet all he could see was the flash of doubt in Jo's eyes as he asked if she really understood who her father was. The answer was no, she didn't. Nate would bet his life on that fact. "She has no idea what she's participating in. No idea that whatever trick they're trying to pull in the next few days is part of a much larger scheme, a much darker one than fulfilling the whims of an aging criminal on his way out. I can't explain it, sir. I just have a gut instinct."

"I'm not sure your gut will be enough to convince a court to grant immunity," the boss drawled.

"Give me a day, sir. To work her for information."

"A day?" the boss replied.

A flurry of activity came through on the tablet.

"Hold on, Parker," the boss said, seeing the same action Nate was. "She's on her phone again."

He read the screen.

She turned on her camera app.

Then her messaging app.

Sent a text—*What do you think?*

The image was loading. Damn things took forever.

"Do we recognize the number she's communicating with? Is it Carter? Ryder?" The boss's scratchy voice came through the line—he was talking to the tech team, not directly into his mic. But Nate shifted his attention to the ten-digit number, reading it twice as his brows pushed together.

Wait a minute—

The phone in his pocket buzzed.

Goddamn that woman.

"It's my phone, sir," Nate grumbled. "Somehow she got my number."

He shifted his weight to reach for the phone in his back pocket.

Before he had a chance to pull it free, a sharply sucked in breath came through the comm.

"Hot damn," the boss muttered.

Leo pounced before Nate could stop him and grabbed the tablet from his lap. He slid it onto the wheel while the image finished loading, then promptly let out a soft whistle as his knee started bouncing with the hilarity he was trying his best to suppress.

What the hell did she do now?

Nate closed his eyes and dropped his head against the back of his seat, squeezing the bridge of his nose with his fingers.

"You better get it over with, man," Leo muttered.

Nate hated when his partner was right. But he was. With a sigh, he picked his head up and looked down at the phone in his lap, just as it buzzed a second time.

I seem to remember you liking the color red...

Jo. Again.

Nate took a deep breath and slid his finger across the screen, unlocking it. Then promptly started choking on his own breath.

Jo.

In a red lace bra and panty set.

No more revealing than her bikini, but it set his blood on fire.

"Breathe, Parker. Breathe," Leo joked and slapped him roughly on the back.

He shut his phone off.

But the image was burned into his brain. The lace hugging her petite waist. The flash of his hands sliding up beneath it. The garter highlighting her long legs. The flicker of those thighs wrapped around him. The curves, too many curves to keep straight. He could spend hours studying the lines of her body. Tracing them. Touching them.

If she weren't a criminal.

Or his target.

Or a royal pain in his ass.

"She's unbelievable," he muttered, tossing his phone to the floor and resisting the urge to stomp on it. Breaking the damn thing would only cost him. "She's really unbelievable."

"You've got that right," Leo commented under his breath, though his tone sounded a lot more appreciative and a lot less annoyed than Nate's.

The phone by his feet buzzed.

Leo opened his mouth.

"I don't want to know," Nate interrupted before he could speak.

His partner plowed on anyway. "Should I wear this under my dress for the gala?'"

"Gala?" Nate perked up and lifted the mic to his lips. "Boss, did you hear that? Gala?"

"I did, Parker," he said slowly.

"Do you think she's telling the truth? Do you think it's a ruse to distract us from Ryder? I can't imagine she gave up their plan, just like that, just to get a rise out of me."

"Unclear, Parker."

Gala.

The gala was at the townhouse they'd been watching. A rich man hosting a charity event. Nothing too unusual, and there hadn't been anything within the silent auction that had particularly stood out to the team as something that would be of true interest to Robert Carter, but was that in itself a clue? They'd chosen it as the least likely option between the three possible locations. So was she throwing them off the scent? Or had she made a mistake? *Or is she just trying to drive me completely insane?*

The latter.

Definitely the latter.

"So, Parker." His boss came through the comm again. "When you said you needed a day to work Jolene Carter for information, what exactly did you mean...?"

Leo snickered.

Nate groaned. "Not...that, sir."

"Professional, Parker," his boss ordered, the command in his voice clear, hardened by age and experience. "Keep it strictly professional. And if you get anything we can use, I'll see what I can do about an immunity deal. Got it?"

"Yes, sir," Nate said, unable to stop his gaze from dropping to the tablet still perched against the steering wheel. He snatched his attention away, turning instead to the window. Jolene Carter, fully clothed this time, walked out of the store, not bothering to turn her face in their direction. But her smug expression let him know exactly what was on her mind.

It wouldn't be there for long.

He was going to turn her.

He was going to give her an offer she couldn't refuse.

He was going to win…as long as it didn't kill him first.

- 13 -

Jo

In need of caffeine, Jo stepped sleepily off the elevator the next morning and stopped dead in her tracks as her mind processed the scene before her. Agent Parker, standing in the middle of the lobby, with a brown paper bag and two cups of coffee in his hands.

"Do my eyes deceive me? Am I still dreaming?" she asked as she sauntered over with a coy smile on her lips. Tilting her nose up, Jo drew in a deep breath, catching the scent of espresso and chocolate in the air—two of her very favorite things.

He offered her a cup, saying, "You seem like a vanilla latte sort of girl."

"Good guess," Jo commented and snatched the drink, then brought it to her lips with a sigh. She was, in fact, a vanilla latte sort of girl. And this was a damn good one.

Coffee addiction somewhat satiated, she slid her gaze to the brown bag in his hands. Jo raised a brow, eying Agent Parker. "Do I smell chocolate?"

The edge of his lip perked up in a lopsided smile that made her heart pinch inside her chest. "Banana chocolate chip muffins from a bakery around the corner from my hotel. The concierge said they were the best in the city."

Jo's eyes went wide. "Gimme, gimme."

A puff of air sounding suspiciously like soft laughter slipped through his lips before he shook his head and nodded in the direction of two chairs in the corner of the lobby. "Want to sit and eat?"

"Hold on," Jo said, narrowing her gaze as she zeroed in on him, looking to his neck, then his wrist, then back into his charming blue eyes, which were for the first time warm as a cloudless sky on a sunny day instead of cool as ice. "No earpiece. No mic. What's going on here, Agent Parker?"

"I came to apologize," he said with a shrug.

Jo eyed him dubiously. "Apologize? The Feds don't apologize."

"Maybe I'm more than a Fed."

"Am I more than a criminal?"

He held her gaze for a moment. Jo stared right back. If they were starting fresh, for a reason that still eluded her, she deserved to know where she stood.

"I'm starting to think you might be," he acquiesced.

Not quite convinced, Jo knelt to put her coffee on the ground and then stepped close to Agent Parker. He watched her curiously but didn't do anything except hold his arms wide as she pressed her palms against his stomach…his hard-as-a-rock stomach.

"I'm not wearing a wire," he murmured, voice amused.

That alone made her intrigue spike.

He's…cheerful. Did I step off the elevator and into an alternate universe? Jo thought as her fingers ran over the defined contours of his abdomen, lingering a little longer than necessary. Okay…a lot longer than necessary. But it had been ages since she'd been around any man besides Thad and her father, let alone a man who looked like this, and smelled like… Jo took a deep breath, sighing. *Clean laundry and a fresh, woodsy soap.*

"Are you finished?" he drawled, looking down at her.

Jo winced internally but kept her hands in place, maintaining her cool. Holding on to his gaze, she ran her palms up his chest, nice and slow, taking her time as an electric bolt flashed in his eyes. Agent Parker licked his lips and swallowed, Adam's apple bobbing, but didn't look away. Jo slipped her fingers around the collar of his shirt, undid the first two buttons, and stepped back with a grin. *Much better.*

"I've been dying to do that ever since I first laid eyes on you."

"Yeah, well…" He paused, coughing under his breath and looking away. But not before Jo caught the spark of something bright in his eyes, a hint at maybe something he'd been wanting to do to her ever since the first time they'd met. Her smile deepened. He motioned back to the chairs. "So, should we sit?"

"Sure…" Jo said slowly, always one to go with the flow, even if the flow was confusing as hell.

They sat. Agent Parker pulled two muffins from the bag and slid one across the coffee table toward her, a peace offering. She carefully peeled the paper away and took a bite, moaning a little bit as fruity sweet banana and sugary cocoa exploded in her mouth, all accented by what must have been a pinch of salt in the batter to bring the flavors out.

"So good," she mumbled with her mouth full, but it had to be said. Agent Parker lifted his muffin as if to toast with it and took a bite, then nodded in agreement. "So," Jo continued when she finally swallowed. "I thought you said something about an apology…"

"I did," he agreed, voice firm but not stern, more like emphatically honest. Direct and confident. To the point in a way Jo appreciated, a way that was foreign to her and her guarded heart. "I'm sorry for saying you were a bad person yesterday. I said it out of frustration, but I don't really feel that way, Jo. You seem like a good person who maybe got caught up in a bad situation. Or maybe just someone who was raised not to know better. Anyway, I shouldn't have said it. I know it hurt you. And I apologize."

"Thank you."

He stared at her.

She stared at him.

He raised his brows wryly.

Jo looked down at her coffee and lifted it to cover her mouth. "I'm sorry too, Agent Parker."

"What?" he questioned, lips pursing. "I couldn't hear you."

Is he actually teasing me? Teasing me!

Who is this man?

"I said I'm sorry, Nathaniel," Jo drawled.

"You can call me Nate."

"Nate," she said, enjoying the way his name sounded rolling through her lips. *Nate. Nate. Straightforward. Simple.* "Well, Nate, I'm sorry for bringing up your father." That sting of pain burned in his eyes once again, dark streaks of sapphire cutting through his irises. "It was wrong of me. I know nothing about him. And as I'm sure you know, I understand the pain of losing a parent, and I can't believe I went there. I never should have, and I never will again."

He nodded his gratitude.

Jo looked away from the intensity of his gaze, worried that maybe for all her hard work, he could still see straight through her. And she wasn't an idiot. He wasn't here out of the goodness of his heart. He had an agenda. There was no denying it.

"So, why exactly are you here, Nate? Not that I'm complaining, of course—just curious why you went from stalking me one day to greeting me with baked goods the next."

"I'm trying to understand you."

She pinched her brows. "Understand me?"

To what end…?

"Yes, Jo. You're a riddle I'm trying to solve, and I thought the best way to go about it would actually be to talk to you. Directly."

"You have to admit," Jo countered. "It's a little unorthodox, for a federal agent and his target to sit and have a casual conversation as…friends."

He shrugged. "It is."

"You don't strike me as unorthodox."

"You do," he stated matter-of-factly, a little challenge in his voice, a dare that—*dammit!*—she wanted to take.

This is exactly what Thad was worried about, Jo argued with herself as she leaned back and took another sip of her coffee, analyzing the man before her.

Thad knows me better than I know myself. He told me not to get too close. Not to play with fire. We can't afford to get burned.

And yet, Jo was intrigued.

Maybe she wanted to understand Nate better too. Because she thought for sure she'd had Mr. Stiff all figured out, but watching him now—collar unbuttoned, sandy-blond hair casually tousled from a breeze, strong line of his jaw accented by the subtle uplift of his lips, a taunt shining brightly in those crystal eyes—Jo was beginning to think she didn't know him at all. And the hacker inside of her demanded to unravel his secrets, to decode the mystery in his eyes, to find all her answers. Breaking and entering was in her blood. If there was a crack in his defenses, she'd find it.

"Okay, Nate," she said, sitting up and putting her coffee on the table. Jo rested her elbows on her knees, leaning forward, leaning into his personal space. "You're in luck, because the only thing I had on my agenda today was exploring New York, and I wouldn't mind doing it with…a new friend. But I want to establish some guidelines, okay?"

He held his hands wide, unconcerned. "Go ahead."

"First"—Jo held up her pointer finger—"no mentioning my father or Thad."

Nate tilted his head, the corners of his eyes narrowing a hair as he examined her. "Okay."

"Second," Jo continued, "no asking me questions you know I can't answer."

"Done," he agreed smoothly.

"Third, no talk about jail, or locking me up, or evidence, or calling me a criminal, or anything like that. No work. Only fun. The way I like it."

Nate nodded. "I can do that."

"Finally," Jo said slowly, leaning a little bit closer, not even trying to hide the mischief she knew sparkled in her eyes, "you have to play by my rules."

"I wasn't aware you had any," Nate answered, leaning forward to put his coffee down on the table, and staying there, so their faces rested no more than a foot apart, close enough for the air between them to heat up a notch…or three.

A sly smile spread across her face. "That's the beauty of it."

Nate clenched his jaw, chiseled muscles ticking twice before releasing. "I won't do anything illegal."

"What do you take me for?" Jo rolled her eyes.

Nate lifted a brow. "Well, I've been banned from mentioning the word."

Touché.

"Nothing illegal."

"Then done." He sat up and extended his hand, offering to seal the deal.

"Done." Jo held his gaze and slid her fingers forward. A spike of fire blasted up her arm as their skin touched, palm to palm. He tried to tug away, but she held on, forcing him to hold her stare. "One more thing."

He sighed and tilted his head to the side, tossing her a not-at-all-surprised and completely expectant look. *Guess I'm more predictable than I thought.*

Jo let him have his hand back, though she couldn't help but notice how her own felt suddenly cold when he pulled away. "Before we begin our grand adventure, I want to establish a little bit of trust. We each get to ask the other a question, one question, whatever we want, according to our previously established guidelines, of course. And we have to answer truthfully. I'm sure you have a whole file on me at the office. You know I have a whole file on you in my securely hidden away computer. I want to dig deeper, even the playing field, stir up some confidence between us."

He scrunched his brows together, unable to hide the curious twitch of his lips. "Who goes first?"

"Me, of course."

Jo took another sip of coffee and leaned back, drumming her fingers on the cup as questions circulated in the back of her mind. She needed something to throw him off a little, to force him to open up.

First kiss? No, she'd gone the salacious route too much already with him. It was what he'd expect. *Most embarrassing moment?*

The edge of her lip curved—it was probably what she'd put him through yesterday. And even if not, she'd teased enough.

She wanted something real. Something deeper.

And then she had it.

"What's the worst rule you've ever broken? Ever? In your life?"

Nate was Mr. Goody Two-shoes, Mr. Black and White, Mr. Secret Agent Man. She wanted to knock him off his high horse a bit. Bring him back down to earth. Back down to where she lived.

Well, maybe not quite that low. But still…

"Hmm…" He put his head back against the seat and looked to the ceiling as he rubbed his thumb over his clean-shaven chin, drawing her attention to his strong, sturdy hands. Though she was sure that bit was unintentional, and the part where her mind wandered to what that thumb could do against her body definitely was.

Jo cleared her throat and shifted her weight.

He dropped his eyes to her for a moment, curious, but then a lightbulb seemed to ignite. "Oh, I know. In sixth grade, there was this kid a year above me who was always picking on all my friends because we were smaller and younger. And one day, I'd had enough. So I planned an elaborate ruse to lure him out to the sixth grader part of the schoolyard during recess, and just launched on him before he understood what was happening. I got in a sucker punch right to the nose before he had a chance to fire back. I think I broke it. Anyway, my dad had taught me a few tricks, so I could hold my own against someone bigger than me. When the teachers finally pulled us apart, I blamed everything on him. They knew he was a bully. I started crying to push my point. So, they sent me to the nurse, but sent him home with a one-week suspension."

Jo stared at him. "That's it? That's your big bad? Taking down the class bully. You were probably a hero for the rest of the year."

"Maybe." Nate shrugged. Then he shuddered, remembering something she wasn't privy to. "I was punished when I got home, believe me."

Jo wrinkled her nose. "You rebel, you."

"Look, we didn't all have the luxury of—" Nate cut himself off, curling his hands into fists as his gaze dropped to the ground. But it wasn't anger written across his face. It was pain.

Jo softened her tone. "Have the luxury of what?"

"I…" He paused, lifting his gaze to hers. There was a question in his eyes, silently asking how much he could trust her, how much he should tell her, how much she already knew. And then he sighed, stretched his fingers, and took a deep breath. "I was twelve when my dad passed away. My mom was inconsolable. My younger brother was already a little rascal, but without my dad around, he got worse. And my sister needed someone she could depend on, someone to be strong. So I became that person to them. I had to grow up, fast. And part of growing up is learning the rules and following them, being a role model. Not all of us had the luxury of youth."

He finished quietly, almost like a confession. Deep in her chest, something stung, a familiar ache. She'd only been fourteen when her mother died, but where Nate's mother had turned weak, her father had been strong. There were no siblings she'd had to worry about. No one she'd needed to take care of. Instead of growing up, Jo had held on to her childhood for all it was worth. In many ways, she still was holding on to the past, onto Daddy's little girl, the one who was too afraid to turn into a woman without her mother around to guide her.

"Okay," Jo told him.

"Okay?" he asked, unabashed surprise in his voice that she wasn't pressing for more information.

"Your turn."

He didn't hesitate. "So, what is it about baking?"

Of all the questions in the world!

"Really?" she blurted, unable to rein in the snort that followed it. Very unladylike. Not at all sexy. Yet it still made him smile. "You're so hung up on my baking. Must have really impressed you with my coopies."

Jo winked.

He arched a brow. "You got a question. I get a question too."

That wasn't a denial.

But instead of retorting, Jo bit her lip to keep the remark in and sighed.

He was right. He'd been open and honest, and he deserved the same from her. That was the whole point of this exercise, after all—to prove to each other they were more than cop and criminal.

They were human.

"I don't really know. I've always loved it," Jo began, blinking quickly to stifle the sudden pools of water in her eyes as her memories rewound, to a place she rarely ever went—the place before her life flipped upside down and turned into what it was today. "All my best memories are in the kitchen. Every Christmas morning, my mom and I would wake up early while my dad put out the presents, and we'd bake a fresh batch of cinnamon buns in the shape of a tree. And the day after Thanksgiving, we'd spend hours making gingerbread men and decorating gingerbread cottages and castles and haunted mansions, until the entire house smelled of allspice and nutmeg. On Easter, she always made the best carrot cake, one I still haven't been able to perfect no matter how many times I try. And when my dad was away on business, sometimes we'd skip dinner altogether and just put a fresh batch of chocolate chip cookies in the oven, then dip them in milk, for the calcium she always said, and eat until our bellies hurt."

Jo couldn't help but laugh at the memory of the two of them curled on the couch, clutching their stomachs in pain, taking just one more bite as a romantic comedy played on the screen. A girl's weekend. Her favorite kind.

She swallowed the clog in her throat and continued, flicking her gaze to Nate's. As soon as she noticed the sympathy and understanding in his eyes, she looked away. Because it was too much right then, too endearing. "I got my first Easy-Bake oven when I was eight, and it's still the best present I ever received. I used it all the time, until the knobs were gray with wear because the pink had rubbed off. But it was the best. And even after my mom died, I couldn't stop. The kitchen became painful at times, an escape at others, but the baking remained. A constant. I always wanted to go to culinary school, but, well..." Jo shrugged and scratched her nails against her empty coffee cup, just to have something to do. "Life happened, as they say."

Her gaze darted to Nate.

His lips were drawn in a line and his brows were pressed together with something almost like worry or concern...maybe even caring. "Okay."

Jo rolled her lips into her mouth, but they spread into a smile anyway. "Okay."

He stood abruptly, grabbed the muffin wrappers from the table, and crunched both of their empty coffee cups in his hands before depositing them into a garbage bin nearby. And then he walked back and stood over her chair, offering her a hand.

"Jolene Carter, I'm at your mercy."

She took the help he offered, letting his more-than-capable biceps pull her to a standing position. "Why, Agent Parker, that might be the nicest thing you've ever said."

Just like that, a silent truce was established.

And maybe something else too.

Something she was too afraid to acknowledge as she shook her hand free and strutted out the door, leaving him to follow in her wake as she led him on what was sure to be both the greatest and most annoying day of his life.

- 14 -

Nate

When Jo said she'd saved this day to explore New York City, she'd meant explore. Good lord. They'd spent three hours on a bus tour—a hop-on, hop-off double-decker bus tour under the relentless heat of the sun with stops everywhere. From Battery Park on the southernmost tip of Manhattan, where Jo had forced him to pose for a photograph with the Statue of Liberty in the background, to Times Square, which had provided nothing more than a headache from the lights and noise, to the Empire State Building, where she'd somehow produced VIP tickets to take the elevator to the top. Nate still wasn't convinced everything about that particular stop had been legal, but he was trying a new thing with Jolene Carter—trust.

Hell, he'd tried everything else already.

By the time they'd hopped back on their eighth tour bus, Nate was pleading for reprieve. And Jo finally relented. They hopped off for a final time near an entrance to Central Park and had been wandering the tree-covered sidewalks ever since.

"So, you were recruited fresh out of grad school?" Jo asked.

Her gaze slid curiously to the baseball game happening in the middle of the field they were walking by, and Nate's followed. Young kids, early teens maybe, judging by their size. A scrawny left-handed batter stepped up to the plate. The pitcher threw. And *bam!* The ball flew over the shortstop, shooting deep into right field. A cheer erupted from the row of beach chairs set up behind home plate, bringing a soft smile to Nate's lips.

"Uh, yeah," he murmured, trying to focus on the question instead of the Little League memories floating to the surface. His father coaching from the dugout. His mother nervously watching from the bleachers. His brother complaining that he was too young to play. His sister obliviously doing cartwheels along the sidelines. His family had spent many a Sunday morning on the baseball field…until suddenly, that all stopped. The fun stopped. For a long time, at least.

Nate blinked and shook his head, turning back to Jo. There was a silent question in her gaze. "Yeah, I graduated with my master's in criminal justice. My mother wanted me to go to law school, but I always knew I wanted to follow in my father's footsteps and join the bureau. So that's what I did."

Jo dropped her gaze to the pavement beneath their feet and then lifted it back up, but this time her eyes were brighter, more intense. Probing. "Can you tell me about them? Your family, I mean? You said you have a brother and a sister?"

They'd been keeping it relatively surface level since leaving the hotel, nothing too personal, nothing too deep. There was a line they couldn't cross, not yet. Not unless he got her a deal and she agreed to it. Jo wasn't stupid enough to incriminate herself. He wasn't stupid enough to give her any ammo she could use against him. But that line was as deep as the Grand Canyon, and there was a whole mess of exploring they could do without having to cross it. If they wanted to. If they dared.

Nate's attention slipped back to the baseball game as another cheer erupted, but the sound made his gut tighten into a knot, coiled and painful and uncertain. He kept his memories on lockdown, carefully stored and bolted shut. Or at least he had, before today. Before Jo and her questions undid all his defenses.

"My mother is a gentle soul," Nate began slowly, returning his focus to Jo and the green of her eyes, a green that was becoming less and less like hard, unbreakable jade, and more and more like a shadowy forest inviting him to come inside and explore its secrets. "Couldn't hurt a fly. My father had always been the enforcer, and my mom the shoulder to cry on. She gives and gives and gives without ever taking. I truly believe there's nothing but love in her heart, no capacity for hate or even anger really."

I had to learn how to do those things for her, Nate silently finished the thought, frowning. He had to hate the people who killed his father so one day justice could be found. He had to get angry when his brother got in fights, when his sister broke the rules. He had to learn discipline and dole it out, because his mother had never known how. But he took those burdens on willingly, before he fully understood them, because even as a boy he knew he never wanted his mother to change. He didn't want to live in a world where her soft heart learned to harden.

Jo studied him.

Nate coughed and kept his eyes forward. "My brother, Chris, was a terror as a teen, but he eventually got his act together. Now he owns his own construction company building houses in Virginia. Married with a little girl and a baby on the way. And Caroline, my sister, only graduated from college about a year ago, so she's still figuring things out. For now, she's working as my mom's interior design assistant and helping her at home." He shrugged, turning back to Jo, who had stars in her eyes. "Just your typical family."

"That's wonderful," she said with a sigh.

Nate snorted.

Jo snapped her head in his direction. "What? It *is* wonderful."

"Oh, sure," Nate commented, unable to completely remove the sarcasm from his voice. "Wonderful. I'm just happy I got them both through college alive."

Her lips twitched, but the reproachful expression remained. "I always wanted siblings, you know. And I guess I did have one, in a way, with Thad." Jo swallowed quickly and looked away. She clasped her fingers by her waist, fiddling with her thumbs in a way that didn't match the confident woman he was used to. And then she looked up, directly into his eyes. "I moved to the island with my dad right after middle school—no friends, really, not much family except for Thad and his father, who were only around over the summer and on vacations. It was, well, a bit lonely at times, you could say. I used to spend hours wondering what the classmates I'd left behind were doing—going to the homecoming dance, to football games, to prom. Applying for college, maybe going to summer camp, or to the movies over the weekend, or the mall to gossip about boys. I mean, I'm fine with how I grew up. Not everyone has a beach for a backyard and anything else they could ever want, but you shouldn't knock typical. Typical is just fine. To some people, typical is the dream."

Jo turned back to the baseball game. Nate kept his eyes on her, studying the subtle downturn of her red lips, the graceful way her fingers lifted to brush a lock of hair back behind her ear. Was that why she'd become so good with computers? At hacking? Because the internet had become her only interaction with the outside world? It was hard to connect this assured, teasing, poised woman with a lost teenager struggling with loneliness and lack of self-worth. Had crime helped her find her way? Given her a purpose? Or was she always meant to be someone else, something else, and life got in the way?

The questions bunched in the back of his throat, but Nate stuck to his agreement—no work, only play. For now.

"What about the girls you were talking to on your phone?" Nate asked.

And then immediately cringed.

The only reason he knew about them was a wiretap on her cell phone. A wiretap he'd ordered. Because he was a Fed. And she was a thief. And it always came back to that in the end.

Jo turned to him with a brow raised in amusement but didn't go for the obvious taunt. Instead, her lips widened into an honest, energetic smile. "McKenzie and Addison? They're the best. Just, the best. The only girlfriends I've had in a long time who understand me. I met them online a few years ago in a chat room about this baking show, and we've been close ever since. Bouncing ideas back and forth, sending each other recipes, boosting confidence when needed, that sort of thing. I hadn't really talked to anyone about my cooking since my mom died, but as soon as I connected with them, I realized how much I missed sharing that part of me with other people, you know?"

Nate nodded. He understood exactly what she meant. No one in his life growing up had understood his drive to join the agency, his desire to follow in his father's footsteps when those footsteps had led him to an early grave. But when he joined the bureau, Nate had felt accepted. Surrounded by so many like-minded people, he understood it was where he was meant to be, what he was meant to be doing.

"But they don't know..." He trailed off, biting his tongue because he wasn't supposed to ask questions she couldn't answer. Not yet.

Jo cut him a sharp look. "No."

And that was that.

Shit.

He hadn't meant to throw off the vibe, to make her shut down. Not when she was finally opening up. Not when he, much to his surprise, was actually enjoying this side of Jolene Carter—the honest, real woman instead of the vixen. Though…the vixen wasn't half bad either.

"You're right, you know," Nate said, hoping to bring her back in. Because she *was* right. In the back of his mind, Nate tried to imagine his life without his brother and sister, without the stress of worrying about them, yes, but without the laughter their antics supplied, the joy their love brought him. One of the happiest days of his life had been standing by his brother's side as he married the woman of his dreams. A close second was sitting in the stands as his sister accepted her diploma, pride a swelling bubble in his chest. He wouldn't trade them for anything. Not even to have his father back. "Typical is nothing to be snide about."

In fact, he really did owe his mom a phone call.

It had been ages since he'd heard the sound of her voice, of any of their voices. Life in the bureau didn't leave much room for anything else.

Jo nudged him with her elbow.

Nate tossed her a wry glance.

They locked eyes and came to a standstill, too focused on one another to move. His feet were heavy, trapped in place by the intensity of her gaze. Deep in the centers of those emerald irises, he could almost see the dream playing through her thoughts, the dream he was too afraid to dare imagine for himself. Of a white picket fence. And children running around a freshly mowed backyard. And a woman by his side, her smooth hand wrapped in his, her head on his shoulder, his arm around her waist, as they watched, at peace, at home.

And then *bam!*

Just like that, a memory invaded.

The same one as always.

Screeching tires. A high-pitched shriek. An inhuman scream crawling its way up his throat. The burn of asphalt scraping against his knees. His hands pressed to a twitching chest. The blood spilling over his fingers, more and more and more, dripping down his arms and onto the driveway, spreading wider and wider and—

Nate lurched his eyes away from Jo, breaking the contact, breaking the memory. He couldn't think about it. Didn't want to. That dream wasn't part of his future. Not with this life. This job. This past. He would never risk doing that to a child, to his child. Never.

"Nate?" Jo asked softly, her voice cautious, maybe the least bit concerned.

He shook his head.

Fingers encircled his, petite and dainty, yet strong enough to squeeze so tight he could feel her touch all the way to his core, a warm embrace.

"Look!" Her voice shifted completely.

Nate groaned, already knowing he didn't like the overly gleeful and enthusiastic tone. "What?"

Jo lifted both of their hands, pointed to a spot in the distance. "Are you seeing what I'm seeing?"

Nate zeroed in on the spot, then proceeded to hang his head in disdain. "Unfortunately, I am."

"A carousel!" Jo exclaimed, even though he could see it same as her and knew exactly what it was.

"A kiddie ride," he grumbled.

"Oh, let's go," she pleaded, dragging him forward as he dug his heels into the pavement. "Come on, I used to love them as a little girl. I haven't even seen one in ages."

"Jo."

That was it. That was all he had.

Clearly, it did nothing.

"Nathaniel Parker, are you really going to deny me the joy of a ride on a carousel? I thought you agreed to play by my rules today. And my rules say age is just a number."

"Can I watch?" He tried a different approach.

Jo rolled her big green eyes in his direction. "Don't be such a grump."

His mouth fell open in mock horror.

Jo grinned. "You're too young and too handsome to be an old curmudgeon."

"I'm not sure if that's a compliment or an insult," he teased but let her pull him forward with a sigh.

They found a place in line behind a pack of screaming six-year-olds. Nate lifted his fingers to pinch his brow, but Jo swatted his arm back down, refusing to let him rain on her parade. She tightened both of her hands around one of his, one small step away from jumping up and down with her excitement. And though Nate kept a staunch frown on his face, it was a struggle as some foreign sense of lightness sprinkled across his chest at the sight of her happiness.

When their turn was called, Jo jumped through the turnstile, rushing to find the perfect horse. "Hmm, white with gold reins. Pink and silver? There are too many options… Ooh! A unicorn!"

She jumped up and held the pole for balance.

Nate stood next to her with his arms crossed. "This is the most ridiculous I've ever felt in my entire life."

She kicked him gently. "Get on the horse."

"Excuse me?" Nate turned slowly in her direction.

Jo angled her head toward the pink horse on the opposite side—still not claimed. "Come on, get on the horse."

"Jo, there is no way I'm getting on that horse."

Her red lips dropped into a pout. A frustratingly good one. "You promised."

"Promised what?"

"To play by my rules. To have some fun, for once in your life."

She stared at him, hard.

He stared right back.

"Come on. Before someone else takes it."

He didn't move.

She slapped his ass.

Nate jolted. "What the he—"

"Nate," she cut in smoothly, wide-eyed and innocent. "Don't curse in front of the children."

Jo reared her hand back.

Nate sighed.

And stepped around her.

And got on the damn horse.

"I want it to be known I didn't go into this willingly."

Jo grinned. "Noted."

The music started, and the carousel began to turn. All around them, children started squealing. Jo gripped the pole for balance as she bobbed up and down, a childlike sense of awe written across her beautiful face. A sight he couldn't look away from. Laughter spilled from her lips as she leaned her head back, auburn hair swirling in the breeze, and let out a little holler.

Jo turned, catching him staring. "One shout. Just one."

He shook his head.

"Don't make me undo another button on that collar of yours," she threatened.

Nate lifted a hand to his shirt. He'd completely forgotten she'd loosened it. But he didn't mind the extra freedom. He was too used to wearing a comm set, needing to cover it up. But today, he was free of those rules. Today, he followed someone else's. So, with a shake of his head, Nate accepted her silent dare. He slipped another button free, let his head fall back, and released a quick shout.

"You've got more in you than that," Jo teased and looked to the mirrors at the top of the carousel, finding his gaze in the reflection as she screamed. "Woo-hoo!"

"Woo…" Nate tried to match her enthusiasm. He really did. He just wasn't born this way.

Jo shook her head, letting her hair whip. "Woo-hoo!"

Nate sucked in a deep breath, thinking about nothing more than wiping that challenging look from her eyes, and let himself go. "Yee-haw!"

Her eyes widened to saucers in the mirror. She rolled her lips in, biting down to keep them from spreading. And then she copied him. "Yee-haw!"

"Woo-hoo!"

"Ride 'em cowboy!"

"Yahoo!"

"Weeee!"

The ride stopped.

The world came tumbling back.

Nate tore his gaze from Jo's reflection, dropping it back down to the people around them. He'd never known six-year-olds had the power to be so judgmental, but yeesh… Nate shivered from the heat of their glares. Jo took his arm and pulled him from the firing squad.

"Kids are mean," he grumbled.

"Total savages." Jo nodded. "Ooh, soft pretzels!"

Nate shook his head. Having a conversation with her was like constant whiplash. "What?"

"Soft pretzels," she repeated, nudging her chin in the direction of a park vendor.

Street food? Why does it always have to come down to street food?

Nate shook his head. "No. This is where I draw the line."

"At soft pretzels?" she asked, face twisting in confusion. But then she shrugged and held her hands up. "I'll let you have this one. See? I can compromise."

Nate snorted.

Jo shook her head and sauntered off. Nate watched her, eyes drawn almost against their will to wherever she was. And then he noticed a man over her shoulder, sitting on a bench, gaze sharp, studying her.

Nate narrowed his eyes.

Why did that man look so familiar?

Where had he seen him before?

Jo walked back. "Sure you don't want a bite?"

"No," he replied, distracted.

And then he remembered.

Earlier today, he was on our first bus.

And then again, I saw him in Times Square.

We have a tail.

Nate put his hand to the small of Jo's back and turned her, gently shifting so they walked in the opposite direction. "Did you notice that man on the bench?"

"What?" she muttered, mouth half full of pretzel.

"That man on the bench?" he whispered. "I think we're being followed."

Jo tilted her head. "I thought he was with you."

"No, definitely not."

Nate gritted his teeth.

A Russian. It has to be a Russian.

Following Jo.

Following us.

"You swear to me you don't know who that man is?" he asked, one more time, looking directly into her eyes, trusting her not to lie.

"I swear."

Her voice didn't falter. Didn't break.

It was firm. And honest.

He had to believe it was honest.

Which meant he'd been right about her—Jo didn't know about the real work her father was doing, the real work Ryder was doing. But even if she didn't know about them, the Russians knew about her.

Nate's chest pinched, tense and burning.

His fingers curled into tightened fists.

His jaw clenched. The nerve in his neck started ticking.

For the first time since joining this operation, Nate wasn't worried about Jolene Carter. He was worried *for* Jolene Carter. For her safety. For her life.

"What, Nate? What?"

He looked down, meeting those probing eyes. *I can get you out of this,* he wanted to say. *I can get you immunity. I can give you a future.* But if they had a tail, the man could be listening. Anyone could be listening. Nate couldn't say those words aloud.

Not yet.

Not here.

And the longer they were together, the more dangerous it would be for her. If the Russians thought she was talking to him, really talking— If they thought she was a turncoat— Nate shivered. He didn't want to start down that road. "You should go."

Her brows pushed together.

He pressed on, harsher than he'd intended. "Jo, you should go, now. We had a fun day. But I have things to do, and so do you. We both knew this couldn't last forever."

"Nate," she started.

"Goodbye, Jo," he said firmly, interrupting her and darting his gaze toward their tail for emphasis, an explanation he couldn't voice.

Stilted understanding flickered in her eyes, but she didn't move. So Nate did the only thing he could to keep her safe. He turned and marched off, leaving her behind.

- 15 -

Jo

Jo watched Nate walk away, resisting the urge to turn and glance over her shoulder. She had noticed a man following them. But who? And why had he spooked Nate so much? And why had fear sparked like lightning across his eyes? Was it for himself...or for her?

She needed to talk to Thad.

She needed answers.

For once in her life, she needed to know.

Jo reached into her purse and pulled out her burner phone. Thad had bought them each one and had slipped hers into the purse she picked up at coat check the day before. The number of his burner was the only one saved into her contacts. Jo flipped the phone open, but paused, hovering her fingers over the buttons, unsure.

Only for emergencies.

He said only for emergencies.

Clearly, this wasn't one.

But at the same time, she knew Thad. And this seemed like something he'd want to know—the mysterious tail, yes, but also the fact that Nate had pulled a one-eighty switch and spent the entire morning with her off the record.

Strawberry Shortcake in the park.

Jo hit send.

He'd know what it meant.

There was an area of the park dedicated to John Lennon called *Strawberry Fields*. And though Jo had always been partial to viewing Pippi Longstocking as her redheaded icon, Thad used to tease her with Strawberry Shortcake instead.

He'd understand.

Jo put the phone back in her purse and took a compact out instead, under the guise of reapplying her red lipstick. But she angled the mirror just so, using it to glance behind and study the man still discreetly watching her. Tall. Dark hair. Hooded eyes. Frown across his lips. Wearing jeans and a black blazer.

She snapped the compact shut—if she held it up for too long he'd notice—and then she continued on her merry way. The man followed. Jo let him, even as the hairs on the back of her neck stood, and made for the meeting spot. Twenty minutes later, Thad found her.

They made eye contact briefly. He walked right past her and Jo trailed him at a distance, until he found a bench to his liking in a crowded part of the park. Thad sat. Jo took the empty spot at the other end of the bench.

"Someone's following me," she murmured, pretending to look for something in her purse. "Not a Fed."

"How do you know?" he muttered.

"Nate told me."

There was a pause. "Nate?"

Jo closed her eyes tight, squeezing. *Idiot.* "Agent Parker."

"When exactly did he become *Nate*?" Thad asked, voice tight.

"I'll get to that," she sidestepped and then leaned back, dropping her head against the bench, pretending to bask in the sunlight so Thad had a view behind her. She let her head fall in his direction so the tail couldn't see her lips move. "Do you see the guy in jeans and a blazer? Tall? Black hair? Medium scruff? He's been following me all day."

If Jo had blinked, she would've missed the way Thad's lips curled or the storm clouds that gathered in his gray eyes, there and gone in a flash, covered with practiced control. But she saw. And what she saw made her stomach drop.

Annoyance.

Frustration.

But most of all—recognition.

He knew who her tail was. Somehow, he knew.

"Who, Thad? Who is it?"

He broke his own rule and looked directly at her. "Forget it, Jo."

Not Jo Jo.

But Jo.

Her chest burned. "Thad, who—"

"Just leave it," he interrupted, turning back to the open field, tearing his gaze away.

"But—"

"Not now, Jo Jo, not here." He lifted a tanned hand to his face and ran it through his hair, sending his dark brown waves into perfect disarray. "I told you back on the island that there was more going on than you knew, and you could've asked me then, but you didn't. And now it's done. We can't talk about it here, on the job. After. I promise, after New York is done, I'll tell you whatever you want to know. Okay?"

For the first time, Jo wasn't sure she believed Thad's promise. And the very idea sent her world off-kilter.

She swallowed and forced a slow breath down her throat, trying not to notice how her fingers trembled against her thighs. "Okay."

"So what's the deal with Parker?" He practically growled the question, overprotective to the core.

"I'm not sure," Jo answered slowly. To be honest, she was still trying to work that out herself. Greeting her with coffee and muffins. Removing his comm. Not wearing a wire. Opening up. Playing by her rules. It didn't follow the Agent Parker she thought she'd come to understand. Yet she liked this new version better. The buttons-undone, hollering-at-the-top-of-his-lungs-in-the-middle-of-a-kiddie-ride Nate. Not Mr. Stiff. Not anymore. "He showed up at my hotel this morning, said he was trying to understand me. He was alone. No mic. No team. I thought spending the morning together might be mutually beneficial."

Thad pursed his lips. "I see…"

The disapproving tone made her eyes roll of their own accord. "I can handle it."

"Can you?"

Jo licked her lips and lifted her face, gluing her gaze to the field splayed out before her. A group of men played soccer. A few girls sunbathed on towels. A coed crowd of performers practiced handstands and various acrobatics. A young couple with a stroller sat huddled beneath an umbrella. A larger family rested with a picnic, mother and father looking on as three kids rolled around in the grass.

Normal.

Carefree and normal.

A memory fluttered to the forefront of her thoughts, persistent even as she tried to force it away. Nate staring down at her, his eyes as deep as the ocean, swirling with unspoken dreams, a wave rising and rising. In that split second before the inevitable crash, before he'd lurched his gaze away and broken the contact, Jo had seen something, something that terrified her because of how much she wanted it. The typical life. The normal life. Her own dreams reflected back, crisp and clear. A Victorian house framed by a white picket fence. A freshly mowed lawn edged with colorful tulips. A front porch with two rocking chairs and a little table between them, just big enough for two coffees and a plate of fresh chocolate chip cookies. The smell of butter and brown sugar still wafting from the kitchen. A little girl licking her fingers as she sat on the lawn beside a little boy still in his sweaty baseball uniform. And a voice by her side, sounding suspiciously like Nate's, droning on and on about the unfair call an umpire made, how rules were rules for a reason, how he was so proud of the way their son had handled himself, like a little man. But there was a secret little smile across her lips, because she may or may not have taken one of the cupcakes she'd brought for the kids from her bakery and smashed it against the hood of the umpire's car unbeknownst to her husband.

In that split second, Jo had seen all of that.

Just like she was seeing it now.

And then she blinked, and in that broken bit of darkness, she remembered she could never have that dream, that life. Her future was one of constantly looking over her shoulder, always covering her tracks, running and running and never feeling safe because of all the bad things she'd done. Sometimes she wondered if it would be easier to just get caught. Serve her time. And then be free.

But she would never do that to Thad.

To her father.

Not after everything they'd both done for her.

"I can handle it," she repeated, sliding her eyes toward her partner for a brief moment.

Thad didn't look convinced. "He's using you."

"Obviously," Jo commented offhandedly. A flare of denial ignited beneath her skin. "But to what end?"

Thad folded his hands behind his head and leaned back, returning his eyes to the field. Jo didn't miss the way his gaze paused on a street artist set up by the other side of the park, canvas half coated in paint. Once upon a time, Thad used to talk to her about his dreams. He'd been studying art history in college with a minor in fine arts, and whenever he was home, he'd go on endless tangents about the people he was studying, the work he was creating, his passion obvious. For a long time, he spoke of owning his own studio and selling his own art, trying to make a career out of it. But when his father passed, he dropped out of college and came home. After that, he didn't speak about his dreams anymore. Only work. Only the job. And until now, she hadn't paused to wonder why, hadn't stopped to question if maybe sometimes, Thad dreamed of freedom too.

He sighed before she could ask and arched his face toward the sun, moistening his lips. "They sent an undercover agent to me once, a few years back. I never told you, wasn't necessary. But she was beautiful. Five-ten. Blonde. Legs for days. A killer smile. The type that made you want to spill your secrets just to keep her around a little while longer. But I knew exactly who she was and what she was trying to do. And I knew it wasn't worth it."

Jo swallowed, clearing her throat and her wayward thoughts, but her voice still came out a little raspier than usual. "Nate's not undercover. I know exactly who he is."

"That concerns me more," Thad whispered, at-ease body completely at odds with the stress in his voice. "Because there's only one reason I can see that a Fed would so overtly court a criminal. To try to turn her. To lay the groundwork for some kind of deal."

Jo closed her eyes as a wince tightened every inch of her body. *Of course. Why didn't I think of that before?* "I'd never tell him anything about you or Dad. You know that."

"Just be careful."

The fact that he hadn't immediately agreed sent her pulse into hyperspeed. What made Thad think he couldn't trust her to keep quiet? Something she'd done…or whatever he was doing behind her back?

"You can't honestly think I would betray you," she tried again.

"I don't." Thad sighed, the strain in his voice obvious, doing nothing to quiet her thudding heartbeat. "But there are other people involved, and they— If they— If you—" He broke off, then unclasped his hands and ran them down his face as though to wipe whatever image was filling his mind away, to erase it completely. "Just be careful. We're so close to the end."

"These people…" Jo said slowly, trying to quell the questions bursting like little explosions in the back of her mind. *Who are they? What do they want? Why are we working with them? Why haven't I heard about them? What has everyone so freaking concerned?* "What if I made them think it was the other way around? That I was using Nate?"

Thad sat up a little taller, a grin pulling at his lips. The sight of that dimple in his cheek puckering to life did more to calm her nerves than any of his words ever could. "Using him how?"

The suggestive tone of his voice was undeniable. Jo lifted a brow, fully aware she would be unable to stop her current self-righteous mood from spilling into her tone.

"For information."

"No judgment." Thad's lips widened into a full smile this time, beaming. "We all have needs, Jo Jo."

Right now, you need a good kick in the ass, Thaddy Bear. She folded her arms indignantly across her chest. "I am an expert hacker, as you well know. If I can get onto Nate's cell phone or his computer, I can easily get access to his files. See what he has on us. See if it's anything real or if they're still grasping at straws."

"Interesting."

Her brows shot up. "Oh, now I get an 'interesting.'"

"With ideas like that..." He lifted his hand to his chin and tapped his pointer finger against his lips as the thought began to percolate. Jo wasn't sure if she liked his reaction or hated it, but all of a sudden, she felt a bit ill. "So how would you play it? Seduce Parker? Get back to his room? Plant the bug when he's not looking?"

Jo shrugged even as her insides flipped, doing somersaults in her stomach. "That would be one way."

Thad nodded. A wicked little gleam sparked to life in his eyes, one that would have been undeniably sexy if she didn't already know it meant he was scheming— scheming about something she was sure she wouldn't like. But if history was any indication, she'd tag along anyway. Jo wasn't sure how to do anything else.

"I like it," he softly announced, sitting straight. Their meeting was nearing an end. "I like it, Jo Jo. If your dad is going to retire after this, it'd be nice to know what sort of safety net we're all working with and how careful we really have to be moving forward. The gala is tomorrow night, so you've got one afternoon to work on Parker— and one night too, if you're careful. See what you can get out of him, and I'll handle everything else on my end."

Jo tried not to focus on the way he'd said, if her father was going to retire, as though it was a question instead of a definite. But she kept her mouth shut.

"I'll leave first," Thad murmured. "You wait ten minutes, okay?"

"Bye, Thaddy Bear," she whispered.

"Bye, Jo Jo."

He stood and sauntered away, liquid smooth, a body made for stealth. But all Jo noticed was the direction he walked in—toward the man who'd been following her. They wouldn't speak, not so openly, but Jo still reached into her bag to take her compact back out. Sure enough, Thad and the mystery tail made eye contact. And a few seconds later, both of them were gone, heading in the same direction, probably to have a meeting much like the one she'd had here.

Questions.

So many questions.

They battled each other for dominance, punching and kicking and fighting their way to the top of her thoughts.

Who?

What?

Why?

Why?

Why?

Jo fell back against the bench and stretched her body out as a sigh rolled all the way through her, a long slow breath that made her muscles turn weak with exhaustion.

Enough.

She'd had enough of her real life for one day. So she pulled out her phone and dove into her internet life instead, the only place she could be the person she so badly wanted to be, instead of the person that she was.

@TheBakingBandit: Best baked good in New York to clear a sullen mood...GO!

@TheGourmetGoddess: Crack Pie or Cereal Milk soft serve from Milk Bar. There are a few locations in the city. Run, don't walk!

@Sprinkle-Ella: Oh no, what's wrong? What level are we working with here? Cheesecake-won't-freaking-set bad? Or do we have another black wedding cake situation on our hands?

@TheGourmetGoddess: Enough with the freaking cake. Black can be really elegant, you know.

@Sprinkle-Ella: Sure, says the girl from New York.

@TheGourmetGoddess: For your information, I grew up in Connecticut. The land of paisley and pastels.

@Sprinkle-Ella: So how'd you end up with such a dark soul?

Jo lifted her forearm over her eyes and shook her head, mood already lifting. In one quick move, she propelled herself to her feet, keeping her attention on her phone as she typed in the name of the bakery McKenzie had suggested. There was one about a twenty-minute walk south—perfect. And though she knew the Feds could easily track her phone when it was on, she didn't care. She needed the distraction. She needed her friends. And without a kitchen handy, she needed to escape in the only other way she'd ever known how—the Web.

- 16 -

Nate

"Nathaniel, is that you?"

A guilty burn instantly scratched down his spine at the overly shocked and excited tone of her voice. "Hi, Mom. It's me."

He leaned back on the bench, closing his eyes to let the still-soft morning sun sink into his skin a little bit. He was in a park around the corner from Jo's hotel, waiting for word from his boss for the go-ahead with the immunity deal. Leo and the rest of their team were tailing Ryder for the day, since the slippery weasel had managed to dodge the beta team three days in a row. And with the gala Jo mentioned happening tonight as well as the auction they were monitoring, they couldn't afford to lose him again.

"Oh, Nathaniel!" The clang of pots and pans came staticky through the receiver. "Just give me a minute. I was in the middle of doing the dishes…"

A *click* let him know his mother had put the phone on the counter and was probably rushing to take soapy rubber gloves off her hands—yellow if they were the same ones she'd had last time he'd been home. Which had been…eight months ago? Nine maybe?

Jeez. I really do need to check in more often.

"Caroline!" a shout came through the line, distant enough for him to know she still hadn't picked up the phone. "Caroline! Your brother is on the phone!"

"Mom?" Nate tried to grab her attention. "Mom, I don't have too much time."

No answer. The phone was still on the counter undoubtedly.

"Caroline!" And then a mutter. "Where is that girl?"

"Mom?" Nate tried again.

"Oh, I'm back," she replied cheerily. "Just trying to find your sister. This house is too big for me now, all by myself."

"You're not—" But he stopped himself. Because Caroline was only there temporarily, and Nate had been the first to leave and rarely came back. He had no room to speak. "She's probably in the shower. It's okay, I'll catch her next time. I was just calling to say hi, nothing important."

"You're always important to me, sweetie."

The edge of his lip pulled into a smile. That was such a typical mom response. "So how are things with Caroline? When you can find her, I mean. Is she learning the interior design ropes?"

"Oh, you know Caroline…" His mother trailed off with a sigh. She was incapable of saying anything mean about anyone. But she didn't have to. He knew Caroline all right. "She has a real talent for picking out and pairing colors and patterns. She could do great things if she just applied herself a little bit more."

Same as always. This wasn't the first time they'd had this conversation or the first time he'd played the part of parent more than sibling. In high school, it had been about her grades and her sports teams. In college, about her ambition. Now in real life, it was about her job. His sister had a good heart, like their mom, but when it came down to it, she was a flake. But she was young. He still had hope she'd grow out of it when she found something she was passionate about.

"I'll talk to her," Nate said, voice resigned.

"Thank you."

"How's Chris?" He shifted the conversation, going through the checklist. "How old is Gracie now?"

"Two in July, can you believe it? And Eve is four months pregnant, feeling great. They stopped by two weeks ago for Mother's Day."

"Did you get the flowers?" Nate sat up. He couldn't always be there, but he always tried to remember.

"Oh, I did, Nathaniel. They were lovely. I must have forgotten to write in all the commotion. Caroline brought a new boyfriend to dinner, and she didn't remember to tell me he was allergic to, oh, what was it again? Oh, strawberries! And I made a pie, and he thought it was cherry, and, well, we had to take him to the hospital and Gracie was crying and…"

Nate snorted. Now that, he was almost sad he'd missed. "Typical Caroline."

"Chris is doing great though," his mom rolled right on, pretending not to hear his comment. "He just sold two more houses this past month and bought another one to rehab. I'm so proud of him."

"Me too, Mom, me too."

If only you saw him in college, puking into the toilet bowl after his frat initiation.

Nate shook his head. His brother had come a very long way.

"So, how are you?" his mother asked. He hated how tentative she sounded. "Where are you now?"

"I can't say."

"What are you working on?"

"I, uh, again, can't say."

She let out a little laugh. "I feel like I've gone back in time and am talking to your father."

He could perfectly envision her sitting at the kitchen counter, shaking her head as she played with the frayed ends of her worn-out lemon-pattern apron—the one his father had picked out when they went on that second honeymoon to Italy, the year he was supposed to retire then told her when they got home that he couldn't. Twelve months later, he was gone.

"But work is going well?"

"Work is great."

"When can you come home? Just for a visit? We all miss you."

"I miss you guys too," he said, the automatic reply rolling from his lips. But then he perked up, sitting a little straighter. "Mom, the investigation I've been working on for a while, we might have finally caught a break. I might be able to stop by soon."

"Oh, that's wonderful," she gushed, voice animated. And then she paused. He could hear her hesitation through the phone. It made his shoulders writhe uncomfortably. "Just...don't work your life away, Nathaniel."

"Mom—"

"No, I know," she interrupted, as though needing to get everything out quickly, just to make sure she actually said it. "I used to have the same argument with your father. You're doing important things, sweetie—I understand that. I just don't want you to wake up one day and wonder what happened with your life. Where the time went. What it all meant. There are other jobs, even ones within the bureau itself. Less dangerous ones. Less time-consuming ones. Just think about it, okay?"

Nate lifted his fingers and squeezed the bridge of his nose. "Okay, Mom."

"I love you, Nathaniel."

"Love you too."

He dropped his hand into his lap and hung up, suddenly drained. Taking a deep breath, he leaned back, closing his eyes, trying to halt the tight bundle of stress beginning to knot its way across his insides.

It always came down to the same argument in the end.

Which was why he didn't call his mother.

Because he couldn't stop. Not now.

Not when he was so close to justice.

If I can get to Jo.

If I can make her see.

Make her understand.

A tingle tickled the back of his neck.

Two hands came over his eyes.

Nate acted instinctually, too many self-defense lessons drilled into his psyche for his mind to catch up with his muscle memory. One second he was on the bench, and the next he was on his feet with his fingers wrapped around two petite wrists, twisting them into a pretzel as he flipped around. He stopped short of lifting a knee as the auburn hair and feminine body finally registered. Instead, his arms jerked forward, and Jo slammed full-force into the center of his chest, her eyes wide as she stared up at his face, which was now a mere matter of inches away.

"Jo!"

"Morning," she said slowly, mirth evident in the buoyant tone.

He didn't move. He was too caught up in the feel of her thighs pressed against his thighs, the way her body fit like a glove against his, how she was the perfect height. She bit the side of her lower lip, drawing his attention to the plush softness of her mouth. If he leaned his head down, one, maybe two inches, he could finally do what he'd wanted to do ever since he saw her cruising toward him on that jet ski, her caution lost to the wind.

"You going to let me go, Agent Parker?" A smile spread across her bright-red lips as she wriggled in his arms, rubbing up against him in all the right—*I mean, wrong*—places. "Not that I'm complaining. But I brought coffee."

Nate released her hands immediately and stepped back. The warm spring air felt like ice compared to the heat of her body—a much-needed cold shower. He resisted the urge to shake his head clear of the elixir that was Jolene Carter.

"Guess I should've known better than to sneak up on a Fed," she murmured as she knelt, reaching for two paper cups on the ground. "Though a little manhandling in the right situation can be fun. Coffee?"

Nate furrowed his brows, still stuck on that manhandling bit. A vivid image snaked into the forefront of his thoughts—Jo, pressed against a wall, his lips trailing a burning path down the side of her neck as he held her hands above her head, captive.

He did shake his head that time.

Get it together, Parker!

"Huh?" he muttered.

"Coffee?" she repeated, offering him a cup. A suspicious twinkle sparkled in the corner of her eye. "I figured you take yours black. Just a hunch."

"Yeah..." He accepted the coffee, being careful not to let their fingers linger. "Thanks."

Jo stepped around him and sat down. He tried not to notice the way the sun gleamed off her smooth skin as she crossed her legs in those short-shorts...tried and failed. Nate took the spot next to her, just to have somewhere else to look, like the dirty city street. Same thing.

Not.

"So, who were you talking to?" Jo asked as she studied his profile, taking her time, tracing every contour with her eyes. "Girlfriend?"

Nate almost choked on his coffee.

"Hot…" He coughed and pounded a fist to his chest. "And no, just my mom."

"What a charmer," she commented smoothly, a little too smoothly. "Good with his hands and remembers to call his mom."

Nate frowned, glancing at Jo. Was she being more forward than usual? Well…sending him a photo of herself in lingerie was about as forward as it got. But something about her tone seemed more goading, more personal. "What's going on here?"

"Just returning the breakfast favor," she said with a shrug, tugging a brown bag from her purse and handing him a bagel. "From a place around the corner."

He eyed it curiously. "You eat things that don't have sugar?"

"I eat things that have walnut raisin cream cheese," she replied in a sing-song voice and then rolled her eyes. "Don't worry, Nate. I got yours with plain."

Jo took a massive bite, giving herself chipmunk cheeks in the process. Not very ladylike, though for some reason he found it incredibly endearing.

He followed suit.

Delicious.

"What did you and your mom talk about?" Jo asked, seemingly casual, though there was a wistful edge to her voice, one he understood completely.

"My brother, my sister," he said, unable to stop himself from adding, "how she thinks I'm wasting my life. The usual."

"Wasting your life?" Jo's face twisted. "But you're a federal agent. Wasting your life would be like, I don't know, running off to join the circus. Or well, I don't know, because if you were an acrobat that would be a totally plausible profession, but you know what I mean."

I shouldn't have said anything… Though to be honest, it was nice to vent for once. "She wants me to settle down. Do something a little less dangerous with my life."

"Ahh." Jo's brows lifted with understanding, but then the edges of her lips curved behind her coffee cup. "Well, I do have a mean right hook."

"Too bad your reflexes suck."

The jibe slipped out before he could stop it.

Jo straightened her spine and scoffed, turning to him indignantly. "I could've knocked you on your ass if I'd wanted to, Nate. I just chose not to."

His brows rose of their own accord. "Oh, I'm sure that's exactly what happened."

"Careful with that tone, Parker," Jo grumbled. "You know I'm not afraid to take a dare when presented."

"One punch," Nate commented, calling her bluff. He turned, meeting her stare head-on. "I dare you."

Her nose wrinkled adorably with unmasked fury.

Lucky for him, Jo was easier to read than a book. Her chest puffed with a deep breath. Her weight shifted. Her hand balled into a fist. Her elbow ticked back just enough. When the punch came, Nate simply lifted his palm and caught her hand midflight, stopping her in her tracks. Bright flames sparked to life in the centers of her eyes, golden glitter burning with unabashed desire. A blink and the fire was gone.

"You were saying…?" Nate drawled, not letting go of her hand as he lifted his coffee cup to take another sip, balancing his bagel on his lap.

She tugged once or twice against his hold, then sighed in what sounded suspiciously like surrender. "So, your mom thinks you should settle down?"

Nate released her immediately.

We're back to this? "I will eventually."

"Ahh." Jo smirked and lifted her coffee to her lips. "The universal male response."

"No, no, I mean it." And he did. He really did. "There are just some things I need to accomplish first."

"Things like what?" Jo asked, covering her half-full mouth with her hand.

Things involving you.

Nate's gaze slid in her direction. She narrowed her eyes as though she could see the answer written across his irises. He let her, not bothering to look away. Because she didn't know it yet, but Jo was his ticket to closure, to justice. She was the key to everything he'd worked so hard to achieve, the break he'd been waiting nearly twenty years to finally receive.

The phone in his pocket buzzed.

Nate and Jo jolted apart.

He slid his cell out and read the message across the screen. It was from the boss.

Deal is a go. Working on official court approval, should have it by sundown. You're free to approach Carter with the terms.

Nate looked up.

Jo carefully studied her bagel, searching for the perfect bite.

You're mine, Jolene Carter.

The thought cut through his mind like a promise. The gala was in less than twelve hours. Her flight back to the Bahamas was in less than twenty-four. Which meant he had hardly any time at all to figure out how to make the impossible happen—how to get her to turn on her father and her best friend. Luckily, he had a plan. A risky one. But one he felt in his bones would work.

Tonight, Jo, you're mine.

- 17 -

Jo

A hungry gleam filled Nate's gaze, and it wasn't aching for the half-eaten bagel on his lap. He wanted something else, something his eyes whispered only she could provide, something that made a molten stream of heat course through her blood, starting deep in her belly, spreading all the way to her toes, bringing a blush to her cheeks—one she tried to hide behind her coffee cup.

Stick to the plan.

The plan. Right—the plan.

Seduce Nate.

Get invited back to his room.

Finally figure out what those hands could do besides stop a girl midpunch.

Break into his computer.

Steal whatever information he had on her father.

And then bail.

Back to business. Back to Thad. Back to the operation she came to New York for. Her dalliance with Nate would be a side-play, maybe a distraction enough to throw him off the bigger scheme of the night.

Easy. Simple.

A little something for everyone to enjoy.

Jo flicked her gaze to those blue, blue eyes laser focused on her. They burned with a heat even fiercer than the one coming from the sun above their heads. She swallowed.

Yeah…easy.

Except, for the first time, she wasn't quite sure who was doing the seducing here. Was Nate falling into her trap? Or was she tumbling headfirst into his?

"Who was that?" she asked, gazing pointedly toward his cell, mildly curious, but more needing to fill the silence.

Nate shrugged and slipped the phone back into his pocket. "No one important."

I don't believe that for one second.

But she bit her tongue.

"So, did you find Ryder yesterday? After I left?"

The question was so casual she almost didn't realize at first that he was talking about Thad. Jo rarely used his last name—he was just Thad. Thaddy Bear on occasion. But never Thaddeus Ryder. Too formal. And she didn't like to remember that for all their history, he wasn't truly a brother, by name or by blood.

She swallowed her bite. "No talk of Thad, remember?"

"Those were yesterday's rules," Nate said calmly.

Her eyebrows scrunched. What was he trying to do? They'd found a balance, a careful one. Why was he trying to ruin it? "So...?"

"So today, I don't have the time or the luxury of following them." Nate's tone was almost comically even, so completely different from the gravity of the words he offered.

Jo turned to him, shifting her weight on the bench. "What does that mean?"

"It means"—Nate met and held her gaze, probing—"did he tell you who was following us yesterday?"

Jo looked to the ground and studied the cracks in the pavement by their feet. Lying made her uncomfortable when it was with someone who mattered. The fact that her skin currently crawled was more telling than any other reaction she'd ever had in Nate's presence. Because it meant she cared, a lot more than she wanted to. "He didn't know."

Nate snorted. "Sure he didn't."

"I trust him." That, at least, was the truth.

"Oh, you trust him?" Nate murmured, voice heavy with disbelief. "You don't think he's ever lied to you?"

"Not about anything important."

"Where do you think he and your father were last week?" Nate asked, innocent enough.

But still, her chest pulled tight. "Florida. Meeting with some...friends."

"Wrong," Nate countered. "They were in Cuba."

Cuba?

Why Cuba?

Why not be honest?

She shook her head, dispelling the questions.

"So what?" Jo turned on him, practically spitting the words. Who was this Nate? And what happened to the sweet, gentle, kind man from yesterday? The one who looked at her as though he understood all the messy pain inside her heart? This Nate was mean and a bit of a jerk, and she was about one question away from ditching her plan altogether and calling it a day. "I hardly think that makes a big difference."

"Okay, how's this one for you?" Nate answered, voice fueled with challenge. "Why did Ryder drop out of college? Maybe that one's a little more important."

"He..." Jo trailed off, trying to read where this was going, to anticipate the surprise Nate was trying to pull. But what could Nate possibly know that she didn't? Why would Thad have lied about this? To her? "His dad died the summer before his senior year, and he went back to school, and I thought he was doing great, but he came home one day and said he couldn't do it anymore. That the things he used to think were important, didn't matter. He didn't want to be so far away from me, from my father. He didn't want to be so alone. And I understood, in a way, how losing someone like that could make his priorities shift."

Nate pressed his lips together and nodded, considering her answer.

Jo stared at him through the corner of her eye.

He kept his gaze straight ahead, lifting his coffee cup, quietly murmuring, "Your dad said he was going to retire that summer, didn't he? Said it wasn't the same without his partner around?"

How the hell do you know that? Jo shrugged, sidestepping the question. Any verbal answer she gave could be used against her father, against her.

"And you never questioned what happened? To change your dad's mind? To change Ryder's? Two big shifts, at the exact same time, right before they started working together?"

"Nope," Jo stated, letting the P really pop. Yet in the back of her mind, the wheels spun. *No, I never questioned it. Because my dad told me he was going to retire all the time, and he never did.* Part of her still didn't believe it now, despite the promises that this job would be his last, their last, the end. Why would she have dared to hope back then? *I was just so happy to have Thad home, so lonely without him, so jealous he was in school when I'd already dropped out to help my father, I didn't question it. I didn't question anything, ever. It was easier to go with the flow, to pretend.* She'd half convinced herself they were vigilante art crusaders rather than criminals, but what alternative did she have? They were her family. They were the only two people she had left in the world.

"So, Ryder never told you who visited him at campus the day before he packed his things and left?"

What the fuck?!

No!

Jo shrugged again, but her throat was tight, and her stomach was in knots. She tried to keep a straight face, tried to keep Nate from noticing the terrified buzz growing thunderous beneath her skin.

"He never mentioned any conversation, any threat, that maybe prompted a shift in priorities?"

Jo sat stock still.

"And your dad? I have some credit card receipts that indicate he was off the island around the same time? Did he tell you who he met with while he was gone?"

No. And I never asked. Because whenever I was left alone on the island, I could forget why I lived there and what my father was doing and I could just be...me. I watched the Food Network, spent hours in the kitchen, sat on the beach with a notebook dreaming up recipes, and did my best to forget. Like I'm going to do right now.

Jo stood abruptly, done with this conversation.

Nate wrapped his fingers around her wrist, firm enough to stop her, but not enough to hurt. "Jo, wait."

"Why?" She whirled around, raising her voice, unable to stop it, unable to hide how much this conversation was affecting her. "Why should I stay and listen to you? What are you even trying to do?"

"I'm trying to force you to ask yourself the questions you've been running from for your entire life." He loosened his hold, but Jo didn't walk away. The ire in his gaze had turned to concern, to caring. For some reason, that hurt worse. Yet her feet were stuck to the ground, trapped, as Nate shifted his hold, sliding his palm down her hand, lacing his fingers through hers and squeezing in a different way, a way that made her heart burn. "I'm trying to get you to see that you've been lied to for years, by the people you're risking your freedom to protect. I'm trying to tell you that there could be another way, another life, a better life…for you."

"Stop." Jo lifted her other hand and pressed her finger to his mouth.

"Why?" he asked, soft lips moving against her skin, almost like a kiss, yet so incredibly different. She dropped her hand away.

"Because I know what you're going to say," Jo murmured, staring at his chest, not able to lift her gaze that foot higher and look him in the eyes. *I know what you're going to say. You're going to offer me all my dreams on a silver platter in one hand and the knife to stab my own father in the back in the other. And I told Thad I could handle it, but if I hear it out loud...I'm not sure what I'll do.*

"I know, Nate. And my answer is no."

"Jo," he pleaded softly. "They're lying to you."

"And I'm letting them." Jo shrugged. "I'm not the innocent girl you've made me out to be, Nate. I know exactly what I'm doing."

He put his fingers under her chin, lifting her face so she had no choice but to look into the deep pools of his eyes. "Do you?"

No.

No.

No.

No.

"Yes."

They both knew she was lying.

The waver in her voice was unmistakable.

But when she wrenched her arm to the side, Nate let her go. And when she turned to walk away, he didn't try to follow.

Instead, he said, "Think about it, Jo."

She didn't comment.

"Think about it. And maybe tonight, you'll have a different answer."

Like hell I will.

But no roaring retort rose to her lips—her throat was too tight and burned too much to let one through. And as much as she wanted to storm off, not gracing Nate Parker with another millisecond of her time, all she did for the rest of the day was think about those questions he'd asked her, and the totally assured, totally confident tone he'd used.

As she sat in a chair at the hair salon.

As she got her nails painted.

As she got makeup applied.

As she returned to her room and changed into that red lace lingerie she had, in fact, bought for the evening.

As she slipped a black ball gown over her shoulders.

As she poked two emerald studs through her ears.

As she carefully arranged the items in her purse.

She thought about Nate.

And Thad.

And her father.

And what in the hell it could possibly all mean.

- 18 -

Nate

The fight went down exactly as he'd planned. The second Nate had sat on that bench, he'd recognized the Russian operative watching from fifteen feet away. A member of the American branch of the Russian mob. A hitman. A murderer. A man Jo clearly hadn't recognized, though he had been eying her closely—too closely. Nate had known he would need to make a splash to convince their audience he was shooting in the dark trying to turn Jo, so he pushed all the right buttons and didn't stop pushing until she walked away. But if he knew her at all, and by now he was beginning to think he did, his words had planted doubts. Doubts that would spin in the back of her mind all day like a strengthening hurricane. Doubts he would capitalize on at the gala later tonight. Assuming he actually managed to find a tuxedo in time.

Black tie.

Why the hell does it have to be black tie?

Nate fumed for what must have been the hundredth time that afternoon as he scoured the clearance section for a tuxedo that wouldn't cost him an entire month's salary. Tried and failed. He'd been to three department stores and four rental places, but it was too late to rent and all the cheap tuxes available for purchase didn't fit his tall, broad frame. He'd never hated his shoulders so much in his life.

A tuxedo!

After all this, a damn tuxedo is going to be my undoing!

Not the Russian mob.

Not Robert Carter.

Not Ryder.

Not Jo.

But a friggin' tuxedo.

The only possibility Leo and Nate hadn't accounted for was one where they'd be watching the gala from the inside. In all the months they'd been prepping for this mission, the plan had always been surveillance. One team on the gala. One on the auction house. One on the museum. Split into three, sitting outside in cars, maybe an undercover agent or two on the inside, but Nate was never supposed to be that person. Then Jo came along and changed all the plans.

She changed everything.

"I'm here, I'm here." Leo's out-of-breath voice interrupted Nate's ruminations. He'd been staring absently at the same rack of miscellaneous black jackets for the past twenty minutes.

Nate turned. "Took you long enough."

His partner snorted. "Fashion emergencies weren't exactly part of the training, Parker. Lucky for you my mom worked in a department store for most of my childhood, so I have a few tricks up my sleeve."

"Tricks to make a tux appear out of thin air?"

Leo grabbed Nate by the shoulders, turned him toward the escalator, and gave him a shove. "Get out of here, cut your damn hair, and let me handle this."

"Wait—" Nate dug his heels into the polished concrete floor, glancing over his shoulder. "How were things going with Ryder?"

Leo drew his brows together. "Something's going down. For a slippery bastard, he's been surprisingly easy to trail all day. When I left, he was making his way to the auction house, not a care in the world. A little too nonchalant."

Nate scowled. "Nothing I hate more than a carefree criminal."

"Unless she happens to be five-nine with red hair and piercing green eyes?" Leo asked innocently. Before Nate could bite back, his partner nudged him again. "There's a barbershop across the street. Give me half an hour, get yourself cleaned up for the event, and by the time you get back, I'll have a tux in hand."

"How—"

"Don't question it, Parker. Just go."

Leo grinned.

Nate grumbled.

But he left. And sat in a chair for thirty minutes, his leg bouncing the entire time, as the barber repeatedly and politely asked him to stay still. When it was done, he gave the guy a hefty tip and practically ran back across the street. Leo greeted him at a dressing room with a tux in hand. Black. Right size. Right cut. His partner slid two shoes under the door, polished but not too shiny, and then hung a bow tie and matching cummerbund over the side, slate gray and sharp.

Nate glanced in the mirror.

Not bad.

"How much will it cost me?" Nate asked.

"Bring it back in one piece tomorrow, and nothing," Leo drawled.

Nate yanked the door open, meeting Leo's smug face with a look of pure doubt. "Are you serious?"

"Like I said, my mom used to work in a department store. I knew the right people to kiss up to. But lunch is on you tomorrow, Parker."

"Hell, throw in breakfast too. Did you find cufflinks?"

"Here." Leo pulled a small bag from his pocket. "One of the guys has a wedding next weekend. He's flying right there from New York, so we have to get these back to him tomorrow too."

"Done."

Leo crossed his arms and gave Nate a once-over. "For a stubborn asshole, you shape up pretty nicely, Parker."

He arched a brow. "For a haughty jerkoff, you give a mean compliment, Alvarez."

"Got your comm?"

Nate pulled the earpiece out from beneath his collar and slid it on. "Got it."

"Mic?"

"On," he said, tugging his sleeve up an inch.

"Gun?"

"Tucked in my cummerbund."

"Now, there's something you don't hear every day," Leo remarked with a smile. "Badge?"

Nate patted his chest.

Leo spread his arms wide. "Then my work here is done. Off to the ball with you, Cinderfella."

"So what does that make you?" Nate scoffed. "My fairy godfather."

"I prefer suave, charming, underrated sidekick, who steals the show and goes on to star in a spin-off that makes three times as much money as the original."

Nate closed his eyes and shook his head. "What?"

Leo gave him a light shove. "Just go. Before the clock strikes twelve and dear little Jolene Carter gives us the slip again. Go get your princess, Parker."

"She's not—"

"Whatever, I don't need to know and I don't care. Do what you have to do to nail these bastards, because we've tried everything else and none of it's worked."

Nate let the protest die on his lips. "Will do."

"And Nate?" Leo asked, voice softer than usual.

He turned to his partner, taking in the somber features. "What, Leo?"

"Between us," he said, leaning in and using his palm to cover the mic attached to his collar, "if your comm happens to go dark, I'll say it was part of the plan."

Nate flinched, not sure what his partner was implying. "Leo, I—"

"I'm not saying anything. I'm just saying…" Leo lowered his chin, giving Nate a pointed look. "If it happens, for any reason. I'll back you up. Okay?"

The grooves in his face all smoothed as his muscles went slack. With gratitude. With trust. With something he wasn't sure he wanted to understand as a little knot in his chest loosened, making his stiff muscles relax.

Nate nodded. "Okay."

As they walked out of the store, Leo tossed a charming smile in the direction of a certain saleswoman who'd been staring at them. She offered them each a little wave as they slipped through the door. Around the corner, a black car waited. Leo took the front while Nate slipped into the back, a spot that was totally unfamiliar to him. But while he was inside, Ben, another agent, would be acting partner with Leo.

They made their way to the gala, reviewing the plan during the drive. Leo and Ben would work surveillance from the outside, letting Nate know if they noticed any issues with the security system, recognized any other attendees to the party, or saw anything out of the ordinary. Nate would be inside doing his best to convince Jo that whatever she was plotting wasn't worth it, that turning herself over to the authorities was her best option, and most of all, that he could save her.

"Boss, you there? We've arrived at the gala," Leo spoke into the comm. "Are the other teams in place, sir?"

"Everyone is good," the boss responded. "Ryder has been at the auction for about an hour and a half. We've seen him take two laps around the items. No bids. No clues yet. But we have eyes on the inside and a team out back. The museum has been quiet. Let us know as soon as you get something."

"Will do, sir."

"And Parker?"

Nate lifted his mic to his lips. "Yes, sir?"

"We're counting on you."

Nate heard the rest of that sentence loud and clear, without needing the boss to finish. *Your father is counting on you.*

His legacy.

His work.

His life's meaning.

All of it sat heavy on Nate's shoulders. All of it would be decided tonight.

He straightened his spine and took a deep breath, quietly adding, *I'm counting on myself.* Then he pushed away his thoughts, his reservations too, and focused on the task ahead. "Yes, sir."

Nate got out of the car and made for the townhouse across the street, where he stood in line with all the other guests decked out in fine garb, waiting to be let inside. He skipped the photo opportunity and handed over his invitation, the one they'd gotten at the last minute after speaking with the charity event planners the day before. One mention of a thief in their midst was enough to have the organization bending over backward to let the Feds inside. They'd put a subtle watermark on his card, not so obvious any of the guests could see, but obvious enough for a woman to step over and take his arm as soon as he presented it at the door.

"If you need anything, anything at all, let me know," she murmured, guiding him past the tables at the entrance and into the meat of the party.

"Will do," Nate affirmed.

"I'll let security know who you are. If you need help from us, all you have to do is ask." Her tone was very serious and completely earnest. It took everything Nate had to keep his expression controlled. The Feds wouldn't need help from her security team—he was sure that whatever measures they'd put in place had already been subverted by Jo, but he didn't want to scare the poor woman.

"Will do," he repeated, trying to ease the nerves so clearly written across her face.

She squeezed his forearm. "Thank god you're here. If anything happens, if anything—"

"Don't worry, ma'am," he soothed, offering a charming smile. "I've got everything under control."

He didn't.

Far from it.

Jo was as much of a wild card as ever, but this woman didn't need to know that.

"Thank you." Her shoulders hunched as her tension broke. "Thank you."

Nate released her with a firm nod, the action more assured than he felt, and spun, taking in the room. The house looked as if it were torn out of a textbook on the Gilded Age—the definition of opulence. Gilt moldings. Detailed woodwork. Crystal chandeliers. Heavy silk drapes. Clawfoot settees and carved mahogany tables.

The formal living room led to a formal dining room to a dark, cozy library. Each room held scattered objects from the silent auction, and he skimmed as he walked by, but nothing stood out. Nothing screamed Robert Carter. Not until he crested the steps to the ballroom on the second floor and saw a painting hanging over the fireplace that hadn't been in any of his files and the woman standing before it.

Ballerinas, clearly by Degas.

And Jolene Carter.

There was no question as to which was more beautiful in Nate's eyes. Jo's hair was piled high on her head, revealing the elegant arc of her neck and the supple curve of her spine, on display in a low-back dress that hugged her every angle. As though sensing his arrival, she turned. Their eyes met, and the room seemed to fade. The job. The operation. The reason they were here. All of it fell away as he held her gaze, for one second, then two. Neither of them turned away. There was no surprise in her expression, but the longer he looked, the more he thought he saw a bit of joy, a brilliant little spark of something bright and burning beneath her skin. And though he couldn't remember a single word he'd planned to say, Nate found himself striding across the room, steps quick and confident, as though pulled by something outside of his control.

- 19 -

Jo

Every thought in her head seemed to flee as Nate approached, a hunter on the prowl, sauntering toward his prey, slow, determined, and absolutely controlled. Jo was frozen in place, unable to break the mysterious hold he had on her, unable to look away. Her pulse sped, making her heart thunder in her chest, but she managed to keep a coy little smile across her lips. He'd never looked more handsome than he did in that black tuxedo with an ash bow tie bringing out the brightness of his eyes. But he'd never looked so menacing either, so very capable of being her undoing.

A waiter walked by, and Nate grabbed two glasses of champagne from a tray, then closed the small distance between them, offering her one.

"Drink?"

Was his voice deeper than usual? The sensual sound made her stomach muscles clench as she lifted her hand. Her fingers grazed against his as she took the flute, a shock to her system, but she managed to find her voice long enough to tease, "I didn't realize the agency allowed drinking on the job. Have I managed to rub off on you, Nate?"

"There's no specific rule one way or the other." The edge of his lip twitched with a smile as he raised the glass to his mouth and tip his head, taking a long sip.

Jo did the same. The bubbles sprinkled down her throat, spreading warmth and lightness to the center of her chest and the tips of her fingers. Her tension eased away. She breathed deeply, trying to focus on why she was there and what she was supposed to be doing, but as her eyes met Nate's over the rims of their glasses and a giggle spilled from her lips, all thoughts of work fled.

"I needed that," he joked.

"Me too."

They both looked away, perhaps because they both wanted to run from the big question hovering between their words—why?

Why was the air so charged?

Why were the stakes rising higher and higher?

Why did tonight feel different?

More intense.

More important.

More real.

Jo's gaze dropped to the floor.

Nate's must have risen to the wall, because a moment later, he asked, "Degas?"

A flare of heat spiked down her spine. But she kept her face blank. "I think so."

"Suddenly, it all becomes clear," he mused darkly.

Jo looked up, finding those baby-blues already fixed on her, the hottest part of the flame. *Ignorance. Feign ignorance.* "What do you mean?"

"Jo," Nate said, a hint of disappointment in his tone that she'd gone the route of playing dumb. "I've been wondering for weeks why the gala, what was so important here? We scoured the auction list, researched each item, brought in art experts to see if there was a hidden gem. But no, all this time, it's been about the house itself, not the event. The event was just a way inside. A way to get to this." He nudged his chin toward the painting. "I can't believe we didn't know it was here."

You didn't know because the homeowner lent the painting to a museum and conveniently forgot to mention to the FBI that it would be returned in time for the gala. A simple slip of the mind—at least, that's what he'll say if questioned. Oh, and that I must have hacked his private emails because there's no other way I could've known his plans. Of course, she couldn't tell Nate that. Instead, Jo raised her brows and held up her hands, mocking the truth he'd uncovered. "You got me. Sound the alarms. Bring in the handcuffs. Arrest me, if you're so sure."

He narrowed his eyes at the blasé tone. "Why else would you be here?"

"Did you happen to see the name of the charity hosting the event?"

Jo could see the wheels turning in the backs of his eyes. "The American Cancer Alliance."

"Ding, ding, ding," she chimed. "And in all your efforts, did the FBI happen to notice that I was invited to this event, plain and simple? I never hacked my way in. I didn't have to."

"Your father is a donor," he said, eyes widening.

Jo's chest tightened. Why was the truth so easy to spin? "He has been for ten years. Under a false name, of course. Though I have to admit, I'm surprised the agency never managed to crack his code. Campbell was my mother's maiden name."

"Your mother..." Nate trailed off, sympathy flashing in his eyes as the truth hit. His mouth parted slightly, yet no words came out.

Yes, her father was a donor. Yes, they'd given money ever since her mother had passed away. Yes, she'd been invited to the event. And yes, the only reason she was here was because it was the perfect cover for the true purpose of the night. Not that she'd tell Nate that. Even thinking it brought a wave of nausea out of hiding, self-induced disgust. The last thing she wanted was for him to see the ugly side to her. Jo liked the way Nate looked at her, as though she were an answer to his every problem—not the problem itself.

She lifted her glass to her lips, letting another gush of champagne wipe the discomfort knotting her insides away, letting the fizzing liquid spin her dizzy. Jo tilted her head back and downed it, then discarded the empty glass on a tray as a waiter walked by. Nate put his half-finished one beside hers.

"Jo—"

She pressed a finger to his lips, cutting him off. "I'm not really in the mood to talk, Nate."

And she wasn't.

Not when everything spilling from her lips was lie after lie after lie. Or even worse, the truth. Every word brought them closer together and farther apart. Her mind and her heart were at war, two opposite forces tugging and tugging against each other, fighting for dominance.

Jo *was* there for the Degas.

She could never tell Nate that.

She'd already done a sweep of the entire townhouse, walked the building, made sure the blueprints she'd studied had been accurate, made sure every door and window was exactly where she'd thought it would be.

She could never tell him that either.

She'd taken a moment to powder her nose in the restroom, using the small tablet hidden in her purse to hack into the security system and plant the final two remaining bugs in place, giving her full access to every electronic in the house—every camera, every door sensor, every motion detector.

Another thing Nate could never know.

But she'd also put a check for twenty thousand dollars in the donation box downstairs, signed anonymous, in honor of her mother. And bid outrageously high on the luxury European vacation available in the silent auction. And found the item she and her father had sent for the event, a lovely three-strand pearl necklace he'd bought for her mother but had never been able to give her. Their twentieth anniversary had been two weeks after she'd passed. There was other jewelry of her mother's Jo would never dream of parting with, but that one piece had always been too painful to wear. The least she could do was give it to a good cause.

But Jo would never tell Nate any of that, even though she could. Because she didn't want him to look at her like the hero she knew she wasn't. His eyes already shone too bright, so full of hope she had to look away.

He slipped his fingers through hers.

"Then how about a dance instead?"

The music had hardly registered before, but now that Nate mentioned it, she became acutely aware of the sound. Soft orchestral strains filled the room, slow and romantic. A few couples had stepped from the outskirts to gently sway hand in hand.

"Nate," Jo said, voice thick. They were entering dangerous territory. Tenuous ground.

And though she'd told Thad her plan was to seduce Agent Parker to steal information, here, now, with his palm pressed against the small of her back as he led her onto the dance floor, Jo wasn't sure she was prepared to deal with the ramifications of that plan. Not when she knew deep down that her heart was in the game, though it without a doubt shouldn't have been.

Nate swept her around to face him, confident and controlled as he held her body close and lifted her right hand. His chin pressed against her temple so they were chest to chest, hardly any space in between. Not asking permission, he stepped. She followed, letting him lead, her body swaying in tune with his, so naturally—too naturally. The fingers resting on the small of her back began to trace the contours of her spine, up and down, then in small circles, sending a tingle up her back and across her skin. Did he know what he was doing? Was he even aware? Jo was too aware. Too sensitive to his touch. Beneath the surface, an electric charge gathered, spiking with heat as tingles shot across her nerves like little bolts of lightning, a storm only Nate Parker seemed capable of creating.

She started to panic.

Jo had to keep things neutral.

Safe.

At a distance.

Plans be damned. At this point, it was pure self-preservation.

"Where'd a Fed learn how to dance?" she asked, using humor as her shield.

Nate wasn't buying it. He pressed his nose into her hair. The warm brush of his breath against her neck sent her nerves into a tizzy as sparks caught fire, one after another after another, spreading down the nape of her neck and across her shoulder. "You look beautiful tonight."

Jo breathed in, trying to get air to her struggling lungs.

Keep it light.

Keep it surface.

"You don't look half-bad yourself," she teased.

He nuzzled closer so they were cheek to cheek. "Did you think about what I said?"

What?

She resisted the urge to physically shake her head.

Where the hell did that come from?

Jo jerked back, just far enough to stare into his eyes, to meet his subtle challenge head-on. "You want to do this here? Now?"

"I'm not doing anything, Jo." Nate shrugged, far too casual to mean it. The left edge of his lip quirked. "I'm just asking a simple question. Did you think about it?"

Yes.

"No."

"You ran a background check on me, right? Before New York?"

She narrowed her eyes, scrutinizing him, but nodded anyway, playing along.

"Did you ever wonder why a special agent in the organized crime unit was investigating an art thief and his daughter?"

Yes.

"No."

He continued as though he didn't hear her response. "The man following us yesterday was a member of the American branch of the Russian mafia. Did you know that?"

No!

"No…"

"Extremely dangerous. Probably the most violent active organized crime unit in the United States today. Involved in narcotics trafficking, arms deals, loan-sharking, murder-for-hire, and don't forget, the occasional forgery. Though, they have other people to help them with that."

Jo shook her head in denial.

He tightened his grip on her hand and dug his fingers into her back as though anticipating her instinct to run.

"I don't believe you."

But she did.

Her gut clenched painfully tight. Because deep down, she did. Bit by bit, things clicked into place. Puzzle pieces and questions she'd pushed to the back of her mind slowly slipped out of hiding, fitting together to form a picture she didn't want to see, didn't want to know, yet couldn't prevent from forming. The meetings her father and Thad disappeared to. The hours they spent together, in planning sessions she wasn't allowed to join. The people who followed her. The paintings that went missing. The money that came in. Most of all, the deep shame that sometimes glimmered in the backs of Thad's stormy eyes, in the backs of her father's green ones, dark and overwhelming.

What do you know, Nate?

What haven't they told me?

What am I part of?

"You're a smart girl, Jo. In fact, I find your intelligence incredibly sexy. So I didn't understand at first why you'd allow yourself to be so willfully ignorant." He paused, letting his words sink in, letting her doubts simmer. Jo swallowed, stepping where he stepped, letting him lead, because she was hanging on his next words, mentally paralyzed. "And then, once I got to know you, understand you, everything became clear. Love."

"Love?" Jo's voice was breathy as she repeated the word.

"Love can make you blind," Nate murmured, then leaned close, pressing his lips against her ear. "Or if you let it, love can finally make you see."

"Nate—"

He cut her protest off by pushing against her waist, sending her spiraling into a circle as the music hit a crescendo. Their fingers clasped tight as he twirled her across the dance floor. His touch was the only thing that kept her from floating away. And a second later, she was back, pressed against his chest, looking up into those understanding eyes, those pleading eyes.

"Don't you want to see, Jo?" He held her hand and released her hip again, so she spun and spun and spun, body a mirror of the turmoil circling inside her brain.

She did want to see.

She did.

But she couldn't.

Because it would make everything fall apart.

Her family.

Her life.

The balance she'd so carefully maintained.

Jo landed back in Nate's arms. She dropped her gaze to his chest, focusing on the little wire hanging from his ear, remembering the mic that had to be hidden by his wrist. Because he was a Fed. The enemy. But when he leaned down, the smell of woodsy soap and something entirely him filled her nose, and it became more difficult to draw that line. With his fingers brushing softly over her spine and his other hand rubbing her palm and his warm breath tickling her neck, everything blurred. Right. Wrong. Loyalty. Love.

"I have files," he quietly pressed. "I have photographs. I have pages upon pages of information. Coincidences that are far too frequent and counterfeits with your father's signature flair. All I need is proof. Concrete proof that will hold up in court."

Her heart pounded so hard she feared it would break free of her chest.

Drumming and drumming and drumming.

His words swirled, a tornado plowing through her thoughts.

Files. Photographs. Information.

Coincidences. Counterfeits.

Files.

Files.

Files.

Jo looked up into his eyes. He stared back.

Screw caution.

The thought sliced like a knife, cutting through her indecision.

Screw my heart.

Screw my fear.

I need to know.

I need those files.

I need to know.

A new plan stirred—not for Thad, not for her father, not for Nate, but for her. For the first time, for her. Because she needed the truth. She needed whatever information the Feds had. She needed to open her eyes. And when she did, maybe then her choice would become clear. At least, she hoped and prayed it would.

Jo licked her lips, took a deep breath, and stepped over that invisible line etched in the sand. "What can you offer me, Nate? What are your terms?"

- 20 -

Nate

A switch flipped in the depths of her emerald eyes. One moment she was fighting, denying, her thoughts a raging storm clouding her gaze. And the next, those irises were clear. Open and seeing. And yet, a little doubt whispered in the back of his mind that this couldn't be real, that it couldn't have possibly been so easy, that this was just another game Jo was trying to play. He'd been prepared for a fight, for resilience, not for this bare, vulnerable honesty now spreading between them.

"Immunity," he said quickly, grip tightening, as though to catch her and keep her in his arms before she had a chance to fly away. "I can offer you immunity."

Her eyes widened with surprise. "Full immunity?"

"Full immunity," he repeated, holding her gaze captive. "You can have the future you want, Jo. All your dreams, they're within reach. You want a bakery? You can have one. You can have ten. You can live the rest of your life without having to look over your shoulder, without having to wonder if anyone is on your tail, if anyone is watching. You can be free. All I need is your signature on a piece of paper."

"And my cooperation." She licked her plush red lips and swallowed, dropping her focus to the floor. The hand on his shoulder tightened, as though she was holding on to him for support, for comfort. Her chest swelled as she drew in a long, deep breath and looked back up. "What would I have to do?"

Nate's pulse raced.

I'm so close.

We're so close.

I can't believe it.

After so long.

After so many dead ends.

He tried not to let his excitement, his victory, leak into his tone, not when he knew that for Jo, the pieces were falling apart, not finally coming together. "We need access to the vault."

She squeezed her eyes tight but nodded.

"And we need you to wear a wire," he added softly. "We need your father on tape talking about his dealings with the Russians."

Her eyes shot open. "No."

"It's the only way," Nate murmured, dropping his chin to study her expression. It was carefully controlled, yet there was panic subtly written in the way her bottom lip trembled, the way her jaw clenched.

Nate stopped dancing.

He dropped his hold on her body and brought both of his hands to her face, then brushed his thumbs over her cheekbones, crossing a line, but in that moment, he didn't care about professionalism. He cared about Jo. So he tilted her chin up, soothing her with his touch, as he tried to do the same with his words. "I'll guide you through it, Jo, every step of the way. I can't promise it will be easy, but I can promise it's the right thing to do. Five minutes, maybe ten, and you'll be free."

She covered his wrists with her palms, not pulling him away, but holding on tight. "He's my father."

"He made his choices," Nate countered. "You deserve the chance to make your own."

"What will happen to him?" Her voice was small. Fragile. Something Nate had never associated with Jolene Carter before. He hated the hurt he knew he was causing, but there was no other way.

"That depends on him, Jo, not on you. We're after much bigger fish than your father. If he cooperates, we could get him an easier sentence, a more comfortable cell, maybe a chance at probation." Nate didn't give the alternative option, but she heard it through his silence.

He jumped in before he lost her completely. "But no matter what, we can keep him safe, Jo. Safe from the people he's working with—people who wouldn't hesitate to kill him."

She took a stilted breath. "And what about Thad?"

It took everything in his power not to wrinkle his nose with disgust. *Ryder.* Nate had no idea what she saw in the man aside from a criminal. "He'll have the same options."

"Jail?" The word was little more than a whisper.

Nate's brows pushed together, but he nodded nonetheless. She deserved honesty. After living in so many lies, she deserved honesty from at least him.

Jo curled her fingers through his, so they held hands against her cheeks. Her eyes were wide with an innocence he didn't quite understand how she'd managed to preserve, shining with a trust he wasn't sure how he'd earned. And yet, the feelings were there, simmering between them. Loyalty. And another word he wasn't sure if he was ready to face, or even knew how to.

"And you'll be there, Nate?"

"Every step of the way." He squeezed her fingers, showing her with everything he had how much he meant his words. "Whatever you need, Jo."

She pulled her lower lip into her mouth, making his chest pinch and his blood boil as it slowly relaxed back into its normal, plump position. "And what about after?"

With his focus on her lips and the heat stirring beneath his skin, the words failed to fully register. "After?"

"After, Nate, will you—"

"Parker, do you have any updates?"

Leo's voice coming through the comm made Nate jolt upright. His hands dropped from her cheeks, and his feet shuffled back, bringing much-needed space between them. Jo's gaze immediately jumped to the wire disappearing beneath his collar.

He lifted his wrist to his mouth. "Not now, Leo."

The words came out as more of a snarl than he intended.

"Ryder just exited the auction. He's headed toward the museum a few blocks away. Do you have eyes on Jolene Carter?"

"I—" Nate cut himself off. Jo stared. At his mic. At his comm. At him. Accusation and something too close to hurt bright and shiny in her eyes. "I have Jo in sight."

She took a step back, tilting her head to the side as though asking him to give her a reason to stop. He couldn't.

"I have to go, Leo."

"Did she take the bait? Are you getting anywhere with her?"

"I have to go."

But it was too late.

Jo moved farther and farther away. By the time he dropped his wrist back to his side, she'd turned and was halfway across the ballroom, walking fast. People watched, stared. He'd been too wrapped up in Jo to notice they'd become the entertainment. He didn't care.

"Jo!"

She didn't stop. She walked straight through the open French doors, into the hallway, and down the stairs, taking the steps as fast as her hip-hugging dress would allow her.

"Jo! Wait!"

When he reached the bottom step, she was already disappearing around a bend. He ran after, murmuring apologies as he bumped into people, flying through the house, concerned with nothing more than keeping that red hair within sight. She slipped into a room, out of another, maneuvering through the crowd and the house as though she lived there, as though she knew every turn, every door, had the entire place memorized. She probably did. Which left Nate more convinced than ever that the Degas was exactly what Robert Carter was after, sending his daughter to do his dirty work. The man was disgusting. Vile. He deserved to be in jail. He deserved whatever he got.

A cool blast of air hit Nate's cheek.

He scanned the room.

There!

Open patio doors.

Nate raced through, skidding into the private courtyard as he spun, trying to find her through the tall shrubs and the crowd that had wandered outside.

Jo. Jo. Jo.

He spotted her at the far end of the courtyard, half hidden in shadow. Where was she going? What was the plan? A second later, he understood, as she opened a door hidden behind a curtain of ivy. Some of the old townhouses on the Upper East Side had service entrances out the back, usually into a communal alleyway. Nate raced for the exit and forced it open as he sprinted into the night. Her dress was dark enough to blend into the evening shadows, but her sun-kissed skin was illuminated by moonlight, the smooth planes of her back a beacon to his eyes.

"Jo, stop! Wait!"

"Why?" she snapped.

Now that he could see her only way out, there was nothing holding him back. With a foot on her and legs in pants instead of a tight dress, Nate finally caught up and grabbed her hand, spinning her around.

"Don't do it, Jo."

"Don't do what?" she spat.

"Ryder is on the move. That's what Leo was telling me through the comm. Ryder is on the move, and you're going to meet him." Nate paused, taking a deep breath.

His grip loosened, giving her the chance to leave, the choice not to. "Don't."

Jo lifted her face, turning to look up at him.

For a moment, Nate swore the stars reflected in her eyes.

"Why shouldn't I, Nate? Give me one good reason."

His throat went dry. "Your dreams. I can make them happen."

"My dreams…" She released a puff of air as the edge of her lip rose with a sad little smile. "I don't need you to make my dreams come true, Nate Parker. I already know I'm the only one stopping myself from achieving them."

He opened his mouth.

No sound came out.

Jo stared at him, giving him the chance to speak, to offer her anything, everything, whatever it took to make her stay.

But he couldn't.

A clog in his throat held him back.

She turned.

He tightened his fingers. "Jo…"

"There's a problem with your deal, Nate," she whispered, not letting go of his hand but not holding on either, just letting it be, letting them hover in an in-between. "The word 'deal' implies an exchange. But the way I see it, I'm giving everything, and you're giving nothing. Immunity? I'm free now. You don't have anything on me. If you did, I'd be arrested already. I can't be the only one risking my life, the only one with something to lose."

"What do you want from me?" he rasped, not understanding.

Jo glanced back toward his face, studying him with her gaze, reading every hard edge, every line, every curve. "Show me you have something to lose."

"I do, Jo. More than you know."

"Like what?"

He balled his hands into fists. "My job. My respect. My justice."

"I'm not talking about that." Jo shook her head.

"Then what?" He didn't understand. "What are you talking about?"

Jo squared her shoulders, facing him fully, no longer trying to run. "Take your comm out."

"I can't. It's against protocol."

Jo arched a single brow. "Take your comm out."

Nate ground his teeth. Was this what Leo had foreseen? Was this what his partner had been afraid of?

The rules...or Jo? The rules... His boss would understand.

Nate plucked the piece from his ear and yanked on the wire leading to the mic at his wrist, pulling the entire unit free from his tux and holding it out to Jo.

"Unplug it."

He held her gaze for a moment, then disconnected all the wires and let the batteries fall to the ground before he shoved the useless set into his pocket.

Jo stepped closer.

She put her palms to his chest.

She leaned in.

"Don't you see, Nate?"

He searched her eyes for the answer to her question but couldn't find it.

"Me, Nate," she whispered. "I want to be your something to lose."

He froze.

Jo didn't pause. She slid her hands over his shoulders and curled her fingers around the back of his head, massaging his scalp in a way that made sparks dance across his eyes.

"It's just you and me. No partners. No teams. No rules. If I walk away right now, I can still have my bakery. I can still have my freedom. I can still have my family. All I lose is you." She lifted onto her toes, pressing her breasts against his chest, her lips to his ears. Her breath was a warm kiss dancing across his skin. "Convince me to stay."

His head dropped onto her shoulder as his muscles gave out, his fight. His voice came out a deep groan. "Jo..."

"Convince me you don't want to lose me either."

Every moment since they'd met had been leading them here.

To this inevitable choice.

One that would have been easy a mere week before but now seemed impossible.

Jo was a felon.

A criminal.

Everything he hated.

Everything he fought to destroy.

And yet, she was so much more. Warm and exciting. Full of wonder and joy. A bright spark igniting a fire within him, burning hotter than anything he'd ever felt before. They didn't make sense. They never would. And yet, being around her felt right, felt perfect for those few seconds when he could forget the world and focus only on them. She made him want to share parts of himself he'd never shared with anyone. Being around her was like riding a bike for the first time—thrilling, exhilarating. He never knew what came next. There was a bit of fear, a bit of risk, but most of all there was a sense of fun, of wonder, of hope, a sense he'd thought he'd lost a long time ago but had somehow found with her.

Being with her would break all the rules.

His life would no longer be black and white.

But maybe there was a different sort of glory to be found in shades of gray.

A different kind of beauty, if he'd just open his eyes and see, if he'd only let her show him.

Nate lifted his forehead from her shoulder.

Jo sighed.

She dropped back to her heels.

She let her hands fall down his chest and started to turn.

In that split second, Nate saw a future where he let her go, let her walk away, let her leave. He saw her slip around the corner, gone forever, no trace left behind. And his world went dark. As though there was no light without her.

"Stay with me."

The words tumbled out before his mind could stop them, propelling straight from his heart and into the world, like a bullet from a gun.

Jo hesitated.

He gripped her upper arms.

Time rushed forward. A single second turned to an hour. The world blurred, moving faster and faster, moving on without them, as they froze, halted in this moment. Those big green eyes were the only things in acute focus. Those eyes and the decision his heart had made long before his mind had caught up.

"Stay with me," Nate said, louder this time.

Confident.

Firm.

Convincing.

Jo opened her mouth to answer, but Nate didn't let her. Whatever her response, it was swallowed by his lips as he lifted her to her toes and brought her face close, bending his to meet it. Their mouths crashed together, as inevitable as a wave against the shore, impossible to fight, impossible to stop, as nature intended, somehow meant to be.

- 21 -

Jo

At first, it had all been a game. Dance with Nate. Seduce Nate. Tell him what he wanted to hear so she could get where she needed to go—to his room, to his files, to her information. But with each passing second, with each consecutive word, the game changed, bit by bit, until his lips finally touched hers and everything shifted. No more rules. No more tricks. No more deceit. Jo realized every confession that had spilled from her mouth had been real, honest, pulled straight from her heart, and it sent her world off its axis, leaving her unbalanced and unsteady, forcing her to hold on to Nate as her anchor in the storm.

She wanted her freedom.
She wanted her bakery.
She wanted her dreams.

And there was no more denying that she wanted Nate Parker too. He was her something to lose, just as she was his. But there was only one way to keep him—betray the other two men she loved.

Jo pushed that thought away for another time and snaked her arms around Nate's back, digging her fingers into his shoulders as she pulled him closer, deepening their kiss, getting lost in it. A groan stirred deep in his throat as his palms slid up her arms and into her hair, fingers gripping her scalp, possessive and commanding, yet somehow gentle and tender. He tilted her head as his lips shifted, peppering across her skin in scorching touches that were too short, too urgent, trailing down her neck until he found that sensitive spot along the curve, eliciting a sigh as her head fell back. His tongue flicked, fast and searing, making her toes curl in the tips of her heels as her vision spotted, overwhelmed by the magic of his touch.

"Jo," he rasped, voice deep and demanding. The warmth of his breath sent a shiver down her spine. "Stay with me."

He captured her lips again, hungry and hard, smashing any protest as she melted into his embrace, muscles turning weak.

I will.

I will.

The answer bubbled at the back of her throat, but before she could say it, a light flashed over them, bright and jarring, the headlights of a car. They broke apart, foreheads pressed together, nothing but ragged breath and a few bare inches between them. Light strains of music and the dull murmur of conversation filled the empty alley, spilling over the wall, bringing her back to reality.

Jo opened her mouth to say she would stay, but instead, a different sentiment spilled out. "Come with me."

Nate blinked, the heady passion clearing from his eyes. "What?"

Jo grabbed both of his hands and took a step backward, tugging him along. "Come with me."

"Where?" He shook his head. Jo could see the rules and regulations and logic starting to flood back into his gaze. "The car is around front. Follow me, and we can find Leo. We can go to headquarters. You can sign the papers. We can—"

"Nate," Jo said, yanking hard on his hands, forcing him to focus on her. Because paperwork and offices and more Feds were the last things she wanted right now. All she wanted was him. Alone. No urgency. No rush. The two of them in a room with all the time in the world. And Jo knew from her snooping that his hotel was about thirty blocks south. "Come with me."

He scrunched his brows but followed, still holding her hand as she wound them through the rest of the alleyway and the gated entrance to the street, far down the other side of the block where no one from the gala would ever see them. Nate turned left, but Jo tugged him right and lifted her free arm. Two seconds later, a cab pulled to a stop on the street corner.

Jo got in.

Nate looked to where his partner must have been waiting, looked at her, looked back, and then followed her inside.

"Fiftieth and Lex, please," Jo murmured to the driver.

Nate cut her a confused glance and then said, "Actually, can we go to 26 Federal Plaza."

Jo rolled her eyes with a sigh. That was the address of the FBI headquarters in New York. A definite no, thank you.

Difficult. Why do men always have to be so incredibly difficult?

She squeezed Nate's palm and leaned close, pressing her lips to his ear, letting her chest rub against his arm. Her free hand landed on his mid-thigh and crept ever so slightly higher as she whispered, "Do you remember the photo I sent you?"

His eyes practically bulged from his head. The red lace panties. The just-padded-enough bra to perk her chest into optimal position. Oh, he remembered. He definitely remembered. At the time, she'd thought she'd only been teasing him with the idea of barely there lingerie, but in the back of her head, she must have always known where the night would lead. Why else would she have spent a few hundred dollars purchasing new undergarments when she'd already had some perfectly acceptable black cotton ones for the evening? Not sexy, per se, but acceptable.

"Do you remember why I bought them?" she continued, nuzzling into his neck, pressing a soft kiss to his skin.

Nate cleared his throat and shifted his weight. "Yes..."

The obvious strain in his voice brought a wicked smile to her lips. "Don't you want to see if I was lying, Agent Parker? If you can catch me *red*-handed?"

She licked him, darting her tongue against his steaming skin for a hot, quick second, as she tightened her grip on his leg. And then she fell back into her seat and crossed her arms, staring at him with a brow lifted.

Nate swallowed.

Slowly.

And then leaned forward to tell the cabbie, "Fiftieth and Lex, please."

The address of his hotel.

As he well knew.

When Nate sat back down, he reached over and tugged her hand free, so their clasped palms rested on the empty seat between them. Jo didn't fight it. In fact, she liked the feel of his large calloused hands in hers, the rough scrape she couldn't wait to feel on other parts of her skin, the way he took charge. He absently rubbed his thumb over her knuckle, shifting and teasing, tracing shapes along her skin. She loved that it seemed to require no thought, no conscious effort, as though touching her was as easy and as simple as breathing, as necessary too. Where his fingers traveled, heat began to boil and stir, spreading up her arms and into the air, filling the small interior with a heat entirely of their making.

The silence stretched.

The tension grew.

Taut and tight.

A passionate kiss in the heat of the moment was one thing, but a decision, a choice, made consciously, fully aware of where it would lead, was quite another. They both knew exactly what they were doing. And somehow, that made every touch burn, every momentary glance sear, every fleeting second stretch, longer and longer. There was a unique sort of sexiness in knowingly choosing each other, something different from getting lost in the moment, something infinitely deeper and infinitely more intense, and it went without saying as the temperature rose between them. Their hands danced. Their eyes met across too far a distance, both gazes full of the heady desire of knowing exactly where the night would take them.

"Tell me about after," Jo whispered. After the interviews. After the paperwork. After the weeks of hurt and confusion, when the whole mess was done, and she was free, and her criminal days were long behind her, and there was nothing tangible tying them together, what then?

This time, Nate understood exactly what she meant. He didn't look down. He didn't back away. He held her gaze, eyes bright and hopeful. "You could stay with me, for a while, if you want to. While you're getting back on your feet."

The moment she handed her father over to the Feds, she'd lose everything. All her possessions would be confiscated as evidence. All her bank accounts would be frozen. She'd be starting over again, no assets, no family, no support system to help her. His offer meant more than he knew. She squeezed his fingers tight, a small smile on her lips. "Oh, and what sort of place does a single federal agent constantly on the move live in? I've become accustomed to a certain standard, you know."

Her tone was teasing.

His expression was too. "Well, we can't all live on private islands. Some of us have to make do with one-bedroom apartments, but I can promise it'll be clean. And I live close to downtown DC. Lots to see, lots to do, enough to keep even you entertained, I'd imagine."

An image infiltrated her thoughts. His bed was probably perfectly made, one pillow, maybe two, because he was a man, after all. The sheets were probably blue. The comforter too. Though maybe there was a red stripe in the mix somewhere—he did have that all-American vibe. If she snooped through his drawers, she would bet anything his clothes were perfectly folded, neatly organized. His kitchen was probably pristine, nothing but take-out boxes in his fridge, the sort of spot begging for someone like her to come around and put it to good use.

Typical.

Perfectly typical.

"I'd need a new computer," she murmured, undertone undeniably goading.

He lifted a brow.

She shrugged. "For applying to culinary school, obviously."

"Obviously."

"But I think it could work," she commented, tone light, though his probing gaze seemed to pick up on the deeper emotions swirling in the back of her thoughts. Could he see the pictures flashing? Jo in an apron and nothing else, waiting to greet him when he got home.

Nate surprising her at the bakery where she worked because he'd just returned from an overseas assignment. Jo curled against his side as he studied paperwork for a new case and she brainstormed the latest rendition of the coopie. Nate kissing the sugar from her cheeks as they stumbled down the hall to that one bedroom they would share.

He rubbed his thumb over her palm a final time as the cab pulled to a stop. "It could work."

Then he dropped her hand and pushed her door open so she could get out while he paid. Nate joined her a moment later, pressing his palm to the small of her back, always teasing with his touch, exploring her curves, roving over her skin, moving, constantly moving, so there was no break in the tingles spreading and sparking with uncontained fire.

Jo held on to the beautiful dream of after as they made their way through the lobby and into the elevator, as they rose higher and higher, alone yet not quite, waiting a tantalizing wait until they were inside his room, no cameras, no people, no one but each other.

They paused just beyond the doorway.

No need to rush.

Nothing but time.

Nate lifted his hand to her cheek and brushed the backs of his fingers against her skin, as though she were the most precious thing in the world, a gift he couldn't believe he'd received, a treasure he couldn't believe he'd found. Jo lifted her hands to gently tug on the knot of his bowtie until it came free. She slid it around his neck, letting it fall to the floor, never once releasing his gaze as she reached back up to slip his jacket off his broad shoulders, feeling his muscles writhe beneath her gentle touch. And then she went for his buttons, slipping the collar loose, then the one below, the one below, down and down and down, until a taunting inch of his skin was revealed from his throat to his navel. They paused, breathing deeply, as though somehow, they both knew it would be their last taste of air for a while.

Jo moved first, pressing her palms to his chest as he inhaled sharply, her touch as burning as his simmering skin, too hot to handle, a fire she couldn't stop herself from stoking. Jo ran her hands up his smooth chest, pushing the shirt from his shoulders, feeling every contour of hard muscles as her fingers gripped his biceps and traced the cut edges all the way to his wrists. His cufflinks dropped to the floor with two soft *thuds*, followed by the silent flutter of his shirt. As she stared at the firm ridges of his abdomen, the deep V disappearing into the line of his pants, Nate reached for her hips, found the zipper to her dress, and pulled it down. His hands slid beneath the fabric, the rough calluses scratching in the right way as his fingers traveled slowly up her sides, grazing the edges of her breasts, not stopping until he reached the straps balanced carefully on her shoulders. Nate pushed them to the side and let gravity do the rest as her dress slid all the way to the floor. His eyes followed, tracing every inch of her body in the moonlight coming through the window, gaze as tangible as a soft caress, turning her blood molten. She sucked in sharply, finding it difficult to breathe.

Those baby-blues found her again, hooded with passion.

The moment stretched as the temperature around them flared.

They were two objects on a crash course, stuck in that indefinite moment before the inevitable, where time seemed to stop and hover, both aware that in a split second everything was about to change, but there was nothing to do but hold tight and give in and ride the wave.

Jo's throat went dry.

Unable to stop her defenses from flaring, she parted her mouth. "Better in person, huh?"

Nate lifted his hand and ran his thumb across her lower lip. "You're beautiful."

"Well—" she started, but the earnestness in his eyes made her pause, overwhelmed.

"You're perfect, Jo," he whispered. "You're perfect."

And just like that, they collided.

No more slow.

No more calm.

Urgent and hungry, throwing caution to the wind, they let the wild spark that had always simmered between them take over. Their kisses were demanding and rough. He clasped the back of her head, fingers digging into her updo, tugging bobby pins loose with the perfect sort of pain, until all her hair tumbled free. Jo undid the buckle on his belt and pushed his pants to the floor before dipping her fingers beneath the elastic band at his waist. With a groan, Nate grabbed her hands and stumbled forward, until her back hit a wall and he pinned her to it, bodies so tight there wasn't an ounce of air between them. He held her hands above her head with one of his, taking charge, taking over, as his lips tasted every inch of her skin, starting from her neck, working their way over the peak of one breast, down her stomach, farther and farther until she gasped for air.

He grabbed her by the thighs and lifted her into the air. Beneath her palms, his biceps flexed, strong and more than capable as he carried her to the bed. They sank slowly down, eyes locked the entire time he pressed her spine into the mattress, then settled his weight on her. Jo went for his waistband again, but Nate grabbed her wrists and held them against the pillow as his free hand dipped beneath the band of her bra, exploring her supple curves, a clear destination in mind, as though he'd spent a lot of time mapping his route and nothing, not even Jo, could steer him off course. His palm sank farther, and the protest died on her lips as bright lights flashed behind her closed eyes. A sigh slipped out instead.

Clearly, Nate had rules for the bedroom too.

Though as his lips dipped to find the spot his hand just vacated, Jo decided she didn't mind these rules.

No…she didn't mind these rules at all.

- 22 -

Nate

Nate didn't think he would ever tire of touching her, running his hands along her curves, connecting the dots between her freckles, marveling at the silky softness, so perfectly feminine compared to his rough hands and hard edges. Jo was sprawled across his chest, her chin resting on her hands, which were folded over his heart. Her auburn hair cascaded down her back, splashing over his abs, a gossamer curtain framing her lovely face. His left arm wrapped around her torso, holding her close, fingers continuing to explore because he couldn't physically force them to stop. His right arm was folded beneath his head like a pillow, holding his eyes at the perfect angle to study the woman casually displayed before him.

He tried to focus on what she was saying, but the more he studied the plump arc of her lips, the more his mind went to other activities, activities they'd already done twice already, but his body seemed to want more. And Nate wasn't exactly complaining about that...

"Nate. Nathaniel. Nate!"

"Huh?" He blinked.

Jo grinned, arching a brow. "You're insatiable."

He shrugged. "Maybe you're just irresistible."

"Well, I am that," she teased, smile deepening. But her head dropped to the side with sleepiness as a yawn interrupted her taunt. "I was asking what you'll be assigned to next. Will you be able to stick around for a while? Or will you just be gone?"

He didn't like the hollow sound of her voice as she finished speaking. "I don't know."

Jo pulled her bottom lip into her mouth, biting it for a moment as her gaze dropped to his chest, but not fast enough. Disappointment flashed in those green eyes, disappointment and gloom. It wasn't the first time Nate had seen a similar response to his demanding work, but it was the first time it hit him like a punch to the gut, painful and in need of fixing. If Jo was about to uproot her entire life to help him, to help the bureau, the very least he could do was try to stick around for a while, to be there for her while she adjusted to what would be a whole new world. He held her closer, prompting her to look back up.

"I can talk to Leo, see what he thinks, but we've been nonstop for the past few years. It wouldn't be the worst thing to lie low for a while, put in some time at the office instead of in the field. If we get—" Nate paused, flicking his gaze to the side for a moment and then back. He was going to say, *if we get your father to confess, if we nail the Russians,* but he didn't want to mention Carter or Ryder, didn't want to see more shadows cloud her eyes. "If everything works out, we'll be doing paperwork for a while to prepare for trial anyway. And by the time that's done, who knows, you'll probably be sick of me."

"Hmm…"

Nate didn't realize the vulnerability laced through his words until she didn't immediately contradict them. But his chest pulled tight as his breath hitched with an acute shot of panic.

"I don't think that'll happen," she confessed softly. And then everything in her expression shifted to mischief and mirth, lips curving, brows raising, eyes sparkling. "If anything, you'll get sick of me. You seem like the type to fold his underwear."

"What?" Nate blurted, unable to stop himself as the typical Jolene Carter whiplash syndrome hit. A protest stirred on his lips, but he shook his head, because he was, after all, an underwear folder. Well, a boxer-briefs folder to be exact, but that was beside the point. "What does that even mean, Jo?"

She shrugged against his chest. "I'm not an underwear folder, Nate. I'm not really much of a folder at all. I'm a piler. I pile and pile and pile until it starts toppling over and I can't pile any longer."

Nate shuddered. The image of his pristine apartment overrun by mounds of clothes, heaps of shoes, strewn without rhyme or reason, without order... "I'll do the laundry," he said quickly, dispelling the horrifying picture in his mind. "You do the cooking, and I'll do the cleaning."

Jo grinned. "That was easier than I thought it'd be."

"What?" He arched a brow, studying her, taking in that self-satisfied smirk. "Are you playing me, Jo?"

She opened her eyes and dropped her jaw in mock horror. "Would I do that?"

Yes. Yes, you would.

"Using my own vices against me," Nate drawled, shaking his head.

"Cleanliness is a virtue," she countered.

"Fine," Nate said, tightening his grip on her waist. "Then you're using your vices against me, which is even worse."

"I never claimed to play fair..." Jo trailed off as she traced a heart over his chest. "I play to win."

Nate snorted. "Okay then, Jo, maybe we should do my favorite thing. Lay some ground rules. So we both know exactly what we're getting into here."

"Ugh," Jo groaned and rolled her eyes in mock disgust…at least, he hoped it was mocking. "Lay it on me, Parker."

"The last woman I lived with was my mother, a decade ago, so I leave the toilet seat up sometimes. You're going to have to get used to it."

She studied him for a moment, as if balancing the options, but nodded with silent approval. "I'm not one of those girls who only eats salad and loves to share food. When I order a bowl of pasta, it's because I want to eat that whole damn bowl of pasta. And if your fork wanders over to my dish uninvited, I can't be blamed for the consequences."

"Noted," he said smoothly, but really, he found a woman who enjoyed eating a turn-on. "Working for the FBI, you get used to hard deadlines and having to constantly monitor the time. If you're running late, or we're running late, I might be a bit of an ass about it. But I'll always apologize later."

"Can I get flowers or chocolates as part of that apology?"

The edge of his lip twitched. "That could probably be arranged…"

"Then I'm in," Jo confirmed. She absently drummed her fingers against his chest as she thought of what to say next. "Ooh! Contrary to what tonight might lead you to believe, I'm totally a morning person. My idea of a late night is staying up past eleven. And if I fall asleep and you try to wake me up, I can be vicious in my catatonic state…or so I've been told."

"Good thing I don't seem to have a problem carrying you around," he said, letting his tone verge into the highly suggestive, so both their minds drifted back to her legs wrapped around his waist, his hands digging into her thighs, her back against the wall. No, lifting her was not a problem in the slightest. In fact, it had been nothing but immensely pleasurable thus far.

The sight of her blush made his blood stir. "Yeah, well… Don't say I didn't warn you."

"Okay, here's a doozy for you." He paused for dramatic effect, waiting until her eyes narrowed with curiosity and her lips puckered. "I don't like sweets."

"What?" She gasped and leaned on her elbows, sitting up. And then she stared at him as though trying to see straight through him. "You're joking."

He shook his head. "I'm not."

"You don't like dessert?"

"Worst part of the meal."

"Cake?"

"Not my favorite."

"Brownies?"

"Too rich."

"Ice cream. You have to give me ice cream."

"I'd rather have a cold beer."

Her nose wrinkled in disgust. "This might be a deal breaker. I can't risk the DNA passing down and having a child who won't eat my homemade chocolate chip cookies."

"Jo," he muttered, worried for a moment that there was true panic in her voice.

"Cookies!" she cried suddenly, and then turned on him, pressing both of her palms into his shoulders. Jo held him down against the bed with all her weight as she leaned over him, closer and closer, so they were practically nose to nose. "Don't tell me you honestly didn't like my coopies."

"The coopies..." He paused while she sucked in a breath and held it. Then he grinned. "The coopies, I loved."

The energy in her smile could've powered the entire hotel. Hell, it could have powered all of New York. "Then there's hope for us yet, Nate Parker."

He couldn't stop himself from closing the distance between their lips and sealing that promise with a kiss. Because for the first time, tonight with Jo, when he thought about the future, his chest wasn't clenched tight in fear. The past had stayed buried. There were no memories of gunshots and blood, of screams and tears, of panic and despair. There was hope. Unfiltered hope. Something he'd never felt before. There was a reason he'd chosen a job that made relationships difficult, that kept him on the road a lot, too busy to think about his own life, too distracted to care. His father's death had put a cloud over his head, one that had been there, gloomy and depressing and constant, for nearly twenty years. And tonight, in her eyes, he saw sun. Brief but glimmering and there. Nate loved his job too much to quit, but he could cut back once the Russians were dealt with, once she helped destroy them, once that long chapter of his life was over. And if she was in his home waiting for him, there was no criminal important enough to keep him away. He had a sense that she would understand—Jo knew this life, from the other side maybe, but still. She understood what he did and why. And she had dreams of her own, goals of her own, that would draw her to late hours and maybe long distances. But they'd already overcome an impossible divide, so everything else was easy. Doable at least, if it meant she'd always look at him the way she was looking at him now, as she broke off their kiss with her eyes sparkling brighter than the skyline outside the window.

"This is going to be fun," she commented mirthfully.

"What?" he asked, unable to stop the sarcasm from leaking into his voice. "Pushing each other's buttons all the time?"

"Well, you can't knock the results..." She eyed him pointedly. "But what I meant was you, me, us. This is going to be fun."

"Fun, huh?" He cocked an eyebrow and tightened his grip on her waist. Jo had just enough time to narrow her eyes suspiciously before he flipped her on her back and rolled over, pinning her to the mattress. She let out a yelp, but he caught it with his lips, letting his hands slowly make their way up her waist, before he settled his forearms on either side of her head and pushed against the pillows, breaking the kiss off with a grin. "For once, Jo, fun is exactly what I have in mind."

- 23 -

Jo

Jo stared at the clock on the nightstand. Nate had fallen asleep forty-five minutes ago with his torso pressed against her back, his arm draped over the dip in her hip, his hand clasping her tight. And though she closed her eyes over and over, fighting for sleep, her mind was wide awake. And her gaze kept slipping back to that clock. Again. And again. And again.

Because it was 2:00 a.m.

And then 2:05.

And then 2:15.

And now it was 2:40.

And she was supposed to meet Thad in fifty minutes. Thirty blocks uptown. Which she'd have to walk as to not leave a digital record of her location. So they could do what they came to New York to do—steal a painting from a rich man so he could cash in his insurance and they could get paid. Only now, Jo knew there was a much darker side to the whole exchange, a much more dangerous and despicable one than she'd ever cared to realize before.

How did it work exactly? Would her father sell the painting to the Russians? Did they pay him a set fee for his work? Did Thad know all the details? And what would the mafia use a painting for? Collateral on a drug deal? To launder money? In exchange for human trafficking? For murder? The very thought made Jo shiver, cold despite the warmth seeping into her back from Nate's body.

Nate.

Nate…

Thinking of him caused physical pain, a burning in her chest, because the past few hours had been the most magical of her life. A living dream. The future he painted—oh, she wanted it so badly she could taste it, a sugary, buttery vanilla cake that was too indulgent by half. But now the high had worn off. With Nate asleep and her mind left to wander, the elixir of his touch had faded, leaving memories that would turn bitter with time. Because she couldn't stay.

She had to go.

She had to leave.

Jo glanced at the clock again.

2:45.

If she didn't get out of here in the next ten minutes, she'd be late.

As though sensing her thought, Nate sighed and shifted his grip, tugging her the slightest bit closer and nuzzling his face against her back. Jo closed her eyes. Why did he have to fit so perfect? Feel so perfect? Say the perfect things? Perfect Nate Parker. With his perfect lips. And perfect hands. And perfect...

Jo cleared her throat.

Focus.

But she couldn't. Her mind kept wandering back to an image of the two of them snuggled on his couch, arms intertwined, her head on his chest, both their gazes focused on the view outside his apartment window. For some reason in her mind it was snowing, which she knew didn't happen all that often in Washington, DC, but it never happened in the Bahamas, and the idea of watching that white glitter float and fall had always seemed so cozy, so romantic. Maybe there was some smooth jazz playing in the background. Jo had made fresh hot cocoa, with marshmallows of course, and the smell of chocolate hovered in the air around them. The idea of that singular moment filled her with so much bliss, because it was ordinary yet extraordinary, mundane yet remarkable, the way all her favorite love stories always were.

Jo blinked.

The scene shifted.

She sat in a hard plastic chair with fluorescent lights shining painfully in her eyes, turning everything a sickly shade of chartreuse. Her palm was pressed against a wall of thick glass, fingers scratching at the impenetrable divide, unable to break through. In her other hand rested a phone, filled with nothing but static, as she stared at her father, a man who now looked old in every sense of the word. His gray hair was wiry and thin, starting to bald at the top. His eyes were empty of all the life she remembered, dull and devoid. His once firm, tan skin was now an ashy sort of gray and limp with wrinkles. *Why?* the silence seemed to ask. *Why did you do this to me, to us, Jolene? Why, pumpkin? Why?* But when this ghoulish version of her father finally opened his mouth, that's not what came out.

I'm dying, he whispered.

And her stomach dropped to the floor, through it, to a bottomless place she hadn't visited since her mother passed all those years before. Because he was sick. And alone behind bars. A place where she couldn't hold him, couldn't save him, couldn't comfort or protect him.

And she'd put him there.

His own daughter.

His own blood.

Jo closed her eyes tight and shook her head, trying to dispel the image, forcing the picture of Thad in a similar position to stop invading her thoughts yet again that night.

The nightmare.

Then the dream.

Then the nightmare.

Then the dream.

Over and over and over they'd circulated. From Nate to Thad to her father. So many futures in her hands— the ones she wanted and the ones she couldn't face.

She tore her eyes open, gaze sliding to the clock again.

2:50.

If she didn't leave soon, she'd be late.

What is it, Jo?

What are you going to do?

2:51.

Sacrifice your father and your best friend for the life you always dreamed of? Stay here, in Nate's arms, and wake up a free woman and a traitor? Or leave, find Thad, go home, and try your best to forget Nate's touch, his words? Save your father and your best friend, and sacrifice yourself?

2:52.

Make a decision.

2:53.

Now!

Jo rolled over, leaving no time to second-guess, and eased gently out of Nate's grasp as he sighed behind her. When she stood from the bed, she glanced down just long enough to see his hand shuffle over the sheets, as though searching for her warm body, for her touch. Jo ripped her gaze away and hobbled in the dark, searching for her bra and underwear hidden in the shadows along the ground. Then for her dress, a mound of fabric along the floor. Another glance at Nate. He was fast asleep, eyes closed, face perfectly relaxed, lips slightly parted. Jo pulled her gown inside out and quietly extricated the thin leggings and long-sleeve shirt sewn into the lining of the material, darting her gaze to the sleeping Fed with every subtle rip. He didn't move. She balled the dress up, prepared to throw it away as soon as she got outside—there were too many memories soaked into the silk for her to want to lay eyes on it again—and then tugged on her clothes. Her purse was discarded near the door. Jo rushed to grab it and slid the clutch open, revealing the small tablet and handful of electronics she'd stuffed inside. She pulled a flash drive free.

Where is it?

Where would it be?

Jo glanced around the dark hotel room, nothing but the glowing lights of New York to guide her. She went for the most predictable place first—the closet. A small personal safe was hidden inside, requiring a six-digit code. Clicking her tongue, Jo thought of her background check on Nate, all the dates she'd memorized just in case. Most people used predictable passwords—even federal agents weren't above that vice. A lot of hacking was just knowing what might be hiding in plain sight. She tried his birthday first. No go. Then his mother's. Fail. Then it hit her, obvious. She typed in his father's birthday. The safe slid open, revealing a small laptop hidden inside.

Jo knelt in the dark, crossing her legs as she balanced the device on her lap. His agency sign-in required a little more expertise, so she reached into her bag, grabbing a different device, this one a password runner that would shift through the millions of possibilities for her in a matter of minutes—a code she'd specially designed.

Voila, she was in.

Jo strained her neck, peering around the corner, back toward the bed, the sleeping body, and the glaring red light of that damn clock.

3:01.

Shit!

She had to meet Thad in half an hour. The walk uptown alone would take that long. There was no time to sit and read the files, to find the information Nate had teased, to understand exactly what Thad and her father were truly up to, how involved in the Russian mafia they were. But maybe she'd known that all along. Maybe that was why it had taken so long to drag herself out of bed. Just another excuse to delay the inevitable.

Jo slid her flash drive into the laptop.

Later. Later, when there's time, I'll read it all.

I won't turn a blind eye.

I won't ignore.

And then I'll make a decision. When I have all the facts.

Right now, she needed to help her family. Because that image of her father dying alone in a jail cell was too raw, too ripe. She wasn't ready to turn it into a reality, not yet, not even for Nate.

Jo sifted through the FBI research, all the data, illegally dragging and dropping everything she found into her drive. Before the information downloaded, a window popped up, requiring fingerprint approval of the exchange. Jo winced, but stood and walked over to the bed. Ever so carefully, she slid the trackpad beneath Nate's open palm, studying his face for any sign of alertness as the print was confirmed. And then just as carefully, she retreated, pulling her drive free, slipping the laptop back into the hotel safe, and shutting the closet door.

Jo knelt, grabbing her dress and her purse, and then paused. Everything within her screamed to press a soft kiss to his forehead, to say goodbye when she still had the chance, but it was too risky. Even for her. Especially for her.

One glance into those baby-blue eyes and she'd drop it all and crawl back into bed, into the safety of his arms, wrapped up in the dreams he spun. Nate couldn't wake. Because she couldn't bear it.

"I'm sorry," she whispered into the night, somehow hoping that in his sleep he would hear, he would understand. "I thought I could, but I can't. I can't. I'm sorry."

Then she turned and slipped out the door.

Gone.

- 24 -

Nate

Goddammit, Jo. Nate waited for the door to click closed before he threw the covers off and launched from the bed.

Goddammit.

Goddammit.

Goddammit!

He knew she would do that.

He *knew*.

And yet, a small part of him hoped she wouldn't. That she'd chosen him, the way he'd chosen her. But that was too much to ask, too much to dream. And in the end, maybe Nate had been prepared for the alternative all along. Why else had he changed the password to his hotel safe earlier that day, to something so easy to guess it was almost embarrassing? And why else had he rearranged his files so they were effortless to access and simple to find? Why else had he overridden most of the FBI safeguards on his laptop, leaving only the fingerprint verification in place?

Because he'd known.

All day. All week, even.

He'd known the night would somehow lead here.

To them being together.

To Jo tearing them apart.

He'd counted on it.

Nate rubbed the sleep from his eyes and fumbled around the room in the dark, grabbing a shirt from the closet, pants from the drawer, his badge from the tux, and his gun from the ground. Then he turned on his phone and waited for the inevitable rush of vibrations as all the text messages he was sure he'd missed came through. He opened the ones from his partner first.

Parker, your comm went dark. All good?

Parker. Boss is pissed. Do you copy?

Told you I'd cover for you. Didn't expect it to be for so long.

Where the hell are you?

What happened?

Are you with Jo? Are you hurt?

If you two are…

Never mind.

I'm going to kill you, Parker.

Ryder just left the museum, nothing happened. We've changed shifts with the overnight team. Call me when you come back online.

He paced around the room, reading the messages for a few minutes, shifting between grunting incoherently and squeezing his fist until it began to tremble. Then Nate dropped onto the edge of the bed, lifted his fingers to the ridge of his nose, and squeezed as the full implications of his evening rendezvous crashed over him. How was he going to explain this to the boss? To the bureau? Hell, to his team? He wasn't a very good liar, but there was no way he could tell them the truth. He'd be fired. Shamed. He'd known she was trouble from the very start—and he'd walked right into the trap.

Goddammit, Jo.

With a sigh, Nate lifted his head, gaze darting to the clock in the corner.

3:15.

He'd wasted enough time already, so he did the only thing he could think of and called his partner.

"Alvarez here." A sleepy mumble came through the line.

"Leo, it's me."

"Shit, Parker," his partner exclaimed, coming alive in a single second. "What the hell happened to you? And what the hell time is it?" There was a slight pause. "Three o'clock in the fu—"

"I know," Nate cut him off, wincing. "I know, and I'm sorry. But something is going down. I'm sure of it."

He could perfectly envision the suspicious way Leo's eyes were narrowing, especially as he slowly asked his next question. "How exactly do you know something's happening, Parker?"

"That's not important. What's—"

"Holy shit! You did, didn't you?" Leo whooped into the phone. Nate couldn't tell if he was pissed or pleased. Probably a little bit of both. "I didn't think you had it in you, Parker, but you did. You and Jo. You did. While I was on a fucking stakeout, trapped in the car for five hours with can't-get-a-word-in-edgewise Ben."

"Leo."

"So how was it?"

"Leo."

"Because I covered your ass, Parker. I had to spin a whole tale to the boss about how the Russians had been following you guys, how you probably had to go dark to get away from them, how you might have gone into hiding."

"Thank you, Leo."

"I think he actually sent a team out after you, to run some recon, see if there was any word of your whereabouts."

Nate dropped his forehead into his palm and squeezed the phone tight in his other hand. *How the hell am I going to get out of this mess?* But that wasn't important. Not right now. "Leo, listen. Jo just left. She thought I was asleep, but I was watching. She had a set of clothes hidden in the lining of her dress, black leggings, and a black long-sleeve shirt. She changed, and she left. And she has to be meeting Ryder. Are the overnight teams still on watch?"

"Yeah," Leo answered, voice stern and focused, back on the job as quickly as that. "We have people parked outside the auction house and the museum, keeping an eye out for any sign of movement through the windows, any sign of wrongdoing. If they see anything, they're ready to move in."

Nate frowned, feeling a deep wrinkle form in his forehead as his brows pushed together. "What about the townhouse?"

"The gala ended, nothing happened. All the items from the silent auction were removed. We figured there was no need to keep watch. It was a decoy."

God, that's exactly what Ryder was hoping we'd do. That must be why they waited so long to act. "No, Leo. No. The townhouse, that's where they're going."

"What? Why?"

Nate lifted his shoulder, holding the phone against his ear as he pulled on his shoes, cutting a glance to the clock again. He was wasting time. Jo had left fifteen minutes ago. Was he delaying on purpose? Was he giving her a head start? Was there a reason his throat was tightening on the words trying to force their way up, the ones that might see her in handcuffs before the night was through?

"A Degas," he finally blurted.

"A what now?"

"Degas! A Degas!" *What the hell was that guy's first name?* Nate shook his head. "The painter. The artist."

"The ballerina guy?"

"Yes!" Nate yelled triumphantly. "Degas. There was a Degas in the townhouse. Right up Robert Carter's alley."

"Shit," Leo muttered under his breath. "How did we miss that?"

"Maybe it was a family heirloom or something, passed down through a will. They must've just brought it in from another location because it wasn't there during recon. Either way, we didn't dig as deeply as we should've. Because that's what Jo and Ryder are after. I'm sure of it."

"Okay. Okay. I'll wake everyone up. I'll call the guys on watch. I'll—"

The line went dead.

Not off, just completely silent.

An unnerving sort of quiet.

And then Leo whispered, "What are we going to tell everyone?"

Nate stood and rubbed his palm over his face.

He knew exactly what Leo meant. And he was forever grateful for his partner's loyalty. His trust. "I'm not going to ask you to lie for me, Leo."

"Parker—"

"Leo—"

"Parker—"

"Leo—" A knock on his hotel door cut him off. "Someone's here. Hold on."

He crossed the room in an instant and took a deep breath, hope a painful thing in his chest as he hovered on the edge, one step from falling. It wasn't her. She was long gone. She left. It wasn't. But…

Nate opened the door.

Leo stood with his arms crossed, a hard look in his eyes. Before Nate had time to process the painful pang in his chest, his partner stormed into the room and shut the door behind them. "You left the townhouse with Jo. She yanked your comm out and tried to make a run for it. You followed her, but you couldn't tell anyone because your phone was in your room and your comm was dead. You didn't want to lose the trail, so you staked out her hotel, working off a hunch about the Degas, and when you saw her leave, you came back here and woke me up. That's what we tell everyone. And I don't want to hear another word about it."

Nate's shoulders slumped as he let out a breath he'd been holding. "I can't ask you—"

"You're not asking," Leo interrupted as he flicked on the lights and took a fresh comm set out of his pocket. "You broke one rule in your entire life, Parker. And I'm not losing my partner because of it."

Nate slipped the earpiece into place but paused before running the mic through his sleeve. "I broke a pretty big rule, Leo."

His partner dipped his chin and tossed Nate a pointed stare. "Who wouldn't break that rule for a night with Jolene Carter?" And then he arched a brow, the move inherently laced with humor. "Now, come on. We don't have any more time to waste."

Nate sighed.

A night with Jolene Carter.

Was that all it was?

All it would ever be?

The very idea made his heart skip a beat. Not in the good way. In the way that felt as if a hand had shoved beneath his skin and a fist had wrapped around his insides, squeezing so tight, so rigid, there was no room to move. His chest burned, throbbing so painfully he couldn't breathe.

Leo put his hands against Nate's back and gave him a hard shove toward the exit. "I only have one request, Parker."

He risked a glance over his shoulder as he opened the door. "What's that?"

"I'll call the guys in the field." They stepped into the hall and Leo motioned toward the room ten feet down, pointing with his thumb. "You have to wake up the rest of the team."

- 25 -

Jo

Speed was the greatest advantage a thief could have—get in and get out before anyone had a chance to notice. Jo was forever grateful for that singular fact as she rounded the corner to find Thad standing in the shadows, arms crossed, eyes a raging storm as they found hers.

"Where the hell have you been?"

Jo stepped smoothly past him. "I'm five minutes late, relax."

"Jo—" But he cut himself off with a growl.

Because, like she'd said, speed. The Feds weren't here—yet. And they had to finish this before they were.

"Did you deal with the cameras?" Jo asked, getting right to business.

Thad shot her a look, like how dare she question him. "Of course."

The step had been simple enough. Jo had hacked into the city database and grabbed screenshots of the overnight images on each of the street cams within a two-block radius of the townhouse. Thad sized and printed the images, then attached them to the lenses. As long as no police officer happened to be watching during that split second when the photo was slipped into place, which really, was incredibly unlikely considering the cams were mostly used to retroactively search for evidence since there were hundreds, heck, thousands of them, they'd be in the clear. The digital timer would keep counting, and it wouldn't be until morning that someone noticed the street still looked like it did at night—dark and empty—instead of swarming with people in bright daylight. Simple, but effective.

Thad handed her a black ski mask. She tied her hair into a ponytail and slipped the cotton over her head to cover her face. She hated breathing in these damn things. They made her entire chin and neck sweaty and itchy, but they were necessary, just in case anyone happened to burst in before they were done. What she hated most of all, though, was the fact that as soon as she pulled the hood over her head, she truly felt like a criminal. And there was no way around that.

"How'd it go with Parker?" Thad asked, voice slightly muffled as he pulled his mask on. "Did you get anything?"

"No, sorry." Jo looked to the ground as she answered. If he saw into her eyes, he'd know she wasn't telling the truth. The flash drive burned a hole in her metaphorical pocket, but she didn't want Thad to know she had it. To know how close she was to uncovering the truth. "How long ago did the Feds leave?"

"About an hour and a half," Thad murmured. "I didn't come out of hiding until I saw them pull away. But that doesn't mean they won't be back."

Jo nodded, trying her best to act casually. He stared at her a moment longer, then stepped out of the shadows and crossed the street, moving swiftly toward the front door of the townhome. She followed his lead. It was late and quiet and dark, at least by New York standards. For all the money and social status, the Upper East Side was one of the easiest places in the entire city to rob. The streets were more residential than commercial. People went to sleep at a reasonable hour. The only big hindrance was the high-tech security systems, but that was why Jo was there. When they reached the front door, Thad pulled a small needle from his pocket, but it was her moment to shine.

Jo glanced up, finding his steely eyes. "Thaddy..."

He tilted his head, curious.

Jo swallowed. Once they got inside, there'd be no more talking. And once they were done, they'd split up, two different hotels, two different flights, two different destinations. If there was anything she wanted to say, she had to say it now. About Nate. About the Russians. About her father. About them. About anything. But the words caught in her throat, too much to explain, too much to think about when the mission required all her focus.

"Good luck."

"I don't need luck, Jo Jo." He put his finger under her chin, tilting her face up, studying her. And then he winked and dropped his hand. "Not when I have you."

Jo rolled her eyes to cover up the twinge of guilt needling her side. And then she took out her tablet and got to work.

My final job.

One way or another, this is it.

The last time.

With that thought as fuel, she typed a few strands of code and cut her way into the security system using the bugs she'd planted earlier. Her fingers moved fast as lightning over her keyboard as she disabled the house alarm, turned off the cameras inside, and shut down the motion sensors. Then she looked up, meeting Thad's questioning gaze with a nod.

He knelt, pushing his needle into the lock. A few turns of his wrist and the door clicked open. They slipped inside and shut it quietly behind them. Even though Thad hadn't attended the gala, he'd studied the blueprints they'd stolen same as she, and he found the staircase easily, moving fast but absolutely silent through the house, a panther on the hunt, stalking its prey. As they crested the steps, Jo spared a moment to glance his way. A thrilled gleam flared to life in the corners of his eyes, one Jo couldn't help but notice resembled the glinting edge of a sword in the sun, lethal and beautiful and terrifying all at once. He zeroed in on the Degas, taking it in hungrily, a starved man finding food for the first time. Art was his drug, his life, his passion.

And his downfall... The thought broke through before she could smother it.

Jo shook her head, dispelling the words. There was no time for that, not now. She put her hand to his forearm, stopping him, as she took to her tablet again, this time to breach the second layer of the security—a backup circuit for the safe she knew was hidden in the office upstairs, the specialized cabinets in the master closet, most likely holding jewelry, and the discreet sensor attached to the back side of the Degas, hidden, she assumed, in the edge of the frame. It had taken her nearly four straight hours two nights ago to figure out an undetectable way in, but now, it only took a few seconds to type the pathway and deactivate the alarms.

Jo tapped Thad twice, his sign to move.

He took a small flashlight from his pocket, no bigger than a pen, and pressed his cheek against the wall, parallel to the frame. There was no more than a centimeter of space between the back of the painting and the wall, but it was enough space to see if there was a third sensor they'd need to disarm. This was the biggest wild card of the entire operation. Some people, the smart cynical kind who didn't trust big security firms to actually do their jobs, sometimes employed a third line of defense. Something as simple as a cheap battery-operated magnetic alarm was oftentimes the most difficult to get around. Jo couldn't hack her way in. They couldn't plan for them. And unless Thad was careful, even touching the frame could flip the switch. Because this job was about insurance fraud, she doubted the homeowner had gone the extra step—he did, after all, want to be robbed—but they couldn't be too sure.

Thad spent thirty seconds checking every shadow for a hidden sensor, a lifetime in this sort of setting. Satisfied, he slipped a small scanner out, one which should effectively desensitize any magnets in range, and slowly passed the small beam around the edge of the frame—just in case.

He found Jo's gaze.

She moved to the opposite side of the frame, hands hovering over the gilt wood, waiting for the signal.

He held up his fingers, counting down.

Three.

Two.

One.

In a swift motion, they lifted the hefty frame from the wall, stepped back, and froze.

No alarms.

No sirens.

No nothing.

Jo exhaled slowly, finding Thad's gaze again as they gently dropped to their knees and set the painting facedown on the floor. Crinkles formed at the corners of his eyes, letting her know he smiled beneath his mask—a devilish grin, she was sure, filled with victory and ecstasy and sin, the sort of high he only got from one of two things. She'd seen it many times before.

Jo stood and walked to the window, checking the time on her tablet. They'd been inside for less than five minutes, but the hard part was over. Behind her, Thad was painstakingly detaching the canvas from the frame so he could roll it up and store it in the tube secured to his back. If they damaged the art, it would instantly lose value, and since he was the artist, this was his area of expertise. But she wasn't worried. He was as meticulous as he was mischievous. He had it under control, especially with her standing watch, allowing him to focus without having to look over his shoulder, trusting her to have his back. Just as she'd always trusted him to have hers—a promise she desperately wished he hadn't broken.

Her mind went to the flash drive. Her hand instinctively found the purse dangling by her waist. Was the bag hot to the touch? Or was she only imagining that phantom heat—a panicked sort of burning to match the one simmering under her skin, an inferno closing in around her?

A *snap* broke her from her thoughts.

Their signal. The only sound they ever used on a job to catch the other person's attention—speaking was too risky given that the homeowner was asleep down the hall.

Jo turned.

Thad secured the cap on the tube. She caught a flash of white from the canvas now resting inside.

That was it.

Months and months of planning, and they were done.

In. Out.

Easy.

Jo stepped back from the window but stopped cold as a flash of light flooded the room. Headlights. She pressed her back to the wall and peeked around the edge of the molding until she could see the street. A car pulled to a stop two doors down. Far enough away to be coincidence. But she knew in her heart it wasn't.

Jo snapped twice.

Thad froze.

Another car pulled to a stop outside. Then one more.

Jo signaled to the window on the other side of the room, and Thad crept over to peer outside. He held out his hand, signaling the number two.

Shit.

Five cars.

Nate woke up. That was the only explanation. He woke to find her missing and knew exactly where she'd gone. And he could've let it go, but he didn't. He came after her.

Shit. Shit. Shit!

Jo closed her eyes, squeezing, as her heart thudded in her chest, beating like a fist against a locked door, trying to break free.

She had to calm down.

She had to focus.

They'd planned for this. Their escape routes had been specifically designed around the possibility of being surrounded. Thad would go to the roof, and from there, the opportunities were endless—the man was practically a monkey. He'd climb into the neighbor's terrace and maybe over one more building just to be safe, and then he'd hide until the street cleared. Jo wasn't worried about him. Not at all. He was a master of the getaway.

Jo, on the other hand, had already shown her cards.

Her exit was out the back.

Into the alley.

Where Nate would undoubtedly be waiting.

If she hadn't taken him out that door earlier that night, he probably would've never known it existed. Not every townhouse had them—in fact, very few did. Jo would've been gone before the Feds even thought to check the opposite side of the block for an exit. She would've been free. Instead, she was trapped, in a web of her own making.

With that singular realization, all her dreams went up in smoke. Her bakery. Her coopies. The image of being nestled in Nate's arms, watching snow fall. All of it. Gone. Poof. Because when he caught her, there'd be no deal. No leverage. No immunity. He wouldn't need it. She'd be caught red-handed, a criminal through and through, with the ski mask to prove it. Which, really, when it came down to it, was no worse than she deserved.

A warm palm landed on her shoulder. Jo spun with a gasp, but it was Thad. Only Thad. He stared at her, trying to understand her panic, when as far as he knew the plan was still foolproof, still a go. And for him it was. There was no reason for Thad to get caught. Not when it was her fault, and hers alone, for getting in too deep.

Boom. Boom. Boom.

A hard knock sounded against the door.

Jo and Thad locked eyes.

The homeowner would be awake any instant. The Feds were about to bust their way in. If they were leaving, it had to be now.

Boom. Boom. Boom.

Instincts taking over, they snapped apart and turned, running for the stairs. Thad raced up. Jo hurried down. No time to think. No time to process. Only to act.

Boom. Boom. Boom.

Footsteps thudded from the bedroom upstairs, but Jo was already on the ground floor, racing for the back exit. And she had no doubt Thad had made it to the roof terrace and was already climbing his way over the divide and into the neighbor's property. She unlocked the deadbolt on the patio doors, slid outside, and crossed the courtyard in a matter of seconds. Her hand hovered over the knob for the exit into the alley. She paused, ripped off her ski mask, and arched her head back, sucking in a long, cool breath of air. Her last, she was sure, as a free woman.

Then she opened the door and stepped through.

- 26 -

Nate

There was a defeated look in her eyes as she stepped through the door, something resigned yet content, something he'd never seen before. Her hair was disheveled. Her movements slow. Her body stiff. They locked gazes across the dark expanse of the alley as Jo quietly shut the door behind her. For a moment, they both remained still. Quiet and still. Was there anything left to say?

She glanced behind him, to either side, her brows pulling together and her mouth dropping as she realized Nate was alone. "No backup?"

The question could've been flippant, but with the shock running through her tone, he didn't think so. If he were being honest, he was just as surprised as she was. Nate had no idea why he'd told the others he was going to do a quick scan of the surrounding streets. He had no idea why he'd shrugged off Leo's offer to provide backup. He had no idea why instead of actually taking a lap around the block, he'd turned into this discreet alley, blanketed in shadow. He had no idea, and yet, even worse, he did.

Because he knew Jo would be here. And he knew if anyone had come with him, they'd arrest her on the spot. And he wasn't sure he could bear the sight of her in handcuffs or the knowledge that all those glorious ideas of after would be gone.

Jo took a step forward, wary. "What are you doing, Nate?"

"I don't know, Jo," he growled, anger simmering, threatening to break free of his careful control. Anger at her for leaving. Anger with himself for letting her go. Anger that after so much time and so much dedication and so much commitment, he was risking it all—a promise he never spoke of, a revenge nearly two decades in the making, his entire career—over something his father would have scoffed at. Over a woman. A woman he'd only known for a week.

But for some reason, Jo was so much more than that.

Somehow, she was everything.

"Why'd you leave?"

Jo sighed, tilting her head to the side, as though the answer was obvious. "Why'd you follow?"

"Because it's my job." Was that the real reason? Or was it because he needed to see her again, to fight for her, to at least say goodbye?

Her eyes softened, as though she heard the struggle in his voice. "Are you here to arrest me, Nate?"

"I don't know." Nate shifted his weight, gaze dropping to the asphalt beneath his feet. He didn't seem to know anything anymore.

Jo stepped closer, hesitant but growing bolder, turning back into a more recognizable version of herself. "Are you going to let me go?"

"I don't know," he said through gritted teeth. As Jo closed the distance between them, his hands formed into fists. She pressed her palms to his chest, sending a different sort of heat into the inferno building beneath his skin, two sides, two warring sides, one tender and one tempestuous, both fighting for the lead. Jo slid her fingers around the back side of his neck, teasing, toying as her nails grazed his scalp.

"Are you going to kiss me?" Her voice was deeper this time, full of an ocean of implication.

Yes.

He leaned down.

No.

He pulled his head back.

Yes.

Again.

No.

Again.

I shouldn't—

We shouldn't—

She—

I—

Nate shook his head, releasing a frustrated breath as the battle reached a crescendo. "Goddammit, Jo, I don't know!"

She folded her lips, rolling them into her mouth and biting down for a moment as the corners twitched. "Then what do you know?"

She was enjoying this.

Enjoying this!

The woman was infuriating.

Absolutely infuriating.

Nate's nostrils flared as he met her amused gaze. "I know you stole my files." The pleasure fled from her features. "I know you just broke into a house and aided in the theft of a priceless work of art in order to make good on a deal with the Russian mafia." Nate shoved his hand into his pocket, then pulled out a set of metal handcuffs. They glinted in the bit of light seeping into the alley from the street. "I know I have every reason in the world to turn you around, place these on your wrists, and take you to headquarters for questioning."

Jo swallowed. So did Nate.

Every muscle in his body trembled gently with the weight of those words, the truth of them. And then his body went lax. Because as soon as he saw that brief flash of fear in her dazzling green eyes, his heart won the fight.

Nate dropped the handcuffs.

They clinked as they hit the street.

"And I know," he murmured, lifting his hand to her cheek and brushing his thumb over her silken skin. "I know I won't use them." She moved her palm to cover his, holding his hand against her face. Nate stared into her eyes and asked again, "Why'd you leave?" But this time there was nothing but vulnerable, brutal barrenness in his tone.

Jo closed her eyes, letting her head dip into his hand. "I'm sorry."

"I know that too, Jo." She'd told him already, in that soft confession before she'd walked out of his room. *I'm sorry. I thought I could, but I can't. I can't. I'm sorry.* An apology made to the empty night, to silence, when she'd thought he was asleep. But he'd heard every word. "What did you mean when you said you can't?"

He had to know.

That was what it all came down to. Was she delaying the inevitable…or was she putting it off completely?

One option he could live with.

The other, he honestly wasn't sure he could.

"I can't..." she trailed off, closing her eyes as though to hide from the truth. Her brows knotted together as her face scrunched with silent pain. "I can't do this the way you want me to do this. I need time. Time to read the files, but mostly, time to talk to my father."

"Jo—"

"No, please, Nate," she said as her eyes popped open and bored into his. "Please, you have to understand. I need to hear it from his lips. I need to see the truth in his eyes. I can record it on my phone. I can do whatever I need to do. But I can't wear your wire and have that conversation when I know the whole world is listening. I can't. He's my father. My *father*."

Her voice caught on the word, breaking.

"I understand. I do. But there's something you need to understand too." Nate paused, taking a breath, stalling. He'd never told anyone this before. Not his mother. Not his siblings. Not his partner. Some of the men at the bureau understood a portion of it—they had eyes and access to the confidential files and were smart enough to put two and two together. But it was different to tell someone, to actually say it out loud and face that day he'd shoved as far into the back of his mind as possible, to remember those last few moments, the darkest of his life, when all he'd seen was red—on his hands, on the grass, flooding down the street, spilling from his father's chest, his own vision curtained by a gossamer red in his agony and anger. Speaking the words gave them life, tossed them into someone else's hands to either protect or throw back in his face. For the first time in his life, staring into Jo's eyes, he understood he'd found someone who'd keep them safe, keep him safe. "There's something I haven't told you, Jo. Something, something I need you to know."

His voice was raw.

Stripped bare.

She squeezed his hand, nothing but concern in her eyes as she watched him, studied him. "What, Nate? What?"

"This is about more than just work for me. It's about so much more than my job. It's— It's— It's everything, Jo." His voice was barely a whisper. Little more than the wind.

Her eyes narrowed as she fought to understand.

Nate sucked in an uneven breath, opening the lock on that door he'd slammed in the back of his mind, over and over and over, burying the memories as deep as he could, which was never deep at all, really, but always there, simmering beneath the surface, informing his every decision. He'd given that day so much power. Too much power. And it was time to let it go. To face the horror and release it. To free himself of nearly twenty years of pent-up pain. If he didn't do this, here, now, with Jo, he wasn't sure he ever would.

"You know my father was an agent," he started slowly, but after that first sentence, everything came tumbling out. "You must know he died on the job. But that's not all, not by a long shot. He worked in the organized crime unit, which back then, was even more dangerous than it is now. The criminals were bolder, less afraid. The Russians were only just getting started in the US. They weren't established like the Italians, but they had ties to the homeland that made them brash and well-armed and eager to cement their place. My father, he went undercover on an operation. He was supposed to retire from fieldwork the year before, but they pulled him into one last job. He was gone for almost eight months. We only saw him twice when the bureau was able to smuggle him away. And then he got the evidence he needed, had one of the kingpins on a recording, more than enough to put him away for life. So the Feds got him out. My family was moved to a safe house, and my father was supposed to join us there until the trial was over. But something happened. No one ever understood how—if the Russians had a contact on the inside, if they managed to break into our databases, if they tortured someone for information. But they knew our location. They knew where we were. And— And—"

God, Nate could see it so clearly.

Like he was twelve again.

Like he'd gone back in time.

Nate was sitting on the grass, throwing a baseball with his younger brother while their sister was napping. She was only a toddler, a little girl, and their mom had wanted them out of the house. When a car pulled down the street, he remembered shouting for his mom.

Dad's here!

Dad's back!

He and his brother dropped their stuff and ran around the side of the house, toward the driveway. The car pulled to a stop. Their dad got out, stood up, and waved with the biggest grin on his face. Nate didn't notice the other car, didn't even see it, not until his father's face snapped to the side, and his eyes widened in horror, but by then, it was too late.

Pop!

Pop!

Pop!

Three shots to the chest, just like that. No time to move, no time to run. His entire body flinched as each bullet sank in, red spray exploding into the air like a gruesome firework display. And then he dropped in what felt like slow motion, wobbling on his feet, falling to his knees, then teetering over, off balance as his shoulder hit the pavement and he rolled onto his back, twitching. And then *pop!* One final shot, just to be sure. That one caught Nate's attention. He whipped around, staring the stranger in his face as he rolled his window up and sped away. Those dark-brown eyes. That coifed black hair. That pale skin. That scruff. That scar on his left cheek. Nate catalogued it all, stored it for safekeeping.

His mother released a bloodcurdling scream.

The man sped off down the road.

Nate ran to his father's side and covered the wound with his hands, but there was no stopping the bleeding. He gripped his father's shoulders. *Don't leave me. Don't leave me.* His father opened his mouth, but there was only the gurgle of death as the life slowly slipped from his eyes. Nate leaned down, pressing his lips to his father's ear, to make sure his spirit would hear. *I'll get him, Dad. I promise. I'll make him pay. I'll make them all pay.* And then he sat in the blood, holding his father to him while his mother shouted his name. But Nate didn't leave until his father's partner finally came and ripped him free.

"They shot him," Nate confessed, sounding like a boy—the boy he no longer had the chance to be. He blinked. The image of that day slowly faded, replaced with Jo, with the worried curl of her lips, the deep sympathy in her eyes. Her fingers brushed his cheek, catching a tear he didn't know he'd cried. He cleared his throat, trying to force back the knot lodged in his neck. "We weren't supposed to talk about it to anyone. The bureau covered it up, made the file confidential, need-to-know. Because they'd failed him. They'd failed us. And the hitman got away." Nate released a bitter laugh. "I knew exactly who he was. I could identify him. I promised my father, I *promised him*, I would make the bastard pay. And he got away, because no one, not even my mother, wanted the truth getting out. She was afraid someone would come after me next. So, we buried my father, and we buried the truth with him. And the Russian? He rose in the ranks."

Jo gasped, shaking her head.

But Nate needed to say it out loud.

All of it.

Everything.

"He's the person your father is working with, Jo," Nate said slowly, deliberately, not a single waver to his voice. Because she needed to understand. "And you are my last chance, my only chance, to do good on the promise I made to my father. To nail him."

Jo opened her mouth.

Closed it.

Opened it. Paused. Licked her lips. "I—I didn't know."

"I didn't expect you to," he said, dipping his head, bringing their faces closer together, forcing her to look at him. "But I do expect you to do the right thing. Not just for me. But for you. For the world. He's a bad man. And he needs to be caught. And you, your father, it's the only way I see that happening."

"I will do the right thing. I will."

Her voice was firm. And he wanted to believe it.

But there was a kernel of doubt, an evil little whisper, murmuring that if he took Jo in right now, he wouldn't have to have faith in someone else. He would know. The cards would be in his hands. The power.

"Please, Nate," she pressed, fingers gripping his shoulders, trying to make him see, make him hear the honesty in her words. "I know you have no reason to trust me, we have no reason to trust each other, not when I snuck out in the middle of the night and you feigned sleep, not when we were both working our own agendas. But I'm not anymore. I promise, I just need time, and the space to do things my way. But I will do what's right. I promise you, I will. I just need you to trust me."

For some reason, against his better judgment, he did. "Go."

Jo blinked, not understanding.

Nate tightened his hold on her cheeks and pulled her closer. He captured her lips with his, greedily, hungrily, taking his fill. Her arms slid around the back of his neck. Their bodies molded together. They kissed like two people in love who didn't care if the world caved in around them.

Because they didn't.

And maybe it already had.

"Go," Nate spoke against her lips, as his grip on the back of her head tightened. He didn't want Jo to move an inch, not a breath farther away, but he tore their faces apart and stumbled back. Because time was running out, and they'd been hiding in this alley too long already. The window of opportunity was closing with every passing second. And he knew, deep in his heart, this wasn't goodbye. He trusted it not to be. "Go."

Jo held his gaze.

For a moment.

Two.

She reached up and traced the edge of his jaw with her thumb.

Then she ran past him.

She ran away.

Nate turned around just in time to see her leave the alley and hang a right. He took a deep breath.

It'll be okay.

I can trust her.

It'll be okay.

Nate didn't know how long he stood there before a shout jolted him back to life.

"Hey, Parker, all clear?"

Leo.

Of course, Leo.

Nate sighed. He hated to lie, but this, even Leo wouldn't understand. "All clear."

His voice sounded convincing, even to him.

"Come on, we're searching the house. So far, nothing. But maybe they left a fingerprint or some DNA behind."

Nate nodded and walked out of the alley, following Leo down the street, toward the townhouse at the far end. An itch on the back of his neck made him pause. Nate turned, scanning the shadows, for what, he didn't know. Regardless, there was nothing there. Just emptiness. A void to match the hollow feeling within.

"Parker, let's move," Leo called, a jibing tone.

Nate turned to face him. "What? A few minutes apart and you can't live without me?"

Leo slammed his hand against his chest, wounded.

Nate snorted and shook his head. He'd promised Jo time, he'd promised her space, he'd promised her trust, so she'd have it. Nate rolled his shoulders and followed his partner down the street to rejoin his team.

- 27 -

Jo

Jo was desperate for sugar.

Desperate.

She was a wild animal on the hunt as she stalked her way through the airport, a snarl on her lips, eyes wide and alert, the ache of an empty stomach propelling her forward. People stepped out of her way. Literally. Which for New York, was really saying something. But she couldn't be stopped. A woman with a sugar craving was a beautiful and terrifying thing to behold.

There were no bakeries in the airport. The coffee shop had already sold out of their chocolate chip muffins. And Jo couldn't bring herself to buy one of the plastic-wrapped cookies that had been sitting on the shelf for god knew how long. Call it snobbish. Call it picky. But after spending the past few days taste testing from some of the best bakeries in the world, she just couldn't. Then, right as she was about to pick up her carry-on suitcase and hurl it at the doughnut advertisement she walked by *three* freaking times, she smelled it.

Jo stopped cold, a predator catching a scent.

Butter.

Ooh, lots of butter.

Cinnamon.

No, better—cinnamon-sugar.

And, yes, a tangy hint of salt.

She was instantly transported back in time, to those long-ago days when her mother would take her to the mall at the end of summer, right before school was back in session. They'd try on all sorts of clothes. Buy a new backpack for the school year. New sets of colorful pens. New notebooks. A special outfit for the first day, a dress, shoes, fun socks, a headband, everything. And at the end, when the exhaustion was ripe and they needed that extra little punch to get home, they'd make a final stop, at the pretzel shop near the exit. Jo would squeeze her mother's hand, tugging with her enthusiasm, practically jumping up and down as they neared. And then they'd split a cup of nuggets, pinky-swearing in an unbreakable mother-daughter pact that neither of them would tell Father when they got home.

She hadn't seen one of those places in ten years.

Not since they moved to the island.

Oh, please. Please. Please!

It was just what she needed to get through what she already knew would be a horrible flight, a horrible day, a horrible conversation waiting when she got home.

Jo spun on her heels, slow, trying not to get too excited, but she couldn't help the squeal that slipped through her lips as her gaze landed on the shop tucked all the way in the back corner of the food court—Auntie Anne's.

Jo made a beeline. The world faded. Everything was blurry aside from that bright, gleaming, oversized image of a soft pretzel hanging from the wall. All she could think was, *Cinnamon-sugar? Or original? Or cinnamon-sugar? Or original?*

Both excellent choices.

She couldn't *really* go wrong.

Hmm…

Jo was still torn when she stepped up to the counter. "Can I please get a cup of cinnamon-sugar nuggets?"

"Su—"

"No, wait! Original. A cup of original nuggets." She bit her lip. *Yeah, that's the right choice. That's…*

"O—"

"No, cinnamon-sugar. Definitely cinnamon-sugar."

The guy behind the counter was doing that customer service glare—the one where he was trying to be pleasant, but his nostrils were slightly flared and his lips a little flat, and fire was shooting from his eyes. Yeah, he was doing that. "You sure, miss?"

Was she?

Was she sure?

Did she know anything anymore?

Okay, why is this starting to feel like maybe, it's not about the pretzels…?

The guy lifted a brow, waiting. The woman behind her in line coughed. Jo tossed a glare—a real one—over her shoulder.

"Yes, I'm sure." She nodded emphatically and pulled out her wallet. "Only…could you maybe put one original nugget on top? Just a little taster?"

He paused to swallow what she was sure would have been a highly frowned upon though probably epic retort. "I'll see what I can do."

Five minutes later, Jo stood by her gate, waiting for first class to be called as she munched on her nuggets. Her unnamed new best friend had given her an assortment of original and cinnamon-sugar, and the salty-sweet mixture was pure perfection to her taste buds. Jo pulled out her phone, eager for a distraction as she waited with the growing horde for boarding to begin, and snapped a pic of her nuggets.

@TheBakingBandit: Try not to be too jealous…

@Sprinkle-Ella: I tried…and I failed. I haven't had those in FOREVER!

@TheGourmetGoddess: Okay, even my mouth is watering a little.

@Sprinkle-Ella: Do my eyes deceive me? What did I just read?

@TheBakingBandit: No one can deny the power of the cinnamon-sugar pretzel bite!

@TheBakingBandit: How's the conference going, btw?

@TheGourmetGoddess: Amazing! Exhausting, but amazing! Today is the last day of the food tents, I'm just finishing my setup now. There's a place a few rows down with the most incredible coffee, so I'm walking over to get some much-needed caffeine before the doors open in an hour.

@Sprinkle-Ella: What are you making?

@TheGourmetGoddess: Felt like my table was lacking a little yesterday, so I stayed up all night putting together a chocolate display of the New York skyline—thank god I brought some molds with me! Finished it off with some spun sugar and some edible glitter, looks great. Pastries are the same as yesterday, mini crème brûlée, assorted macaroons, and éclairs—my favorite! Wanted to go traditional French with a flair, shifted some of the flavors around so they were more surprising, but with so many reviewers and masters in the room, I didn't want to go too far outside of my comfort zone.

@Sprinkle-Ella: Yum! Sounds amazing! I know they'll all be impressed!

@TheBakingBandit: Ugh, your éclairs! I still can't get that freaking recipe you sent me right even though I've tried a million times. My inside always ends up too runny.

@TheGourmetGoddess: Send me a pic next time you make them! You might not be poking the hole right to let the steam out. Took me forever to get that part just so.

@Sprinkle-Ella: Send us some photos from the conference! Sounds so exciting! I have to go. Meeting with some clients. Woman wants a perfect princess wedding cake overflowing with buttercream flowers. My dream!

@TheBakingBandit: Welcome back to the land of color!

A call for boarding jolted Jo from her phone, pulling her back into the real world. She quickly finished saying goodbye and shoved another nugget into her mouth before sliding her ticket from her purse. First class boarded, well, first, so it wasn't long before she was at seat 1A, getting situated. Jo always loved the legroom of the front row. The only downside was it meant she had to put her bag in the overhead compartment, so before she sat, she took out everything she thought she might need for her flight—her computer, her charger, the flash drive that still felt hot to the touch, a bag of M&M's, a Snickers bar, a diet Coke, and the rest of her pretzel nuggets.

With a deep breath, Jo sat down, unable to stop her legs from bouncing, her heart from pounding, her insides from twisting into tightly bound knots. The *click* of her seat belt sounded more like a lock sliding into place. The curved walls of the plane closed in. There was nowhere else to run, nowhere else to go. The computer on her lap might as well have weighed a thousand pounds for how thoroughly it held her down, held her trapped. Jo arranged the items on her lap. Rearranged them. Her fingers twitched. Her movements jerked. Her entire body fidgeted with unease.

Stop.

Jo curled her fingers into fists, clenching for a moment, before gently flattening them against the leather seat. She lifted her gaze and turned her head, searching for some sort of distraction. Almost immediately, she locked eyes with the man sitting across the aisle, judgment etched into his features. He'd been staring at her. Legit staring. Thick brows. Dark hazel eyes. Cleanly shaven cheeks. Hair buzzed close to his scalp. All of it turned on her with unabashed disapproval…unless she was just imagining the slight curl to his lips, the subtle sneer?

Jo held his gaze and lifted a nugget to her mouth, careful to lick every speck of sugar from her lips as she took her time chewing.

Go ahead and stare, asshole.

I paid for my seat, same as you. And I'll do whatever I damn well please, especially when I'm in a crisis.

Jo narrowed her eyes, not at all in the mood.

He coughed and looked away, straight ahead at the gray wall.

Yeah, that's what I thought.

"Can I get you anything?" a flight attendant asked, holding a tray of water, wine, and orange juice.

The man just grunted, his deep voice resembling tires on gravel, rude and gruff. Jo looked up, meeting eyes with the flight attendant, sharing that look that only two women could possibly understand when a man was being a complete jerk. Jo rolled her eyes. The stewardess tried to stifle a smile. And then Jo took a glass of water from the tray—hydration was key when consuming the amount of sugar she'd planned on consuming to get through reading these files.

"Thank you."

"You're welcome."

The man was still staring as the flight attendant walked by, but this time it was subtler, out of the corners of his eyes, just creepy enough to make Jo's hackles rise. His arms were crossed over his chest and he hunched low in his seat, legs stretched as far out as they could go. His gaze was cast low, locked on her lap, on her carefully arranged selection of sweets.

Or is it? Jo swallowed, glancing back toward her thighs, mind going to the black laptop and the flash drive resting on top. Could he be staring at those?

Don't be silly.

Jo took a deep breath and tried to force her unease to the side. That man couldn't possibly have any idea what was on that drive, what she had taken, what her family had done. These were her fears, her insecurities, the ones she'd tried to suppress all day, coming out of hiding, plaguing her in plain sight, no longer willing to be ignored.

The man was just a man.

He was probably leering at the sliver of skin exposed by the slit in her long dress. No doubt wondering how she ate what she ate and looked the way she looked—Jo had questioned it herself a million times. Good genes and a six-mile run every day was all she'd ever come up with.

She let her head fall to the other side, gaze slipping out the window. The skyline of New York was visible beyond the wing of the plane. Her mind wandered to the men she'd left behind. Nate. Thad. Two opposite ends of the pole. One no doubt dealing with the painting they'd stolen the night before, on his way to make a delivery before slipping off the grid for a few days. The other no doubt with his team, torn down the middle by his heart and his head, by the trust he'd given her and the trust he owed to his colleagues, his partner, his family.

His father, Jo thought with a sigh, munching on another nugget, salty this time, buttery and tangy, a jolt to her system, just as Nate had been. Her heart pinched as she remembered the story he'd confessed the night before, words she somehow knew he hadn't told anyone else. The promise any boy would make to his father, but only a man like Nate would fight his entire life to uphold. A good person. A loyal one. Someone who followed through on his word. Someone Jo wasn't sure she deserved.

I promise.

The two words haunted her.

I will do what's right. I promise you, I will.

The plane started to move. To turn. New York slipped away. But the memory lingered, grew, expanded. They shot down the runway. Jo's promise shot across her thoughts.

Racing.

Speeding.

Lifting.

Because she wanted to do the right thing. For once in her life, for this man whose trust she didn't deserve but somehow earned, for her dreams and her passions and her conscience, she wanted to do what was right. But she still wasn't completely sure she could.

Jo looked away from the window as it turned a blinding white. The plane bounced as they catapulted through the clouds. Up and away. To another world. Alone. Her focus latched on to the little seat belt symbol above her head, waiting for it to turn off. Her eyes burned. Her hands trembled. With a *ding* the light blinked out. A muffled voice came over the loudspeaker, announcing that the use of portable electronics was allowed.

Jo slowly finished her nuggets.

Each bite taking longer and longer.

Until there were none left., no more reason to delay.

She glanced to the passenger at her side, sure he'd been watching her, but his eyes were closed, and his head was tilted back. She swallowed the queasy feeling in her stomach and opened her can of soda. The *snap* and *pop* followed by a soft bubbling fizz made her nerves settle. Jo took a long sip, letting the ice-cold liquid slip down her throat, sharp and bursting. And then she lifted the top of her computer and slid the flash drive in before clicking a file at random.

Federal Bureau of Investigation
Organized Crime Division
Subject: Robert Carter

Jo ripped her M&M's open and forced herself to keep reading and reading and reading, until the world faded and time drifted away, and everything she thought she'd ever known fell out from underneath her.

- 28 -

Nate

"So we have nothing?" The disgust in the boss's tone was evident. The fury was too. He slammed a wad of stuffed manila envelopes against the conference table, making everyone jump. "Months and months of work, gone. What the hell happened?"

All the men and women around the table shifted uncomfortably in their seats. The boss was not an intimidating man based on looks alone. A little short. Starting to bald. Tanned face leathery from too much sun and full of wrinkles. Broad shoulders with muscles that had begun to turn soft. But the knowledge in his hazel eyes and the iron in his voice, a voice that had chided them all many times before, were enough to make Nate's blood run cold.

"Anyone want to tell me how this operation got royally fucked? Anyone? No?" Nate froze when that shrewd gaze landed on him. "Parker? What the hell happened with the daughter? I thought we had a lead?"

He cleared his throat, sitting straighter. "We might still have a lead, sir. I haven't ruled it out."

The boss arched one thick brow, staring at him with disbelief. "Let me get this straight. She turned down your offer of immunity. Ran away from you. Helped Ryder steal the painting. And then vanished in the middle of the night. And what? You think it was an elaborate ruse? Tell me what I'm missing here, Parker, because I'd really love to know."

It took every ounce of self-control Nate possessed to not glance at Leo across the conference table. But he was trained in interrogation tactics, and he knew body language could give away far more than words ever would. "That's correct, sir. I have a hunch—"

"A hunch?" the boss roared. Nate didn't flinch. "A fucking hunch? Parker, you got played. We all got played."

"I think she just wanted time, sir, to do things her own way. Jolene Carter isn't the type to be bossed around or cornered into anything."

Well, that was mostly true. But somehow, Nate highly doubted the boss wanted to know that the only time Jo didn't mind being dominated was in the bedroom. He clenched his teeth as images of their night flooded his thoughts, the sound of her sighs, the feel of her skin, the weight of her body as she straddled his—

"Parker?" the boss said loudly, giving Nate the distinct impression it hadn't been the first time.

He tried to swallow the sudden tightness in his throat and other places away. "Sir?"

The boss stared at him for a moment and then scoffed, turning to another agent. "Samuels, do we have locations? An update? Anything?"

"Nothing new, sir. Jolene Carter was spotted at the airport. Spent a lot of time circling the shops. She picked up a few cookies, put them back, but there were no notes underneath. An agent followed her to a few food stores and coffee places, no purchases but some candy and a soda. No obvious interactions. The only person we saw her talk to was the cashier at a soft pretzel place, and that was a routine order."

The corner of Nate's lip lifted. *Sounds like Jo.*

"Her plane," Samuels continued, scrolling a tablet for more updates. "Looks like it took off about forty-five minutes ago. Scheduled to land in two and a half hours. Our agent saw her board and waited for the doors to close before leaving. A ground crew searched her checked luggage but there was nothing of interest, and we didn't have enough evidence for an arrest to seem worthwhile."

"And Ryder?"

Samuels winced and glanced at the floor. "Nothing, sir. No one has seen him since he gave us the slip outside the museum last night."

The boss grumbled incoherently. A vein pulsed in his forehead. "How is that possible? Have we checked the street cameras? Anything?"

"All the cameras within a few blocks were tampered with, and we have men searching all the others, trying to locate a man of Ryder's description at around the time of the theft, but so far nothing. He disappeared."

"He's not a fucking magician," the boss growled.

Might as well be.

"So we've got no prints, no hair follicles, no DNA?" the boss said, turning to one of the forensics guys for confirmation, which he gave, reluctantly. "And we've got no video footage, no way to tie the bugs in the security system to Jolene Carter, and no way to place either of them at the scene?" He glanced at the tech team. Again, a silent, hesitant nod was the only response. "And Ryder has vanished off the face of the earth like a fucking Houdini?"

No one bothered to respond. Judging by the boss's tone, the answer wouldn't have been received kindly.

"Well, what the hell *do* we have, boys and girls?"

"The homeowner has given us everything he has on the painting..."

Nate tuned it out. He'd heard it all before. And it was all crap. Fluffy, shiny, bulked-up and well-packaged bullshit. All they had was Jo. And it would be hours, hell, days before he heard from her, if he ever did again.

The phone in his pocket buzzed.

Nate's entire body jerked into motion as he hastily silenced the vibration. Leo shot him a hopeful look across the table, but there was no way it was Jo. Not so soon. He knew better than to hope, so he shook his head at his partner.

The phone buzzed again.

What the hell?

He silenced the call, but this time pulled the cell out of his pocket far enough to read an unknown number across the screen.

Spam?

Now?

Really?

He shoved it back into his pocket.

Thirty seconds later, the fucking thing buzzed again.

"Oh, for god's sake," he grumbled as every eye in the room turned in his direction. "Sorry, sir."

"No problem at all, Parker. I wouldn't want a little thing like an international crisis to get in the way of your busy social life. Answer it. I don't mind."

Nate squeezed his eyes shut for a moment. The boss was in rare form. "Really, sir, it's nothing."

"Humor me," he drawled, voice dry and devoid of any hint of amusement.

Nate sighed but did as he was told and lifted the phone to his ear. "Parker here."

His voice came out deep enough to make Leo hold a fist to his lips to cover up his laughter. He glared at his partner as he waited for a response, any response. But there was only static. Heavy breathing and static.

"Who is it, Parker? We're all dying to know."

"No one, sir," Nate said. "Wrong number."

Just as he pulled the device from his ear, he heard it.

Pop! Pop!

A sound that haunted his nightmares.

A sound that followed him around in his waking hours, at the practice range, on the job.

A sound that defined his life.

Gunshots.

Oh god. Jo. Jo!

Nate jumped to his feet, clutching the phone. "Hello? Hello? Who is it?"

More static.

Heavy breathing. The pounding of boots. Scuffs and scrapes he couldn't identify.

Just as he was about to say her name, a man's voice came on the line, controlled in a way that was completely at odds with the noises that had preceded him. "Agent Parker?"

"Yes. This is Agent Nate Parker. To whom am I speaking?"

Leo reached across the table with a cord. Nate stuck it into his phone, and the call transferred to the comm set in the middle of the room, putting the unidentified man on speaker. Everyone's energy shifted, on alert, on the job. No more joking. No more reprimanding. Just business.

There was no response.

Just more running. More breathing.

"Hello?" he tried again. The boss signaled everyone else to shut up and not say a word. He started pointing to various agents, signaling with his hands. Working together long enough meant they didn't need words. The tech team launched into motion, messaging the agents back at their desks to get tracking on the call immediately. "This is Agent Nate Parker. To whom am I speaking?"

"I think you know," came the smooth reply.

Everything snapped into place. "Ryder? Ryder, is that you?"

The boss's eyes bulged. Leo smirked, as if he'd known Nate had a plan all along. But this wasn't it. This had never been it.

"Ryder!" he shouted again, smacking his hand against the table in his frustration. "Where—"

"Jo is in danger," Ryder interjected, cutting him off.

Nate's entire body went still, everything except for his heart, which pounded against his rib cage, a beast turned rabid.

"I can't get to her in time. You need to save her."

Click.

The line went dead. It happened so fast that for a second, no one moved or spoke.

"Did we get a location?" The boss broke the silence. Nate heard his voice as though it had come from somewhere far away, slow and muffled. For a moment, he wondered if he had slipped into a dream, because that was what it felt like, out of body. His mind was disconnected, drifting away. The boss was on a boat above the water, and Nate was under the surface, sinking fast, unable to process as the oxygen stopped flowing to his brain. All he heard was—

Pop!

Pop!

Pop!

"I want agents on the ground immediately. Call the local precinct. Have them send patrol cars. Warn them there's an active shooter, armed and dangerous. Their goal is to stall until we have Feds on the scene. This might be our only chance to get Ryder."

Ryder?

Nate shook his head.

Ryder?

He came alive in a single second. "What about Jo?"

Everyone paused, turning to the boss for guidance.

"What about Jo? Her plane won't land for another two hours, and we have Ryder on the ground now, possibly injured. I don't give a fuck about Jo."

"Sir—"

"Parker."

Nate was one word away from leaping across the table and wringing his boss's neck, consequences be damned. "Sir—"

"Nate's right. We need Jolene Carter," Leo stepped in. Their eyes met across the table and in a second, Nate and his partner had an entire conversation. Leo was on his side. Leo wanted to help. Leo was the voice of reason, whereas Nate was about to explode. "Without the daughter, we have no leverage on Robert Carter. Even if we get enough to arrest him, we need something to hold over his head, something to use against him. The only way we'll get him to talk is with the promise of his daughter's freedom and her safety. We need her. Alive and unharmed."

I need her, Nate thought, the realization a knife to his chest. *I need her. Alive and unharmed and in my arms immediately.*

The boss considered it for a moment. "Fine. Parker, Alvarez, you're on the daughter. Everyone else, I want you working on Ryder. Let's move it, people."

Needing no more prompting, they all raced from the room. Nate and Leo ran to the temporary desks that had been set up for them in the New York office, and hurriedly signed on to the clunky desktop computers.

"Do we request an emergency landing?" Nate asked his partner, his right knee bouncing at an uncontrollable rate as he spun in his chair. "Somewhere in the States? We could have local police waiting?"

Leo scrunched his cheeks, thinking. "Eh, I don't know. If there's a hitman on the flight with her, an emergency landing might spook him into action. We both know he wouldn't need a gun to make his move. Bare hands might be enough, especially if he acted fast enough, during landing when everyone was belted in."

The idea made Nate queasy. "What then?"

"Let's get to the Bahamas as fast as we can. My guess is they'll try to hit Jo and her father at once, kill two birds with one stone, and destroy the evidence on the island. They must suspect foul play to have gone after Ryder. They'll want to wipe the slate clean. But we can get to her first if we play this right. I know we can."

"I'll search for flights to Nassau," Nate said with a firm nod.

"I'm already calling Air Traffic Control to see if they can stall Jo's flight until we get there to intercept it."

"One's leaving from Newark in forty-five minutes." The flight was sold out, and they'd never make it in time. But that didn't matter. *Sometimes, it's good to be a Fed.* "I'll call the airline on the way to reserve seats. Tell Air Traffic Control they need to hold the flight."

"Will do. I'm being transferred. Book a boat for when we land, just in case we're too late."

"Already on it."

They went back and forth a few more times. Within five minutes, they hastily rushed out the door with nothing but their guns, badges, and wallets as they hailed a cab. Nate didn't give a damn about the suits hanging in his hotel closet. The shoes. The belts. The boss would have someone grab them. All Nate cared about was Jo. Was getting to her in time.

Pop!

Pop!

Pop!

The memory made him flinch. He couldn't be late—he wouldn't be late.

Not this time.

Not with her.

Not again.

- 29 -

Jo

When the wheels touched down in Nassau, Jo jolted in her seat at the impact. She blinked a few times, clearing the water from her eyes, but couldn't clear the daze. Her mind was a jumbled mess.

Russians.

And hitmen.

And arms deals.

And money laundering.

And human trafficking.

And those were just the words. The pictures that had come with them—

Jo shook her head and lifted her fingers to her lips, coughing as she fought to contain the physical manifestation of her disgust. Nate had been right. These were bad people. Horrific people. And her father had helped them. Jo saw the evidence clear as day. Some of the artwork she'd helped steal had been used as collateral payment for illegal arms deals with terrorist organizations, some for things even worse than that, things she couldn't bear thinking about. Forgeries she'd seen her father create in his studio had been used to cheat and steal and lie. All the meeting dates had lined up with trips her father and Thad had taken, telling her they were going to the mainland for supplies. All the proof Nate needed was right there in his files, but Jo was the missing piece, the person who could tie it all together and confirm his suspicions. After finally opening her eyes to the truth, she knew exactly what she needed to do.

Jo followed the horde blindly off the plane, struggling to keep her mind focused on the reality around her and not the fireworks exploding like bombs inside her brain. She waited for her checked bag. The passengers around her grumbled about the delay. Apparently, the flight had taken about an hour longer than expected—a long route due to some unforeseen weather they'd had to fly around. Jo hadn't noticed a thing. She didn't even notice her bag on the conveyor belt until it slid right by and out of reach, forcing her to wait another few minutes for it to circle back around.

"Jolene!" She recognized the voice immediately. Only one person called her by her full name.

Jo spun, finding her father hastily rushing through the crowd, gaze locked on her. "Daddy?"

As soon as the word passed through her lips, Jo heard the naiveté laced through it—the youth and the innocence she'd tried desperately to hold on to ever since her mother passed away. Jo had wanted to remain fourteen forever, wanted to stay that little girl who didn't need to face the fact that her mother was gone, that her father was a criminal, that her typical, normal, simple life had been nothing but a sham.

But her eyes were open now.

She was seeing things clearly for the first time. And she was a woman, not a girl, who needed to make things right. "I mean, Dad, what are you doing here? I thought I was supposed to meet you at home? Who's watching the island?"

His eyes were dark with worry as they shifted left and right. A deep wrinkle was etched into the curve of his forehead. Not pausing for a beat, her father walked to her side and gripped her biceps hard, tugging her to the side. "We have to leave, pumpkin."

"My bag—"

"Not now," he said, yanking her behind as he pushed through the crowd.

The hairs on the back of her neck stood with the sudden sense of being watched. Jo let her father pull her forward as she glanced behind, finding the face of the man who had been sitting beside her on the plane, still studying her carefully. Only now, she took note of the awareness in his deep-set hooded eyes, the lack of bags, the fact that she hadn't heard him speak.

Is he one of the Russians?

Are they watching us?

Jo tripped over her feet and stumbled forward. Her father helped her right her balance, and this time, they moved as one through the crowd. Jo didn't argue. She did as he'd taught her, not needing him to say when to duck into a store, when to cut a corner, when to hide around a bend or take a route that led in circles. They eventually made it to the parking lot. Her father hot-wired a car and they jumped in before easing onto the street, doing the same thing on the road as they'd done on their feet. In about twice the time it normally took, they made it to a boat dock—a different one than her father typically used. But Jo recognized the yacht at the end of the slip. *My Susanna.*

What would her mother say to see them now?

If she'd known what they'd become?

What Jo had become?

She shook her head—those thoughts were better left for another time—and followed her father onto the gleaming white deck, hastily making for the helm. He took the captain's seat, and Jo filled in as first mate, a spot she'd taken many times before. But never again.

"What's going on, Dad?" she asked as they glided out of the port and into open sea. For the first time with her father, Jo's voice was stern and demanding, not childish and carefree.

He kept his gaze locked on the horizon. "Don't you worry, pumpkin. I've got it all under control."

Ten days ago, that might have worked.

Now, it wasn't nearly enough. "I said, what's going on?"

He looked at her then, scrutinizing the thin line of her lips, the hard edges carved into her face, the unspoken demand. Something shifted in his features. One instant he was the commanding, suave, confident man she'd always known. And then he blinked. And swallowed. And suddenly he seemed old. Tired. His shoulders hunched ever so slightly. His eyelids dipped to a droop. He released a resigned sigh.

He knew.

One look and he knew.

But Jo pressed the point anyway. "I know everything, Dad. You, Thad, the Russian mafia. What the hell were you thinking? Why? And what is going on?"

"Thad…" He glanced back at the horizon as he swallowed a tightness in his throat. "Thad called. The meet didn't go as planned."

Jo's heart leapt into her throat, clogging it with dread. "What? What happened?"

"Something tipped the Russians off. Thad sensed a shift in his contact, so he ran before they had a chance to act. Last we spoke, I heard gunfire in the background. But Thaddeus is quick on his feet, as smart as anyone I've met. I'm sure he got out. He must have gotten out."

The repetition of that thought did nothing to quell her nerves. Instead, Jo collapsed into her seat, all her muscles giving out at once.

Thad.

Oh my god, Thad.

Are you okay?

Are you hurt?

Are you—

Jo shook her head, unable to conceive of a life without her best friend—her brother—in it. The world blurred, and then strange bits and pieces came together to form a clear scene, one she didn't know how to face.

"It's my fault," she confessed softly. The realization made her flinch.

Her father darted a glance in her direction. Jo closed her eyes and squeezed against the pain, the doubts, the fear.

"It's my fault, Dad. They were following me. I was meeting with— I was talking to— I— I—" Jo opened her eyes and found her father's. They were so similar, the deep green of an old dollar bill or a palm leaf in the shade. But had either of them truly seen each other until this moment? Ever noticed all the minute differences that would tear them apart? "I made a deal with the Feds."

He didn't move.

Didn't react.

He blinked twice and remained silent, waiting for her to continue. Every other inch of him was frozen.

"An agent approached me, and I don't really even know why, but I listened to what he had to say. And he told me, about you, about what you were doing. He let me take his files, everything they had on you. He offered me immunity to get you on record, on a wire, to hand you in. And I said no. I wasn't going to do it. But I have to, Dad, don't you see? We have to. Together."

"Jolene..." His tone was a strange mix of defiance and resignation, of fight and surrender, and it trailed off into silence, as though unsure which side should win out.

"They are *evil*, Dad. Evil. How could you— What in the world—" She broke off as her voice cracked. But one single word was all she needed to say. It came out rough and demanding, as hard as the diamond engagement ring she knew he still wore around his neck, the one belonging to her mother. "Why?"

He stood from his chair and knelt before her, taking both of her hands in his, looking up into her eyes so she couldn't look away, forcing her to listen. The lines of his face were protective and caring, fatherly in a way that brought her back to the last time they'd sat like this, in a sterile hospital waiting area, when he told her that her mother had died. He'd sent her from the room so she wouldn't hear those ragged, gurgling breaths, but Jo had listened with her ear pressed to the door, her eyes straining to see through the frosted glass, holding on for dear life to those last moments. It felt the same now. Like an end of something. The end of her youth perhaps. The end of believing her father was a hero. The realization that he was a man, just a man like any other, who had made mistakes—grave, terrible mistakes.

"We did it to protect you," he said softly.

"Protect—"

"Let me finish, Jolene," he scolded, voice gentle but not to be disobeyed.

Oddly, that conviction calmed her, because it reminded her of the father she knew, the one she loved. Jo shut her mouth and did what she was told, something completely against her nature—she listened.

"When Thad's father died, I was planning to retire. Thad was about to graduate college. You know this, you remember. I saw that you'd held yourself back, remained home out of worry for me, out of loyalty to me, and I knew I had to let my old life go. Give you and Thad both a chance to be better, to be different. I was all set to cut off ties with my contacts, some friends, some not, and I left the island to do just that. But when I landed in the States, I was intercepted by members of the Russian mafia, thrown into a van, bag over my head, gun to my neck, and taken to a meeting point. When I got there, they told me Thad's father, the partner I'd worked with all my life, had been working with them on the side. I had no idea. At first, I didn't believe them, but the proof was right before my eyes. Photographs. Phone logs. Messages. And they told me they'd killed him because he'd been about to go to the Feds."

Jo gasped. "But the car crash—"

"Deliberate. They messed with his brakes in a way that was undetectable by the cops, made to look like a malfunction, not foul play. But it was murder. And then they told me I had a choice—finish the work my partner had started or watch my only child, my daughter, die."

Jo's mouth dropped open, but she was too shocked to speak.

"They knew I'd rather be killed than work for them, but they knew I would never risk your life, so I agreed. And when I got back to the island, Thad was there. One look in his eyes and I knew he'd been offered the same deal. So we kept you out of it as best we could and did what we were told, to keep you safe. Always to keep you safe."

Jo took a long, uneven breath, hating the question that had come to mind, but unable to stop herself from asking it. "Am I safe, Dad? Are you? Is Thad?"

No.

They both knew the answer.

Jo could see her father teetering, one foot balanced on the edge as he fought not to fall one way or the other. "This was supposed to be the last job."

"Do you really believe that?" She squeezed his hands, forcing him to listen. "Do you really think they would've ever let you go?"

He held her gaze but didn't say a word.

"Let's end this, Dad. The Feds will keep us safe. I—I trust them. We'll never be able to make things right. We'll never be able to reverse the horrible things we've been a part of. But we can stop it. Here. Now. We can stop them. All it will take is one phone call."

Please, she added silently. *Please, Dad, please.*

But she couldn't bring herself to beg. Not with her father. The small part of her still holding on to the belief that he was a good man deep down wouldn't let her. He had to make this decision for himself. Jo's choice would be the same either way—either her father would confess or she would confess for him, no matter the consequence.

He lifted his palm to her cheek. His hand was warm from the sun, soft the way it always had been, loving. Jo covered his fingers with her own, feeling the wrinkles on his hand she hadn't noticed before, noticing the silver sheen of his hair, the deep grooves around his eyes. But when she met his gaze, he didn't look old. He looked lighter. Full of a bright glow nothing could dampen. Freed from a weight that had made the years longer.

"Will you ever forgive me, pumpkin?"

Jo squeezed his hand as a tear spilled from the corner of her eye. "Of course, Daddy." She couldn't stop the endearment from slipping out. "I love you."

He nodded. Jo could see the walls come up, the defenses refortify. He stood from the floor and went back to the captain's chair, where he sat tall, with dignity, with newfound strength. "Make the call, Jolene."

Like father, like daughter. Jo wiped the salty droplet from her cheek and took a deep breath, pushing the emotions back as she straightened her spine and reached into her purse for her phone, getting back to business. She'd completely forgotten to turn it off airplane mode when she'd landed, too wrapped up in her thoughts, so she did so now, waiting for the signal to connect. As soon as it did, her phone began to buzz with missed calls, voicemails, and messages. Half were from Thad and half from Nate.

Jo clicked on Thad's first, then put the receiver to her ear. She flinched at every gunshot, holding on to the calmness in his voice as he warned her to run, not an ounce of accusation in the tone, only fear—fear for her, not for himself.

Oh, Thad.

Jo sighed when the line went dead, a heavy weight in her chest. But there was nothing else from him. No messages. No more calls.

He's alive.

He's alive.

He's Thad.

He's the king of the getaway.

He's fine.

He's safe.

Jo wanted to believe it, but deep down, she didn't. Deep down, there was nothing but a pit of dread, a chasm growing wider and wider by the second.

She didn't bother to read Nate's messages. She needed a distraction now, immediately.

"Jo?" His voice sounded rushed.

"Nate." She breathed the word, so it sounded almost like a sigh of relief. Just hearing his voice made everything seem a little easier to manage. Her father glanced over, frowning at her tone, at the affection she hadn't bothered to veil.

"Jo! Are you all right? Are you safe? Leo and I are here. We're in a boat, on our way. I must have just missed you at the airport. I thought I— I thought you— I thought—"

"I'm okay," Jo soothed. Her gaze darted out the window, to the island only a few hundred yards away. "I'm almost home. My father picked me up. I think, maybe, someone was on the plane watching me, but we got away before he could do anything. We're fine."

"Ohthankgod." It came out in a whoosh, one connected thought. Jo smiled, perfectly able to envision how he must have been sitting, his thumb and pointer finger squeezing the ridge of his nose, all stress and hard lines, until her assurance forced the tension away, finally letting his firm muscles release. "Are you sure the island is safe?"

"I don't see any foreign vessels," she said slowly, skimming the shoreline for anything out of the ordinary. Jo glanced to her father. "Dad, has the alarm been disturbed? Were the motion cameras alerted to any activity?"

He shook his head. "No. I've been checking the system every ten minutes since the moment I left. No one's been inside the house."

"Once we get inside, they won't be able to touch us," Jo told Nate. The glass was bulletproof. The vault acted as a safe room. Hidden cameras would give her a view of the entire property. Steel bars could be dropped in front of all the entrances at the push of a button. And she could dispense tear gas from the air ducts if she needed to. The island villa wasn't just a home—it was a fortress, designed for this exact purpose. "You don't have to worry. And, Nate, I have good news."

Her father pulled into the slip.

"What?" Nate asked over the line, hesitant.

Jo followed her father out of the cabin and leapt over the edge of the boat, onto the dock, happy to have solid ground beneath her feet, happy to be home safe. She signaled him to keep walking, that she'd take care of the boat. As she tied the rope, phone squished between her shoulder and her ear, she said, "My father agreed to confess."

"He did?" The shock in Nate's tone was evident.

"I'll explain everything when you get here, but I promise, he's not as bad as you've made him out to be. He'll tell you everything you want to know. He just wants all of this to end. For me to be okay."

The pause on the line made Nate's doubt obvious. He cleared his throat. "I may have forged your signature on the immunity plea when I got back to my hotel last night, so the deal we made with you will still stand either way."

"Nathaniel Parker," Jo teased. "I didn't know you had it in you."

Somehow, she could hear his smile through the line, could perfectly envision his wide lips, his straight rows of teeth gleaming white against his tanned skin. "Clearly, you've been a bad influence."

"Fun," Jo corrected, humor flooding her system for the first time in what felt like days. "I prefer, 'a fun influence.'" She squeezed the knot on the second rope tight and stood from her crouched position, turning to face the house. "Speaking of fun…"

The innuendo was sharp.

Nate laughed over the line. The sound was like a perfect bite of cake, sweet and sugary, sending a sense of comfort to her core, a warm embrace that brought back memories of better times. Jo took a step down the dock, unable to control the grin widening her cheeks, and watched as her father stepped up to the back door and put his hand on the knob, twisting.

Bam!

The world exploded.

For a second, everything stopped, a snapshot of time. The flames halted, froze midbillow, angry, red, and bright enough to blind. Her father's silhouette flickered, already coming apart at the seams. Debris hovered, glass and wood and rock, static in midair. Nate's soft amusement lingered in her ear, so at odds with the scene on display before her.

And just as quickly, it rushed forward.

The force of the blast smacked her in the center of the chest. Jo flew off her feet, catapulting backward. Her body hit the water hard, headfirst, turning her vision to a night sky blinking with fractured stars. There was no up or down, just crashing waves and rolling water and confusion as she sank beneath the surface.

- 30 -

Nate

"Jo!" he screamed as the line went dead. Nate jumped to his feet, fighting for balance as their speedboat vaulted from crest to crest, darting through the waves. A single second was all it took to spot the onyx swirl of smoke blossoming on the horizon. The sound of the blast hit a few seconds later, a muffled, muted version of the one that had interrupted Jo's call. Nate gripped the phone in his hands as his entire body shook.

Jo.

Oh god. Jo!

Jo!

"Leo, how far are we? How long?" The words came quick, years and years of training drilled into his system, instincts kicking in to stifle the panic and maintain his focus. Nate was no longer the little boy who cried over his father's dead body. He was a man—armed and trained and dangerous in his own right. And he would not lose this fight. He refused.

"A few minutes," Leo answered, voice deep with unspoken sympathy but laced with determination—the same grit flowing through Nate's nerves, turning them to steel.

"Make it one."

Leo revved the engine.

Nate leapt over the protective glass, leaving Leo at the wheel, as he crept forward and crouched behind the cushioned seats at the bow of the ship. They'd grabbed bulletproof vests from the local police who'd been waiting for them at the airport. Two coast guard ships were five minutes behind, and a chopper was supposed to be on its way. But for now, he and Leo were alone. So Nate slipped his gun from his belt and unclicked the safety, then got into position, leaning his elbows on the boat for stability.

"We should wait for backup," Leo called over the roar of the wind.

Nate shook his head as the island loomed before them, nothing but smoke and rubble, so out of place against the glistening aqua waves. A twisted view of paradise. "There's no time. Pull right up to the beach."

He heard the *Pop! Pop! Pop!* before he saw the shooter.

Bullets ricocheted off the side of the boat. One hit the glass, cracking it down the middle but not breaking through. The speed and power of the blast told him it was an assault rifle. Nate's pointer finger twitched against the trigger of his Glock 22. Not an equal match, not by a long shot. He swallowed, calming his nerves, reminding himself that in the game of size versus skill, skill almost always won out.

As soon as the barrage ended, he lifted his head over the edge of the bow. Two men were on the beach. No protective gear. No cover. They thought their weapons made them immune. Nate would teach them different. He fired four shots in quick succession, two at each man, watching them drop. Another ran out from the tree line. Nate got him in the chest.

A distraction.

The mobsters were nothing but a distraction.

Where's Jo?

Where's Jo?

She wasn't at the house.

She was still by the boat.

I heard waves in the background right before the blast.

Another round of shots was fired from an unseen location. Nate hit the deck. Leo cursed behind him. Pieces of the boat exploded into the air, stinging his cheeks as they peppered down, a plastic rain. The motor groaned as Leo pressed down as hard as he could.

They rammed into the beach, slamming into the sand before coming to a sudden stop. The shots paused. Nate peeked over the edge, scanning the beach, but there was nothing. No one. He traced the line of the dock. Studied the water. And then he saw her.

Jo!

A body, floating facedown in the water.

The red hair spread like a fan across the surface was unmistakable. Not thinking, just acting, Nate leapt over the side of the boat and ran into the surf. He dove beneath the water as another spray of bullets was released, carving swirling currents through the blue expanse to either side of him. One nicked his leg, a stinging kiss, but not enough to cause real damage. Another lodged in the back of his vest, hitting hard enough to expel an agonized groan, but he kept pushing with his arms, kicking with his feet. He kept going. Leo returned fire, providing cover as Nate surged to the surface for a deep breath. The weight of the vest slowed him down, so he unclipped it, not caring about the risk. From their spot in the woods to either side of the house, the Russians didn't have a great shot at the water. At least, that was what he told himself as he cut beneath the pier for cover, swimming through striped shadow until he reached the end. Ignoring the blasts of bullets and the guttural shouts as he surfaced once more, Nate focused his attention on one thing.

"Jo," he said as he flipped her in the water. Her skin was cold, pale. Her chest wasn't moving. Her eyes were closed. Nate kicked with his feet, keeping them both above the surface as he held her nose and forced breath into her lungs.

No response.

He tried again, but he needed leverage. There was nothing he could do here, from the water. They needed to get on land. He needed to force the liquid from her lungs, get her blood pumping. And even then…

No. Nate shook his head, trying to remember what he'd learned in basic training. The brain could go up to five minutes without oxygen before permanent damage occurred, sometimes even more, depending on the conditions. Five minutes was a lifetime. He couldn't have been that far behind. And she might have found a moment to take a breath. Her heart might not have stopped right away. He could save her. He would save her.

Jo is strong.

She's a fighter.

So am I.

Water sprayed like a fountain to their right as bullets sliced through. Nate clutched Jo to his chest and kicked with his feet, hauling them both to the yacht a few feet away. Unlike Leo's boat, which was chipping apart like wood through a chopper under the relentless assault,

Robert Carter's yacht was still pristine, completely at odds with the devastation around them. It wouldn't be that way for long.

As soon as the Russians realized what he was doing, the bullets came. Nate hastily climbed the ladder at the back made for swimming and pulled Jo up behind him. The wound in his calf screamed as he put weight on the leg, but he didn't stop until they were far enough away from the open air to be safe. Muffled *thumps* pounded the side of the yacht. They'd break through eventually, but for now, it didn't matter. All that mattered was Jo.

Nate held her nose and blew two deep breaths into her lungs, watching her chest rise and fall with the force. Then he folded his hands over her heart and pumped thirty times.

Nothing.

He repeated the action again.

Still nothing.

He closed his eyes as his body went through the motions, mind racing over everything he'd been taught, everything he'd learned. The important thing was to keep her blood flowing, to keep her vital organs from dying, her brain from damage. Resuscitation could wait as long as he kept everything else in her body alive.

It took a second for the sound of an alarm to register. Nate darted his gaze toward the side, finding the coast guard was almost there.

The bullets stopped.

The Russians ran.

Nate kept performing CPR, over and over and over, Jo's body twitching beneath him.

"Come on, Jo," he murmured.

Nate blinked, and it was his father beneath him, the blood pouring over his hands, spreading across the grass, spilling down the drive.

He blinked again, and it was Jo, face at peace and eyes closed, almost in sleep, except she wouldn't wake.

His father.

Then Jo.

His father.

Then Jo.

"Not again. Not again!"

Nate blew air into her chest.

He forced her heart to beat.

His blood dripped onto the carpet. His muscles ached. His chest burned. But he wouldn't stop. Couldn't stop.

"Parker!" Leo's voice.

Nate had no idea how long he'd been there, kneeling over Jo's body, willing her back to life. There was only one thing left he could think to try. One thing that might jolt her heart back into motion. "Take over."

Leo got into position immediately. Nate jumped to his feet and ran inside the cabin of the yacht, making for the hull, searching for the symbol he knew had to be somewhere—a red box with a white cross.

There!

Nate ripped open the latch and grabbed the first aid kit before running back to Jo and Leo. He fell to his knees as he dumped the kit over, letting everything fall to the floor in a jumbled heap. Scissors first, he cut her dress from her body. Then he grabbed a towel and dried her torso and limbs. Leo kept performing CPR as Nate laid out the towel. The two of them gently eased Jo from the puddle of water she'd been lying in, moving her to dry ground. Nate pulled the portable defibrillator from the mess, then attached two pads to Jo's exposed chest. He and Leo, still sopping wet, stepped back. He pressed the button.

Jo jolted, back arching for a moment.

She stilled.

"Goddammit, Jo. Come on!"

Nate waited for the device to charge.

He pressed again.

One moment stretched to a lifetime as he waited for the charge to hit her heart, to bring her back to him.

Please.

Please.

Jo.

I need you.

I love you.

Her body lurched as the volts of electricity sank beneath her skin.

Nate froze.

Jo came back to life, convulsing as coughs forced their way up her throat, and she vomited a mess of liquid onto the carpet. Nate was by her side immediately, rolling her over as gush after gush of water spilled from her lungs. He rubbed her back, murmured soothingly, pulled her wet hair away, until it was over and she breathed heavily on the floor, blinking with confusion, but undeniably alive.

"Jo," he said, searching her face for recognition, for understanding. He didn't know how long she'd been under, what sort of damage might've been done. "Jo, are you okay? Do you know who I am?"

The fog lifted, and her eyes cleared to bright emeralds. "Nate?"

"Oh god, Jo." Nate blurted the words like a confession as he pulled her into his arms, pressing her cold body to his chest to give her warmth, needing her close, needing her beating heart pressed against his so he knew the gentle rhythm was real. He buried his head in her neck, pressing soft kisses to her throat, in time with her thrumming pulse, as her arms came across his shoulders and held him close. He leaned back far enough to press his palm to her cheek. And then he kissed her, soft and slow, gentle and tender, taking his time because they had it, not pressing too hard because she was the strongest woman he'd ever met, but in that moment, she felt so impossibly fragile all he wanted to do was keep her protected.

Jo pulled back, keeping their foreheads pressed together, and held the back of his head in her hands. "What happened?"

Nate sighed, not sure where to begin.

Jo's gaze dropped, and she jerked back. "Nate, why am I naked?"

Okay, I wasn't going to start there…but that's as good a place as any.

"You—"

"And why is Agent Alvarez watching from the corner like a creepy lecher with an oddly goofy smile on his face?"

Nate arched a brow and turned on his partner, who was, in fact, standing a few feet away, grinning like a buffoon as he hugged his arms around his torso and unabashedly watched their reunion. At least he was, until Jo's words registered and he had the decency to flinch back to life and turn away.

Nate looked back at Jo. "Because Leo's a softie at heart. And he's never fully grasped the concept of boundaries."

"I resent that, Parker."

"It's true—"

Jo gasped and lifted her fingers to her lips in shock, silencing Nate midsentence. Her muscles went slack. His arms were the only things keeping her upright.

"The house… The explosion… Daddy…" Her voice cracked and broke off, catching in her throat as the memory of those last few moments rushed over her, making her tremble. She looked up at Nate, the most hopeful look in her eyes. All he could do was shake his head and watch as her world crumbled. Jo closed her eyes tight, squeezing them so hard her entire face wrinkled with the motion. Moisture leaked onto her lashes, pooling at the edges, silently spilling down her cheeks. For this pain, there was nothing he could do to help but hold her and tell her it would be okay. Which he did, as many times as it took for her to open her eyes again. They were shiny and wet but determined and resilient.

"Is Thad…?" A whisper was all she could manage.

"He called me to warn me that you were in danger. He's the only reason I got here so fast. But he hung up before we could fully trace the call. Our men scoured the area but didn't find anything except for stray bullets. The Russians were gone. So was Ryder. But we have no way to know if he got away or was caught, at least not yet."

Jo nodded silently, taking it all in. Before either of them could speak, boots thudded on the deck outside the cabin. Nate whipped his head around, reaching for his gun, but it was the coast guard. It was the good guys.

"Here!" he shouted, lifting a hand to catch their attention. "She needs help."

Two men raced deeper into the yacht, a stretcher held between them. "We have a chopper outside, ready for a medevac to Nassau—"

"Jolene Carter, age twenty-five, United States citizen, in good health, no known allergies or disorders." Nate launched into the rundown immediately, not bothering to let them finish as he moved out of the way to reveal Jo huddled against his chest. The men rushed over and took Jo from his arms to strap her to the stretcher. She was weak enough not to protest, but held on to his hand the entire time, refusing to let go. And Nate held right back. There was no way she'd be leaving his sight—not anytime soon. "Hit by the blast, possible head trauma, no visible sign of burns. I wasn't there to witness, but I heard through the phone. We got to her a few minutes after the explosion to find her unconscious in the water. I began CPR immediately in the water and moved to the boat to begin chest compressions. We ran the defibrillator twice before a successful resuscitation."

The emergency responders nodded along, checking her vitals. "And the blood? Where's the wound?"

Blood?

Wound?

Nate pushed his brows together, staring at the floor, noticing for the first time that a wet ruby trail painted a gory path from the edge of the boat, all the way inside, spreading into a pool around his body. And then he remembered.

"Oh, the blood! The blood is me."

"What?" Jo shouted, sitting up in an instant, eyes wide.

"I was hit. I'm fine."

"You were hit?" she shrieked, finally overwhelmed by everything that had happened, and taking it out on the only person there who could survive the heat. "As in shot? As in a bullet? Why the hell didn't you say anything?"

Nate squeezed her fingers with one hand and then used his other to gently force her back down against the stretcher so they could finish strapping her up. "Because I'm fine. I've been wounded on active duty before—"

"You have?"

Only his palm against her shoulder kept her from leaping to a seated position again. "I'm fine, Jo, I promise. See?"

He shifted his leg so both of them could see, trying to prove his point.

Bad idea.

Horrible.

Adrenaline must have been pumping through his system, because he could hardly feel any pain, but the wound was a mess. Skin ripped apart. Blood spurting.

Like something out of a horror movie. Nate hastily shifted his calf out of her sight, but it was too late. The damage was done.

"Oh my god!"

"Jo—"

"We're going to have a conversation about this, Nathaniel. Don't think we won't."

He rolled his eyes. "Not now, Jo. You need to get to the hospital."

"So do you!"

Nate glanced at the paramedic, searching for backup, but the man was already coming at him with a strip of gauze. Hands immediately landed on his shoulders, and before he could mutter a protest, Nate found himself on his back with his leg raised and resting on Leo's knee as a bandage was applied to stop the bleeding.

"It didn't hit bone," Nate argued, fully aware he never would've been able to run around in search of that first aid kit if he'd shattered a tibia. "Just muscle tissue. It looks worse than it is. I—"

"Shut up," Jo and Leo said as one, and then looked at each other, smirking.

Oh, great. That's just wonderful.

"She needs immediate medical attention," he said. But at that exact moment, another stretcher was brought in by two different paramedics.

"So do you, sir."

"Oh, for the love of god," he muttered as they strapped him down. "I'm fine."

The victorious look on Jo's face would have been comical if it weren't turned on him. "Safety first, Agent Parker."

Words to live by.

Words he *did* live by, until about eight days ago.

Nate sighed, stuck in a web of his own making. Before he could respond, the paramedics lifted the stretchers, forcing him and Jo apart as they carried them from the yacht, down the pier, and into the chopper waiting on the beach.

When they were settled inside, Nate let his head fall to the side so he could watch Jo. Her gaze was hard to read as she looked at the charred remains of her home. He couldn't decipher which memories raced through her head. Good. Bad. Or unimaginable. So instead, he reached out and took her fingers back in his, squeezing tight, trying to give her all his strength, however much of it she needed. She turned toward him, watching him as though he were her only tether to the earth, as though without him she might float away. But her grip remained loose in his, as though she wasn't sure if she wanted to stay or go. All Nate could think about was bringing a speck of joy back to her eyes, a sparkle of mirth.

He rubbed his thumb over her skin, tracing a pattern as he spoke. "I have to admit, Jo, when I envisioned riding off into the sunset with you, it wasn't on matching stretchers. Horseback, maybe. A red convertible, even better. My old beat-up Ford truck would've worked fine. But a medevac chopper? That wasn't high on the list."

Nate watched his words land, waiting for her response. *See now, that just shows a lack of imagination...* Or maybe, *in my dreams, we weren't so much riding off as sitting on the couch, sharing a cake made for two...or three...or ten.*

But she didn't say any of that. She held his gaze, somewhat somber and subdued, even as the slightest smile wobbled on her lips. "I'll take what I can get, Nate, as long as I'm with you."

The blades began to churn, roaring loudly, picking up speed as the pilots settled in their seats and prepared for takeoff. Paramedics slipped foam buds into their ears, muffling the sound. The world shifted to an oddly peaceful sort of silence as the chopper lifted and the air cleared of smoke, and there was nothing but blue sky all around them.

Nate and Jo looked at each other.

They didn't need to speak.

Not with words.

Jo laced her fingers through his and held on firm. Nate did the same. And it was enough. More than enough, as they silently promised each other forever.

- 31 -

Jo

Two Weeks Later

Jo kicked her flip-flops off and took a step forward, moving from the sidewalk to the beach. She wriggled her toes in the sand. Amazing how no matter where she went, it felt the same. Sometimes smooth. Sometimes rocky. But always comforting, always cathartic. The sound of softly lapping water filtered into her ears, a soothing rhythm. A faded pink sliver cut across the horizon, the last remnants of dusk as night fell. The moon glittered on the flowing black surface, lighting her path in the dark. Jo clasped the urn to her chest, not sure if she was ready to let go.

"Are you okay?" Nate murmured from behind. The deep, solid sound of his voice was reassuring, her anchor to the shore, her new rock, steadfast and constant.

Jo glanced over her shoulder, finding his eyes, holding on to the love and sympathy swirling within them. "I'm okay."

"Do you want me to—"

Jo shook her head.

No.

Nate had already done enough. He'd saved her life. He'd convinced the FBI to recover her father's remains. He'd followed through on his promise of an immunity deal, giving her the opportunity to see all her dreams come true. He'd done everything within his power to ease the pain, to take away her hurt. And this was something she needed to do by herself.

So she turned and took a step, and another and another, until she felt the cool kiss of water against her toes, and then she kept going until she was up to her knees. The world was different out here, surrounded by bright twinkles and deep shadow, the flow of the river pushing against her balance, the surface rippling, the shore so seemingly far away. There was something magical about it, almost surreal.

When they'd deposited her mother's ashes in the ocean outside their private island, it had been broad daylight. Nothing but sun and turquoise water and white sand. The total opposite of this final goodbye with her father, on a small beach at the edge of the Potomac River under cover of night. But it made sense in a way. Her mother had been the serene, graceful beauty of the sunrise, her father the stark, vivid drama of the sunset, but together, they'd made the day complete. And now, they'd be reunited, somewhere in the vast sea, somewhere beyond understanding.

Jo opened the lid of the urn.

She gently turned it over, letting the wind and the current carry the ashes out of sight. There hadn't been much recovered at the scene, so the process was quick and painless in a way Jo hadn't expected it to be. Oh, her chest burned. Tears slid silently down her cheeks. Her hands shook. And yet, there was something hopeful, a small part of her that thought maybe it was better this way. Her mother was no longer alone, waiting. Her father was no longer alone, wanting. They were both at peace. And the alternative had been the rest of his life behind bars, an atonement he probably deserved, but one Jo was glad to not have to witness.

He'd come to her rescue.

He'd apologized for his sins.

Then he was gone, too fast to feel anything at all.

The explosion had killed him in an instant, but Jo liked to believe he hadn't died in vain. The Russians had wired the entire exterior of the house, so all their personal possessions had been completely destroyed. The vault, however, was underground and untouched by the fire due to all the precautions her father had painstakingly taken during its construction. The priceless works and heirlooms he'd stolen were in the process of being returned to the families and museums from which they'd been taken. And thanks to his precise recordkeeping, the bureau had more than enough evidence to begin making arrests, against the Russians but also against a number of shady criminals her father had worked with over the years. Though he'd done a lot of bad things in his life, Jo hoped that in the end he'd be remembered for being good—a good person, a good husband, and a good father. She at least would always think of him that way.

Jo replaced the lid on the now-empty urn and tucked it against her hip, holding it with one hand, using the other to clasp the rings hanging from a chain around her neck. They'd been recovered in her father's remains. Two wedding rings, scorched black, but undamaged. The agents on the scene had slipped them into an envelope and kept them off the record, handing them to Nate on the sly so Jo could keep a little part of her past. The rest was gone—lost to the explosion or confiscated by the government. Jo had nothing—at least, that was what a lot of news outlets were reporting, what some people kept telling her, what she kept reading.

A small smile quirked her lips.

I have Nate. I have these rings. I have my dreams. I have a future. I have everything I could possibly need.

Well, except one thing.

Thad.

No one had heard from him or seen him. And while the evidence in her father's vault had been invaluable, Nate said nothing convinced a jury like an eyewitness. So, the bureau was scouring the country looking for him. And Jo was positive the Russians were doing the same. But she held on to the belief that Thad was okay. He was in hiding. And somehow, someway, when it was safe, he'd find a way to contact her. A way the Russians and the FBI would never anticipate. A way only she would understand.

Jo sighed.

Slowly, she walked out of the water and up the beach, back to where Nate was patiently waiting, leaning against his crutches for support. The gunshot hadn't inflicted any permanent damage aside from what was sure to be a wicked scar, but the recovery would be slow. She'd never tell Nate, but Jo was secretly overjoyed to have him stuck in the office and not out in the field, so he could come home to her every night and kiss her goodbye every morning.

"So how does it feel to break the law, Agent Parker?"

It was the first thing that had come to her lips, and in typical fashion, she'd spit it out without thinking. But it was easier to joke than to feel. She needed a break from her emotions. And, well, it was the truth—

scattering ashes in an inland waterway, especially without a permit, wasn't quite legal. But just this once, Nate had agreed to look the other way.

Literally.

He jolted when Jo spoke and snapped his head around to face her, a grin dancing across his lips. "I don't know what you're talking about. I'm just out for an evening stroll on a moonlit beach with my girlfriend. Very romantic."

Jo arched a brow and stepped closer. "Girlfriend, huh?"

"We rule-followers like the use of a label every now and again, to keep things organized." Even with crutches, Nate was quick. He darted his hand out, grabbing the edge of her shirt, and tugged. Jo fell against his chest, no other place in the world she'd rather be. "You have a problem with that?"

Though she'd normally retort, Jo melted into his words and his embrace, all the fight and all the bravado gone from her body in one fell swoop. "No."

Nate's features softened, humor turning to empathy in an instant. He lifted his hand and tucked her hair behind her ear, then gently brushed his fingers over her cheeks, wiping the tears away. Words danced in the depths of his eyes. *I'm sorry. What can I do? How can I help? Are you okay? Will you be okay? I want to take your pain away.* But he didn't say any of it, because he knew her, and he knew she didn't want to hear it. Instead, he pressed a soft kiss to her forehead and murmured a single word. The perfect one.

"Home?"

Jo leaned back and found his eyes. "Home."

They made their way to the car, and Nate eased into the driver's seat. Jo didn't bother to protest. The last time she'd tried to point out that someone recovering from a bullet to the calf might not be the ideal driver, she'd gotten a gruff, *I got shot in my left leg. I only need the right one to drive.* And to be honest, all she wanted to do now was hold his hand and zone out until they got home.

Home.

What an odd concept. Two weeks ago, the only home she'd known for the past ten years had been blown to smithereens. And now, only fourteen days later, another spot had already claimed the title. But that was something loss had taught her—home wasn't a place, not really. It was a person. Home had once been a farmhouse in the countryside, until the day her mother's laughter disappeared and took all sense of belonging with it. Then home had become an isolated island in the middle of the sea. But without her father's presence, that house would never have felt the same. And now, home was a small one-bedroom apartment in the middle of Washington, DC, a bachelor pad slowly seeing signs of a woman's touch. But really, home was being wrapped in Nate's arms, safe and loved and warm. That was all she wanted as they parked and made their way to the front door. To be surrounded by Nate. Loved by him. To escape for a little bit beneath his touch. In her mind, they were already in bed, tangled in the sheets, finding solace in each other's—

"What the hell?"

Jo blinked, dispelling the image as Nate's blurted words brought her back to reality. "Wha— Oh."

She followed him through the front door and winced, taking in the utter disaster that was the apartment. Cardboard boxes and bits of Styrofoam were scattered across the living room floor. Bags of flour and sugar and chocolate chips sat open on the kitchen counters. Butter had melted into a puddle, dripping over the edge and onto the ceramic tiles. Cooling racks were stacked two feet high on the dining room table, overflowing with baked goods.

"The, um, KitchenAid I ordered arrived today…" Jo trailed off when she realized Nate wasn't listening but was instead frozen in horror, eyes wide, mouth open, steam practically coming out of his ears. *Damage control. ASAP.* "I meant to clean it," Jo started again. Nate still didn't move. She bit her lip and lifted one of her feet, dragging the tips of her toes back and forth across the wooden boards. "But I was on a roll, creative-wise I mean. And I was so nervous about tonight, about how I would feel, I couldn't stop. And then you called to say you were out front. And I just grabbed the urn and left and, well, completely forgot to warn you..." Jo swallowed. Was he having a heart attack? A panic attack? A— "Nate?"

Jo put a hand to his arm. As soon as she touched him, he sucked a long, measured breath through his lips, then held it for a few moments before releasing it just as steadily, just as controlled. He gradually shifted his head, turning it toward her in slow motion.

"Jo."

An apologetic smile rose on her lips. *Please find me adorable and cute.* "I made coopies, your favorite. The brownie ones are brand new. They're just over there, on the end of the table. Or chocolate chip. A classic. You can't go wrong with chocolate chip. Or, um, oatmeal raisin? Though, those still need a little work. Ooh! The birthday cake ones are delicious."

"Jo." He drew the O out into a sentence all its own.

"I know..."

He turned back toward the mess. "Look at this place."

"I'm sorry."

Panic sizzled beneath her skin. All she wanted was to lose herself in Nate's arms, to forget the hurt for a little while, to forget it all—and dammit, she would!

Jo did the only thing she could think of.

She stripped.

While Nate was busy darting his gaze around every splotch of dough on the counter, Jo yanked off her T-shirt and pulled down her shorts, then unclipped her bra and stepped out of her panties. She kicked her flip-flops into the center of the kitchen—hell, at this point, it couldn't be any messier—and said, "Nate."

"Jo—"

"I'm naked."

He spun so fast she was worried he might get whiplash, nothing but empty air spilling from his lips.

"I'm naked."

"You already said that."

"I felt it needed repeating."

"You make a good point." Nate drank in every inch of her body. Jo smirked. "But you can't win every argument this way, Jo."

She opened her mouth in admonishment. "This is the first time I've done this!"

"I'm just saying..." Nate scanned her once more, then he swallowed, throat tight.

Jo swayed her hips, sauntering closer, never one to fight fair, especially if her tactic was proving effective. The flames in his eyes turned to an inferno as she leaned into his chest, whispering, "I think I'll take my chances."

Nate stared at her, a war playing behind his eyes.

Then in one fell swoop, he groaned, let his crutches fall to the ground, and grabbed her by the waist to toss her over his shoulder.

"Nate!" she gasped in surprise.

He didn't respond. He just turned and made for the bedroom.

"Nate, your leg!"

"I'm fine," he muttered, even as he started to limp.

When he grunted and began hopping down the hallway on one foot, Jo couldn't help it. She covered her lips with her hands, trembling as her entire body jerked in what had to be the least seductive motion in the history of dating. But it was Nate. And she loved him. And she loved this. And it didn't matter that they fell onto the bed in a jumbled heap. It only mattered that they were there, together, laughing until they were crying, then kissing the tears away.

* * *

Thank you for reading!

I hope Jo and Nate stole your heart, the way they did mine. If you have a moment, please consider leaving a review. Even a few words can make a huge difference in someone deciding to give my book a chance.

While this love story is complete, there are more *To Catch a Thief* adventures to enjoy!

Don't miss the next two books in the series—*Stolen Goods*, following the love story of devilish thief-on-the-run Thad and daydreaming cake designer Addison, and *Off the Grid*, following the love story of badass pastry chef McKenzie and charming federal agent Leo.

Both are available now!

About The Author

Bestselling author Kaitlyn Davis writes young adult fantasy novels under the name Kaitlyn Davis and contemporary romance novels under the name Kay Marie.

While she's been writing ever since she picked up her first crayon, she spends more time these days with her "mom" hat on than her "writer" hat - and she wouldn't have it any other way! But she does squeeze in as much writing (and reading!) as she can. Storytelling is a vital part of who she is, and she can't thank her readers enough for keeping this beautiful dream of hers alive.

Connect with Kay online:

Website: www.KayMarieBooks.com
Instagram: @KayMarieBooks
TikTok: @KayMarieBooks
Facebook: Facebook.com/KaitlynDavisBooks
Goodreads: Goodreads.com/Kay_Marie
Bookbub: @KayMarie1